A Very Funny Murder Mystery

Murder Mystery

A British Comedy Spoof

by Paul Mathews

Clinton Trump Detective Genius series
Book 1

Cover illustration by Alex Storer
www.thelightdream.net

A tremendous tale for stable geniuses everywhere

Chapter 1

Lady Edith Peculiar sat bolt upright on her bejewelled dining throne, disengaged from polite chatter about weeds on the village green, boisterous roosters and whether capital punishment should be reintroduced for apple scrumpers, and surveyed the guests at the latest gathering of her country ladies' curry club. Practically every female from the higher echelons of Upper Goosing society was sitting at Peculiar Manor's impressive oak dining table on this hot and spicy August evening. Of course, one or two had yet to prove their social worth – such as that curious red-headed Russian, Svetlana something-or-other, who poured milk into her teacup before the Earl Grey, used American English in her RSVPs and displayed an inexplicable aversion to digestive biscuits. But one had to give newcomers a chance. And not just those from overseas and big cities. Allowances had to be made for country folk who'd moved from places where the residents' maintenance of their front lawns, taste in lounge curtains and the colour and style of their motor vehicles, waterproof jackets and garden gnomes weren't quite so important to the maintenance of village equilibrium. Yes, having spent over fifty years at the heart of this community, Lady Edith was well aware that new arrivals took some considerable time to adapt to the quirks and quibbles of English country life. And no village was quirkier, or more quibbly, than Upper Goosing.

She suppressed an unexpected burp with all the grace and decorum one would expect from someone who was a fifth cousin four times removed of Her Majesty Queen Elizabeth II. Lizzy would be proud of her. Maybe she would send the reigning monarch an invitation to the next curry-club evening? A well-prepared Indian meal would bring memories of the great British Empire flooding back. And it would help take Lizzy's mind off the current state of the world and all those awful presidents she was forced to meet nowadays. Lady Edith sniffed the cumin-scented air and congratulated herself. A royal visit would be a wonderful surprise for the ladies, cement her status at the top of the county's social tree and be a change of scenery for Her Majesty who must be awfully bored of Buckingham Palace, Windsor Castle and all the other oversized royal residences by now. Peculiar Manor was a bijou country property worthy of any monarch.

Her thoughts were disrupted by the clump of heavy footsteps approaching the door. The police must have arrived.

The dining room's solid-oak doors burst open like a pair of breached floodgates. Before any of the curry ladies could drop their naan breads in surprise, the investigative torrent that was Detective Inspector Clinton Trump surged into the dining room, submerging it with his six-foot-two-inch manliness. Instantly buoyed by his presence, bosoms bobbed, eyebrows floated, lips rippled and cheeks flushed.

'Good evening, ladies,' announced Clinton, in an accent as clipped as his magnificent blond bouffant.

'Good evening, Inspector Trump,' chorused the ladies, in devoted harmony.

Clinton unpeeled his raincoat and tossed it to a star-struck maid, who simpered spectacularly before staggering to the cloakroom.

'I'm sorry this super sleuth couldn't arrive any earlier. But the Goosing bypass was absolute *murder*.'

'Rush-hour traffic?' enquired Lady Peculiar.

'No. Diversions. Our old friend Dr Black was found battered to death with a candlestick in Brokenshire Central Library. The constable redirecting traffic informed me.'

Lady Peculiar clutched her pearl necklace. 'How awful.'

'Yes, added a good thirty minutes to my journey. But fret not. The Lower Goosing force are on the case. They've combed the scene, collected evidence and, I'm pleased to inform your ladyship, as a result of their investigations, they've come up with a name.'

'So, they've already identified the perpetrator?'

'Oh, no! They rarely do that. What I meant was, they've settled on a nickname for Dr Black's murderer.'

Lady Peculiar struck a thoughtful pose. 'Dr Black. In the library. With a candlestick. Hmmm. Finding a nickname that neatly summarises their misdeeds, in order to fire the public imagination, maximise publicity and create the possibility of appearing in a true-crime documentary on the BBC in twenty years' time is a tricky proposition, inspector.'

Clinton nodded. 'But Lower Goosing's finest have done it. And they're calling him … the Monopoly Murderer!'

Her ladyship cocked an aristocratic eyebrow. 'The *Monopoly* Murderer?'

'Yes. Dr Black was the *only* general practitioner serving Upper and Lower Goosing, your ladyship. Quite simply, he had a complete monopoly on the treatment of your, my, and everyone else's medical predicaments.' Clinton sighed superbly. 'The man was a clinical genius. There wasn't a replaced hip, slipped disc, hiatus hernia or freak accident with the vacuum cleaner he didn't know about. And now all that knowledge has been lost in a well-placed swing of an ornamental candle-holder.'

An elderly voice came from the back of the room. 'I'm visiting Brokenshire Central Library tomorrow, inspector. Should I be worried?'

'No, no, madam. The traffic should be flowing normally by then.' He tossed his head terrifically. 'But enough of deceased doctors and dastardly diversions. I hear on the brilliant-detective grapevine there's been a death at Peculiar Manor.'

Her ladyship nodded. 'That is correct.' A murmur swept around the room and she turned to address her guests. 'Forgive me for not sharing this news with you earlier, ladies, but I didn't want to spoil the main course for anyone.' She turned back to the inspector. 'My butler and stand-in cook, Jepson, has departed this world in the most ghastly of fashions.'

'Not another one minced to death?' asked Clinton, glancing at the recently widowed butcher's wife.

'I haven't the foggiest idea. I was halfway through the venison vindaloo when my maid alerted me. It's unforgiveable to abandon curried game in polite company and, therefore, I haven't graced the scene with my presence just yet.'

'Then why do you say it's ghastly, your ladyship?'

'The timing, inspector.'

Clinton raised his eyebrows. 'I'm afraid this is one of those rare occasions when South East England's greatest detective doesn't follow.'

'Jepson was bumped off just after preparing the main course, my dear. That means ...' She almost choked on her words. '... we're not having any pudding.'

A collective gasp engulfed the table.

Clinton rubbed his stubble. 'No pudding? This is deadly serious.'

'Yes. But we curry-loving country ladies are made of stern stuff. We shall soldier on – and proceed straight to the coffee and after-dinner mints.'

'I'm extremely glad to hear it. You should never let untimely death interrupt your dinner plans.'

'Quite.'

'Please, your ladyship, take me to Jepson's body.'

'All in good time, inspector. Won't you have something to eat first? I can highly recommend the pheasant korma. I shot the birds myself.'

'Thank you. But this detective only has an appetite for one thing, Lady Peculiar. Getting to the bottom of Jepson's death. And my gut instinct tells me this could be murder.'

Her nostrils flared. 'Really, inspector? What leads you to that hasty conclusion?'

'I've no idea whatsoever. My gut never reveals its sources. But it's rarely been proved wrong.' His eyes flashed cleverly. 'And there hasn't been a murder in Upper Goosing for almost two months, so we are rather overdue one.'

An Eastern European voice called out. 'It one month and twenty day since last murder.'

Lady Peculiar glared in the voice's direction. 'Thank you for the clarification, Svetlana.'

Clinton expanded his chest so impressively, a woman three metres away began hyperventilating. 'I really must see Jepson's body, your ladyship. You see, it's an essential part of attending any sudden death. Someone dies; that means there's a body and we, the police, are called to come and examine the scene and help determine whether the death was due to natural causes or if foul play is involved.' He nodded brilliantly at the guests. 'And, much as I'd love to spend the evening chatting with you good ladies, it would be remiss of me to skip the examination of the body.'

'Of course, inspector.' Lady Peculiar scanned the room. 'However, as hostess for the evening, I'm going to remain here and take my coffee and mints. The body is in the kitchens.' She turned to the other ladies. 'You all know this manor like your own homes. Do we have a volunteer to show the inspector the way?'

Several shoulders were almost dislocated as the arms attached to them shot up.

Clinton pointed at the butcher's widow. 'How about you, madam? You strike me as the type who can stomach a potential crime scene – a situation that possibly features a selection of well-carved body parts, lashings of human entrails and a large dollop of bodily fluids.'

'That's very perceptive of you, inspector,' purred the object of Clinton's attention. 'I used to work occasional shifts in my husband's shop, when he was away on butchering business.' She smiled demurely. 'So, I know how to handle a meat cleaver.'

'Tremendous! Then this investigative genius shall be in safe hands.'

Lady Peculiar nodded in appreciation. 'That's most kind of you, Mrs Savage.'

'Please, it's Ms Savage now, Lady Peculiar.'

'My sincerest apologies, Ms Savage.' Her ladyship bowed her head. 'But, you see, one still hasn't come to terms with your husband's untimely demise. Such a shocking way to go – accidentally falling into his own mincing machine while trying to create the perfect sausage.'

'I think, in a strange way, it's what my husband would have wanted, your ladyship. He was so dedicated to his mincing.' She covered her face with her hands and started to sniffle. 'And now he's gone to the big sausage factory in the sky.'

Lady Peculiar coughed regally. 'Come, come, Ms Savage. The first rule of curry club is never shed a tear around the dinner table – even if you have suffered a recent grisly bereavement. These regular gatherings are a place for us to cast off our troubles and discuss the important matters of the day. Issues such as the best shotgun to pack on a duck hunt. The quickest way to throttle a goose. And how to skin a rabbit with nothing more than a dessert spoon and the teeth God gave us.' She wagged a finger. 'You will have to be strong, my dear. And take comfort in the bumper life-insurance payout.'

'I'll try my best,' sniffed Ms Savage, removing her hands from her face. 'And we've managed to get the mincing machine working again. There are still a few shards of bone in the mechanism. But—'

'But nothing the human digestive system couldn't handle, what?' Lady Peculiar chuckled drily. 'That's splendid! We're making partridge keema on Friday. I'll pluck the birds tomorrow and have them sent to you to put through your mincer. And there'll be no complaints from me if anyone cracks their teeth on a sliver of tibia, fibula or anything else!'

'Certainly, your ladyship.'

'Textbook stuff!' boomed Clinton. 'Now, onwards … to the scene of the crime!'

Chapter 2

As Detective Inspector Trump was escorted along the marble-floored corridor towards the kitchens by the butcher's widow, he steeled himself for what he – and his vital organs – knew would be a murder scene. 'Have we much further to go, Ms Savage?'

She stopped by a portrait of a young deer and quivered slightly. 'I'm sorry, inspector, but I'm feeling a little giddy.'

Clinton halted in his tracks and peered into her eyes. 'How giddy, exactly?'

'Rather giddy.'

'On a scale of one to ten, how giddy do you feel?'

'With ten the maximum level of giddiness?'

'Yes. Though, if you were a ten, you'd be kissing marble by now.'

She touched her temple. 'I would say I'm a six and three quarters on the giddiness scale.'

'Really?'

'Really.'

'Well, it's the first time this phenomenal detective has ever encountered a giddiness level of that specific magnitude. I wonder what's brought it on.'

'Possibly the prospect of the shocking sight that might await us in those kitchens.' She flung her right palm to her forehead. 'It seemed so easy to agree to accompany you when you were standing proud in that dining room, telling me how wonderfully I would handle the deathly scene. But now, as the moment of macabre truth draws near, I can feel the cold hand of fear gripping my innards.'

'Maybe that's the curry. Lady Peculiar's venison vindaloo has been known to bring Bulgarian shot-putters to their knees when she overdoes the chilli peppers.' He flicked his head. 'Whatever. I'm still confident you'll handle seeing a man whose face may be more battered than an Irish rugby player's earlobes, whose limbs could be at angles even a Romanian gymnast would baulk at, and whose entrails might be splattered wider than a spaghetti bolognese caught in a tornado.'

Ms Savage's eyes glazed over. She moved her lips but uttered nothing.

Sensing a damsel in imminent distress, Clinton sprang into action. He shepherded her into the nearby study with a speed and deftness that would have been the envy of every Border collie in Great Britain.

Fortunately, the study was empty. Clinton guided her to a sofa and they sat down.

'Take all the time you need, Ms Savage.' He leant forward. 'Once you've composed yourself, you can provide me with directions to the kitchens and I'll take it from there.'

She gasped for air. 'No, inspector.' Another gasp. 'No, I don't.' And another. 'Want you to.' One more gasp for luck. 'Go alone.' Finally, she was gasp-free. 'I want to be there with you – for moral support.'

Clinton chuckled politely. 'You're too kind. But my morals are strong enough to support themselves, Ms Savage.'

'I understand, inspector.' She turned away. 'But I do rather enjoy your company.'

'So do I.'

Her gasps were back. 'You do?'

'Yes. That's why I never married.'

The gasps were gone again. 'Ah. You mean you enjoy your *own* company.'

'Absolutely love it. And my faithful felines, Clouseau and Columbo, ensure I never run out of intelligent conversation.'

Ms Savage smiled. 'They're very lucky cats.'

'I like to think so. Though they've just been castrated, so they might want to disagree with you on that point.'

13

'Quite. But castration was possibly a pleasant experience compared to having to socialise with some of the ladies around that dining table. For example, that *awful* amateur-dramatics woman who thinks her club is the centre of the village universe.'

'You're referring to Jayne Trill?'

'Yes, that's her.'

'She's not all bad. Once you've known her for a decade or two, you'll start warming to her.' He checked himself. 'Well, at least not dislike her quite so much.'

'And if Pattie from the post office asks me one more time if I'm interested in buying a set of European Murder Destination of the Year 2015 commemorative postage stamps, I think there might be another murder in Upper Goosing. And the victim will be stamped to death.'

'Pattie's just a tad eccentric, that's all. Like most of our residents. And, while the culinary company at your curry events may not be the finest, I've heard the food's top drawer.'

'That's true. But the meetings have become increasingly chaotic. People coming and going as they please while Lady Peculiar sits on her throne surveying her curry kingdom.'

Clinton stroked his chin. 'Who left the room for an extended period this evening?'

'As far as I remember, myself and Lady Peculiar were the only two ladies I could say with any certainty stayed in that dining room. Everyone else, at some point, popped out to powder their nose, take a phone call, adjust their dress or throw up in the flowerbeds.'

'Did you know Jepson at all?'

'He was an acquaintance, shall we say. I don't know if you're aware, but his first job was as an insurance salesman. He was very helpful when I needed advice about taking out life insurance for my late husband, Horace. In fact, Jepson recommended the policy and witnessed it for me.'

'When was this?'

'A couple of months ago.'

'What fortunate timing!'

'Yes, it was.' She gazed down at her high heels. 'Some people might say it was … suspiciously good timing.'

Clinton's head jolted back. 'What? Which people?'

'Just … people.'

'Then those people are talking twaddle! That type of thing only happens in madcap murder-mystery novels set in ridiculously titled fictional English villages and starring quirky detectives and even quirkier suspects. It doesn't happen in real life! Take it from me, South East England's greatest detective. Now, tell me, when did Jepson last make an appearance in the dining room?'

'He served the main course around seven o'clock.'

Clinton checked his watch. 'It's almost nine o'clock now. Using my outstanding detection skills, I can deduce he's been dead no more than two hours.' He stared into her eyes and took her hand. 'Forgive me for not asking since you sat down – how is your giddiness now, Ms Savage?'

She placed a hand on her head. 'Still the same.'

'It's not even dropped a smidgen to six and a half?'

'No. I know because I was a definite six and a half on the giddiness scale when the police informed me about my husband being tragically minced.'

'You weren't a nine or a ten or somewhere in between?'

Ms Savage blushed. 'We weren't the perfect couple, by any stretch of the imagination.' She cleared her throat. 'I'm not sure Horace ever forgave me for going vegan for a month to raise money for the local orphanage. Or for washing his white uniform with my red thong and turning his workwear a delicate shade of pink. Or, for that matter, for the most heinous of crimes for a butcher's wife – forgetting to remove the giblets when I cooked his prize turkey last Christmas.'

Clinton bowed his head. 'I know *exactly* what you mean. My late uncle Archie was a master butcher with a mean streak. He terrorised this village with his overly fatty pork loins, undersized sausage and overzealous boning.'

'What happened to him?'

'His wife bumped him off when I was a small boy. He made my aunt's life a misery. She stunned, killed and butchered him, then fed him to the pigs. Poor creatures. They had indigestion for weeks. And the resulting pork chops were only good enough to sell to American tourists.' His eyebrows shimmied. 'It was an open secret among the movers and shakers of the village. But the local chief inspector of the time was very understanding. My uncle had recently sold her a pack of lamb chops that was three weeks past its sell-by date. The scenes of crime officer had been forced to turn vegetarian after a bad experience with some of my uncle's chipolatas. And the doctor who signed his death certificate had once found a cat's ID tag in one of my uncle's beefburgers. So they all decided to sweep it under the carpet.'

Ms Savage's ears pricked up. 'Oh, did they?'

'Yes. Different times. Different law-enforcement ethics. It was the last occasion a butcher was murdered in Upper Goosing and I suspect it will stay that way for many years to come. People simply don't butcher butchers. Possibly because they have such huge hands. Therefore, I won't have to worry about nabbing any butcher butcherers.'

Ms Savage heaved a relieved sigh. 'That's reassuring to hear.'

'How's that giddiness?'

'Three and a half and falling.'

'Superb! Another couple of minutes and we'll get moving again. Assuming you still want to accompany me, that is?'

Ms Savage smiled. 'Yes. I'm feeling a lot less nervous now.'

Chapter 3

Detective Inspector Trump strode through the kitchen doors with all the purpose of a pensioner patrolling a pound shop. But it wasn't a dead body that greeted him. It was a live one. And it belonged to the Major – long-time companion of Lady Peculiar, permanent resident of the manor, and British army veteran.

'Ah, inspector!' boomed the Major, standing to attention and delivering his trademark salute. 'I was rather hoping you would be selected for this mission, sir.'

'Major, what a pleasant surprise!' oozed Clinton, as they shook hands. 'It's always an honour to visit Peculiar Manor. Even if it is the consequence of someone's life ending prematurely.'

The Major pig-snorted. 'We have a saying in my old regiment – untimely death is as good a reason as any to catch up with old chums.' He guffawed a little too loudly for polite company. 'I've already cleared my diary next week for the funeral. It'll be front-row seats in church for her ladyship and myself. And Jepson had no family we know of, so we'll be masterminding the wake. That'll mean first dibs on the cheese and pickle sandwiches for us.' He brushed his tweed jacket. 'And I'll see if I can commandeer that Fiat Uno of his that's been languishing on our drive for months. Might take a trip to the undertaker's in it. See if they need any help with the embalming. Little hobby of mine, you know. Rabbits, mostly. Managed a badger once. But I dare say I could do a good job on something larger.' He looked Clinton up and down as if inspecting a parade-ground recruit. 'If you ever need embalming, just let me know.'

'I certainly will, Major.' Clinton turned to his companion. 'Have you met Ms Savage? She kindly showed me the way here.'

The Major shook her hand with gusto. 'Pleased to formally meet you, madam. We've only encountered each other in the post-office queue. And what a queue it is, these days, eh? It was snaking out the door when I went to collect my copy of *Bayonets and Battlefields* last Thursday. Hunkered down on one of their chairs; nodded off; woke up; lost my bearings; saw the queue; heard a Russian woman taking our village's name in vain; put two and two together and made the Soviet Union; thought I was back in the Kremlin on another black-ops mission.'

'What a wonderful story, Major. But I'm afraid this inspector needs to get down to his brilliant business.'

Oh. Jolly good.'

'Let's kick off with an easy question. Was it you who found the deceased?'

'Affirmative, sir. I'm always banned from those ladies' curry extravaganzas. I'm a man, you see. But I wanted to sample some of her ladyship's venison vindaloo. So I advanced down here in orderly fashion and, lo and behold, I find our butler has gone AWOL from this world. One of the serving staff popped her head round the door a moment later and I ordered her to inform Lady Peculiar of Jepson's demise.'

'Where's his body?' asked Clinton.

The Major slung a glance over his shoulder. 'I popped it in the freezer for safekeeping.'

Clinton's head lifted in surprise. 'He's in the *freezer*?'

'Yes. Bit of a tight squeeze. But I managed to jam him in between a couple of partridges I bagged last week at the nature sanctuary. Beautiful birds. Ideal curry material.'

The inspector frowned. 'Why did you move the body, Major?'

'Well, I had to, dear boy, in order to get the bowl of mango chutney off his head.'

Clinton's eyes twirled in astonishment. 'I'm sorry. Did you say "bowl of mango chutney"?'

'I certainly did. Poor Jepson was face down in several litres of the perfect poppadom accompaniment. Drowned in it, I'll dare say.'

Clinton's voice deepened. 'The stickiest of sticky ends.' He didn't notice Ms Savage's admiring smile. He was too busy admiring his ready wit.

The Major waved an arm. 'Chaps don't go around drowning in mango chutney. I learnt that in the army. Our regiment consumed ten gallons of the stuff a week while we were deep undercover in India. And, while there were one or two incidents involving new recruits being covered from head to toe in the stuff while they slept, then covered in chicken feathers, none of them ever drowned in it. So, in my military view, we're dealing with a murder.'

The inspector felt his tummy rumble. 'My guts were right.'

The Major pulled a notebook from his pocket. 'I almost forgot to mention. I found this beside the body. Fortunately, it's chutney-free. And it appears to be a joke book of sorts.'

Clinton took the book and read the cover. '*Jepson's Jokes*.' He flicked through it. 'Most of the pages have been torn out. I wonder why he had it on his person.'

'I might be of some assistance here,' announced Ms Savage. 'You see, Jepson was something of a comedian in his spare time. A stand-up comedian.'

The Major frowned. 'Well, he was sitting down when I found him.'

'No, Major, what I mean is he moonlighted at Planet Mirth – the comedy club. I saw his act on a number of occasions. And he was one of the most humorous professional butlers I've ever seen.'

'Really?' huffed the Major. 'He was about as funny as a snake in a Sherman tank in my company. Never had a good word to say about her ladyship or this manor. Crossed swords with Edith on a number of occasions. Most recently after she instructed him to cover culinary duties while the cook took six weeks' leave. Jepson eventually obeyed orders – begrudgingly – but he swore to never do it again.'

'And he was true to his word,' noted Clinton.

'There's something else that might be important, inspector,' added Ms Savage. 'There's a stand-up comedy contest at Planet Mirth next month – The Big Titter. It guarantees the winner twelve months of comedy gigs. Jepson mentioned it at the end of the last show I attended. He asked us to come along on the night, vote for him, and help propel him into a new full-time career.'

'Thank you for informing this phenomenal detective of that fact, Ms Savage.' He glanced at his watch. 'It's getting late so, if you'll excuse me, Major, I'll be on my way.'

The Major's moustache twitched. 'Don't you want to inspect the body?'

'Well, you've described the scene in detail. The corpse is chilling nicely. And I don't want to disturb your frozen partridges. So, I'll leave the ambulance service to collect the body and our scenes of crime officer to comb the kitchens for clues. Statements can wait for another day. That will allow me to get home by ten o'clock, feed the cats before they start clawing at my cheese plants, slip into my favourite silk kimono, fix myself a white-wine spritzer, order a takeaway, and put my feet up in front of a wildlife documentary narrated by Cameron Diaz.'

'Sounds like the perfect evening in,' cooed Ms Savage.

'Oh, it is. Now, I shall pop back to the dining room for a quick chat with her ladyship and then prepare to solve this case before the weekend.'

The Major raised his bushy eyebrows. 'You think you can crack it in the next three days, old boy?'

'Yes, Major. I need to have this case all wrapped up by Friday to remove any risk of being bothered about it at the weekend. The annual Goosing Golf Open is on Saturday and, as champion for the last three years, it would be a criminal offence to miss it!'

Chapter 4

As the ladies of the curry club sipped their coffee and indulged in the after-dinner mints, the Peculiar Manor dining room was positively sizzling with chatter about the evening's disastrous development – the pudding not turning up. But several questions about Jepson's death were also being raised by hushed voices. Could this really be a murder, as the inspector had suggested? If so, who would want to kill Jepson? Did he have any enemies? Had he fallen into bad butlering company? Did his death mean the next curry evening would have to be cancelled? And lastly, and most importantly, did anyone have his recipe for mango chutney?

Lady Peculiar rushed in – appearing unusually flustered – and addressed the room. 'One apologises for the extended absence. One had to make an urgent call.'

'Is everything alright, your ladyship?' asked chairwoman of the Goosing Players, Jayne Trill. 'Only you seem a little hot under the pearl necklace.'

'This lady is maintaining her usual temperature; thank you very much for enquiring, Mrs Trill.'

'Sorry to press home the point, your ladyship, but, as the village's leading amateur actress, I am rather an expert on non-verbal communication. And, from your expression, I would guess that you've just received bad news. If you have, perhaps you should share it with the room – to avoid any unfounded gossip about it somehow being connected to your butler's death.'

Lady Peculiar twiddled her necklace. 'It was business. One's own business. And one never discusses one's business at the dining table. One minds that business oneself and doesn't burden other people with it. While respectfully allowing others to mind their own business and nobody else's.'

Jayne smiled with all the warmth of a vulture at a funeral. 'I'm not sure normal rules of etiquette apply when there's been a suspicious death.'

'We don't know if it's suspicious,' snapped Lady Peculiar, not noticing that Inspector Trump and Ms Savage had entered the room.

'I'm afraid we do, ladies,' announced Clinton, with a spectacular head toss. 'There has been a murder at Peculiar Manor.'

Her ladyship cut through the low murmur that greeted this news. 'How can you be so sure, inspector?'

Clinton lowered his voice to the appropriate octave for startling revelations. 'Jepson was drowned … in a bowl of his own mango chutney.'

Jayne chortled. 'Got himself in rather a pickle, didn't he?'

Lady Peculiar ignored the terrible joke. 'You're sure he didn't have a heart attack and simply fall face down into it?'

Clinton flashed a reassuring smile. 'I hadn't considered that possibility. But let's presume for now that I'm right and there has been a murder because I'm in rather a hurry. I must get back home and feed the cats. Now, the local ambulance service are on their way. And a scenes of crime officer will also be attending – given this village's murderous reputation we always send one along to a sudden death. They'll be arriving shortly.'

'Will they be needing anything, inspector?' asked Lady Peculiar.

'Yes. The paramedics messaged me a couple of minutes ago. They asked if there's any leftover vindaloo they could nab.'

'Of course. We're always happy to grant curry favours at Peculiar Manor. Should one prepare a new bowl of mango chutney for them?'

'No need. I'm sure there'll be plenty of it left after evidential swabs have been taken. No point letting good mango chutney go to waste. Now, I shall need a very quick word with you before I depart, Lady Peculiar. Let us retire to the hallway for a few moments. The rest of you can finish your coffee and after-dinner mints in butler-free peace.'

'Don't you want to take any statements from us?' asked Pattie from the post office.

'No, no, no. That's just what the murderer will be expecting us to do. Criminals are clever beasts. Let's keep this one on their toes and be as unpredictable as we possibly can.'

'Do you think it could be someone in this room, inspector?' asked Jayne, staring at Lady Peculiar.

'Again – something I haven't really considered. But I don't want to rule anyone out at this stage. Or rule anyone in. Or, indeed, rule anyone in between in or out. Now, your ladyship, may I escort you to the hallway?'

'Could one make a quick telephone call first, inspector?'

'Of course, your ladyship.'

'Splendid. We shall meet in the hallway in two minutes.'

Lady Peculiar disappeared through the double doors.

Ms Savage moved alongside Clinton. 'Do you need me for anything, inspector?'

'Not tonight, Ms Savage.'

'Please, call me Josephine.'

'Not tonight, Josephine. Maybe tomorrow, when my felines' stomachs are fuller, my mind is clearer and the air is less-filled with venison vindaloo and its after-effects.'

'Forgive me if I sound boastful, but I obtained a Master's Degree in Advanced Criminology from Brokenshire University last year.'

Clinton tapped his chin. 'Criminology, you say?'

'Advanced criminology. My dissertation, *Committing the Perfect Murder*, is apparently still talked about in Sicilian academic circles.'

'Really?'

'Yes. I thought I might be able to add another pair of unofficial eyes to your investigation. You could pick my brain over elevenses tomorrow at the Tourist Trap café.'

'That sounds like a tremendous idea. Welcome aboard the Trump detection train!'

'I'll scribble it in my social diary,' purred Ms Savage, her cheeks almost collapsing with the weight of her smile. 'It's a lot clearer since my husband's tragic mincing.'

Clinton tugged his tie. 'You see, some good always comes of tragedy. Just like with Romeo and Juliet – they departed this world in the most heartbreaking fashion. But at least old Shakespeare got a play out of it.'

'Were Romeo and Juliet real people, inspector?'

'Real. Not real. As long as you steadfastly believe in something, what does it matter if there's very little empirical evidence for it? And I believe very strongly that Shakespeare based much of his work on reality.' He patted his bouffant. 'Who knows? If the great bard were alive today, maybe he'd be writing a play about South East England's greatest detective?'

Her smile was mischievous now. '*The Comedy of Murders*, perhaps? *The Merry Widows of Windsor*? Or *Much Ado About Garrotting*?'

Clinton's eyes crinkled in amusement. '*A Midsummer Night's Drowning* might be more appropriate after this evening's events.'

They shared a chortle before Clinton bid Ms Savage and the rest of the curry ladies goodbye. Then he proceeded to the corridor, where Lady Peculiar was speaking on her phone. She didn't notice his arrival and continued her conversation.

'He was a ghastly butler. Loathed being told what to do. One doesn't want anyone of his ilk ever working here again.' She paused to listen. 'Because of a solemn promise one gave to one's husband on his deathbed. Lord Peculiar was in tears; begged one to keep Jepson on after his death because of the help he gave with the insurance claim after the fire. What could one say? But this lady shan't be shedding any tears for that damn butler.' She turned and spotted Clinton. 'Anyway, one shall be in touch again. Goodbye.' She slipped her phone in her handbag and forced a smile. 'Apologies. One has to recruit a new butler and the employment agencies are already being difficult.'

Clinton nodded. 'A good butler must be very tricky to unearth, your ladyship.'

'Yes. Quality butlers are rarer than honest politicians.'

'Let's not stray into politics, your ladyship. It's an old Trump family tradition – handed down from generation to generation – never to speak of it.'

'And why's that?'

'I've absolutely no idea. We don't speak about politics so, to my knowledge, no one has ever asked why. Now, onto my questions.'

'As you wish.'

'I'll be very brief. My first question is about Jepson. Were you aware of a joke book he was compiling?'

Lady Peculiar's chest lifted and she expelled a huge sigh. 'One was very aware. It was a constant distraction from his work here. One of many.'

'Did anyone else express an interest in this joke book?'

'Nobody with whom one is acquainted. Jepson wasn't renowned for his sense of humour. It baffles one how he ever made it onto the comedy stage. But he'd been requesting more and more evenings off to perform, so one can only assume he struck a comedy chord with some of the more easily pleased locals.'

'Noted, thank you. Moving on, did he have any enemies? For example, anyone bothering him at the manor? Debt collectors, former business associates, ex-wives or Jehovah's Witnesses who simply wouldn't take "get lost" for an answer?'

'He was unmarried, extremely frugal, never answered the door to religion salesmen, and his only business before butlering was insurance – but he was a one-man-band, if one remembers correctly, so he had no partners to speak of.'

'Wonderful. And finally, were any of your curry ladies absent for an extended period during dinner?'

'It's hard to say. But Ms Savage was sitting at the other end of the table, and one is fairly sure she never left one's field of vision. One always remains on one's dining throne for these events and tonight was no different. As for the rest, many of them came and went but one can't be much more helpful than that, I'm afraid.'

'Excellent! That should keep my superintendent happy for now. Thank you, Lady Peculiar. I shall be on my way.'

'If one may ask a question, inspector, will your deputy be joining you on the case?'

'Detective Constable Dinkel? No, only I possess the necessary sleuthing skillset to handle a high-society mango-chutney drowning. Dinkel doesn't have my years of tact and diplomacy to draw on. The sensitivity to know when's the right time to ask difficult questions of people in close proximity to a murder who are experiencing a cocktail of complex emotions; questions which – if put to them inappropriately – could lead to lasting mental trauma, provoke an angry response and end their cooperation with any investigation.' Clinton paused to think. 'Did *you* bump him off?'

Her ladyship's face didn't flicker. 'Did *one* kill Jepson?'

'Yes. Pardon me for postulating, but I overheard you speaking ill of the butlering dead just now.'

She breathed out with all the coolness of a Hollywood psychopath. 'No, inspector. You have the word of a lady. One did not murder Jepson in cold blood.'

'Superb stuff!' roared Clinton, breaking into a huge grin. 'Between you and me, your ladyship, I never suspected you for a nanosecond. But that overheard phone conversation gave me a nice lead in to the classic "Did you commit the murder?"-style question. And far too many detectives these days leave all that nonsense right to the end. Doesn't look good on the old CV. I can tell my superintendent tomorrow I've already eliminated a key suspect. That will keep him off my back for a while.'

Lady Peculiar chortled in understanding. 'You are a very clever man, inspector.'

'I won't argue with a lady of such eminent social standing as yourself. Now, I must shoot off. Felines to feed.'

'Farewell, inspector.'

He skipped to the door. 'Oh, and one last thing.'

'Yes?'

'I strongly recommend you clean the freezer tomorrow.'

Chapter 5

Inspector Trump's grey tabby cat, Columbo, stared with his one functioning eye at his feline flatmate, Clouseau the ginger tom, who was contorting himself on the lounge rug in an effort to check his nether regions for the umpteenth time that day. He was trying to see if his testicles had magically materialised from wherever the vet had disappeared them to last weekend. But Columbo wasn't bothering himself with any cat-tastic gymnastics. He had already resigned himself to never seeing his cat jewels sparkle again. Life had gone on as before when he'd lost that eye in a kitten fight, and after the tip of his tail had been bitten off by Clouseau when he'd mistaken Columbo for a giant rat during a power cut. They would cope perfectly well as a two-testicle, rather than a six-testicle, family unit. This was a peaceful and predictable household – one that most tomcats would give both testicles and their right paw for.

Columbo stretched his claws as Clouseau searched again for his two long-lost brothers, and his thoughts wandered. Testicles were overrated in his opinion. Females seemed to do pretty well without them. Anyway, it wasn't as if either of them ever got to meet any lady cats. And their human never invited females of his own species to the flat – except some older ones who usually popped in with food or drink and spoke in that strange language Columbo and Clouseau were too lazy to learn – although they recognised essential words like 'tuna', 'milk', 'pigeon' and 'vet', as well as a handful of well-worn phrases such as 'I expect you're both starving' and 'What do you fancy, eh? Chicken, beef, lamb or rabbit?' So, with their owner generally shunning female company, he and Clouseau obviously weren't missing much when it came to the opposite sex.

However, what the cats were missing was tonight's dinner. Their human was late. This happened occasionally. Maybe it had taken him longer than usual to track down the food that filled their bowls. You would think he would improve as a hunter as time went on. But he didn't. He was getting worse. Always the same four flavours – and the tins kept getting smaller. That was humans for you: the more they did something, the less successful they were at it. While Columbo's mind was on the subject, there was another thing he'd noticed – his human was expecting more and more feline fuss when he returned triumphant from his regular foraging. He even expected praise when he came back empty-handed. Still, overall, he wasn't a bad human to have around the place. He was just a bit self-centred – the type who'd arrange for your testicles to be removed but stubbornly insist on keeping his own.

Columbo's thoughts were interrupted by the sound of a key turning. The hunter had finally returned.

'Evening, chaps!' called the human. He ditched his jacket on a peg in the hallway and wandered into the lounge. 'I expect you're both starving.'

Columbo stared unblinking. There was one other observation he'd made about humans. They had a real knack for stating the obvious.

'What do you fancy, eh? Chicken, beef, lamb or rabbit?'

Clouseau wasn't listening. He seemed to have dinner plans of his own.

Columbo didn't bother responding. No matter how many times he meowed – at different volumes, speeds and pitches – his human only selected his preferred option twenty-five per cent of the time. And you didn't need to be Schrödinger's cat to work out what those results meant.

The human's voice rose an octave. 'No welcome home for daddy, boys, after ten hours of dazzling detecting?'

There wasn't.

The human mewed in disappointment and served the cats their dinner.

With his belly full, Columbo decided now was a good time to chill out, blank his mind and let his human do the thinking.

Back in the two-legged world, Clinton slipped into his pink silk kimono, poured himself a white-wine spritzer and ordered an Indian takeaway.

'Yes, a chicken tikka masala with poppadoms on the side, please, my good man. No. I'll skip the mango chutney this time. Cash on delivery alright? Superb. Goodbye.'

Then, as he often did on returning from the scene of a crime, he allowed his thoughts to meander in directions that more logical detective minds might not countenance. He parked himself in his leather armchair, picked up Clouseau, plonked him on his lap, started stroking him and focused on his latest case.

Lady Peculiar hadn't been too convinced of Jepson's comic abilities. But could his killer have been a psychotic stand-up rival with a desire to carve out their own comedy career – at any price? That would certainly explain why the pages of his joke book were pilfered. Had Jepson recently stumbled upon a seam of humorous gold that would guarantee him first prize at The Big Titter – only for someone else to snatch away his twenty-four-carat comedy nuggets?

Clinton glanced at a recent copy of the *Goosing Times* sitting on his coffee table and read the lead headline:

CLIFF RICHARD CANCELS FÊTE APPEARANCE DUE TO 'SUMMER HOLIDAY'

There were three smaller headlines lower down the front page:

FURY OVER PIN-THE-TAIL-ON-THE-DONKEY FAIR FIASCO

CROQUET TEAM IN CRISIS AS WOODWORM STRIKES ANTIQUE MALLETS

SHEEPDOG GALA IN DOUBT AS FARMERS FEUD OVER WHOSE SHEEP TO HERD

Yes, entertainment was a cutthroat business alright. But Clinton had absolutely no idea who Jepson's comedy rival might be. No other comedians or comediennes came to mind. That was no reason to throw out the idea, though. Twenty years as a top detective had taught him never to toss his hypotheses too early. As far as he was concerned, logic was often the enemy of deduction. Too often the illogical was overlooked. Every avenue had to be explored – even if it was an avenue with no pedestrians, traffic or lights on in the houses.

However, with white-wine spritzer now surging through his veins, and the excitement building as both his takeaway curry and the wildlife documentary narrated by Cameron Diaz drew nearer, the urge to venture down this particular avenue soon faded. This was a very funny murder mystery. And it would be an even funnier murder mystery if it was one motivated by comedy rivalry.

After a short period of woozy, thought-free contentedness, Clinton's mental attention turned to his favourite hobby – golf. Thanks to the triple-first Oxford mathematics graduate in human resources completely messing up the police holiday rota, Clinton hadn't been able to take a day off since June. Playing golf, like solving murders, was something that needed to be done regularly. If one failed to practise, a killer could walk free, vital evidence could be overlooked or, much worse, you could end up three-putting on the eighteenth green. Yes, at this time of the year, his golf swing would normally be in rude health, his putting in good shape, his long game lean and mean, and his fairway strut the talk of Goosing golf club. But it had been three weeks since he'd last graced his local course and he'd played his worst eighteen holes of the year on that outing. If he was to retain his title, he would have to practise – murder or no murder.

His guts rumbled, reminding him that they'd been proved right today and deserved a reward. With perfect timing, the doorbell rang. That must be his Indian takeaway. He licked his lips in anticipation and made a promise to himself to solve the Jepson case by Friday, win Saturday's tournament, and then eat a lamb madras on Sunday as a celebratory treat. And the poppadoms with it would be smothered in mango chutney.

Chapter 6

The Upper Goosing post office was eerily quiet for a quarter past eight on a Wednesday morning. By now, the queue was usually snaking past the scenes of Upper Goosing limited-edition prints, through the miniature ceramic postmen, postwomen, postcats and postmice, and all the way to the mini mountain of European Murder Destination of the Year 2015 souvenir hats, T-shirts, mugs, cups, saucers, teapots, tea towels, tea cosies, shortbread and piggy banks that dominated one corner of its well-stuffed interior.

It was possible everyone would avoid the post office this morning, thought Pattie Quirk the postmistress. That was often the villagers' knee-jerk reaction to getting wind of another murder – the culprit might still on be the loose, wanting to buy a newspaper to see if his deadly deeds had been reported, post a cryptic letter taunting the local police, make use of one of the highly popular 'no questions asked' post-office boxes, or simply select his next victim from the queue. She glanced at the village-scene prints in the aisle opposite. One beautiful vista of a sunrise over Peculiar Manor stood out. It retailed at fifty pounds. Maybe she should double the price – in case the murderer did want to pop in and grab a memento of their fatal visit. This village's tourist industry was built on its reputation for untimely death. Why shouldn't she sell souvenirs to killers as well as tourists?

Pattie's dreams of murderous profit were interrupted when her first customer of the day charged through the door so abruptly it almost fell off its hinges. It was her friend Jayne Trill. Time for a gossip while business was as dead as a Peculiar Manor butler.

'Hiya, Jayne!' squealed Pattie, almost knocking over her commemorative-stamp display.

As the door slammed shut, Jayne careered up to the till. 'Pattie, my dear. So good to see a friendly face. I didn't sleep a wink last night. What about you?'

'Fits and starts. First time I've been that close to a murder.'

Jayne tossed her head dramatically. 'Oh, I've been involved in so many murders I've lost count, my dear. I've even been the *killer* on a couple of occasions.'

Pattie's mouth fell open as she digested this news. Then her eyes lit up. 'Could I interest you in a high-quality print of one of your murder scenes? They're, erm, one hundred pounds each. But I could do you a special deal – two for a hundred and ninety-nine pounds, fifty pence.'

Jayne's eyes filled with mischief. 'I didn't commit the murders in Upper Goosing, my dear.'

Pattie frowned. 'You went to Lower Goosing to kill someone? Why would you do that? It's an awful place – full of vintage bed and breakfasts, cheap restaurants, modern cafés, fish-and-chip shops, classic British pubs, big-name retailers and easy-access car parks. And their buses always run on time. So, if you turn up at the bus stop five minutes late, like I always do, you've got to wait ages for the next one. I mean, what kind of public transport service is that?'

Jayne tittered triumphantly. 'I was being jocular.'

Pattie's forehead crinkled. 'You were being what?'

'I was jesting.'

Pattie strained to think. 'Is that like jousting?'

'Metaphorically speaking: you could say that.'

'I could say what, Jayne?'

'I was joking, Pattie, dear! This drama queen was referring to her starring roles in several murder mysteries performed by the Goosing Players.'

'Oh.' Pattie forced a smile. 'Very, erm … funny.'

'You didn't for one second think I could really take another man's life, did you, Pattie?'

Pattie's smile morphed from forced to unsure. 'Man or woman's life – no.'

'Oh, if I was to murder someone, it would most definitely be a man, Pattie.'

'Your husband, Graham, you mean?'

'Most probably. But I have no desire to clean the dishwasher, wash clothes, mop floors, disinfect toilets, vacuum carpets or remove hair from clogged plugholes myself just yet. So, while Graham's physical and mental faculties are more or less intact, he's worth a lot more to me alive than dead.'

'And he does a lot of jobs for your drama group, doesn't he?'

'One or two. He's the lighting technician, sound engineer, props man, publicity officer and set designer. The latter involves holding the stepladder when we're constructing the set. And I'm normally at the top of it – which always worries me because his hands are rather small.'

'You've got big hands. Why don't you hold the stepladder?'

Jayne sniffed the air. 'Some people were born to hold stepladders and others were born to climb them.'

Pattie pondered. 'I've never been up a stepladder.'

'That doesn't surprise me.' Jayne thought of something. 'Oh, yes! And if we're really short-handed, Graham plays the dead bodies.'

Pattie laughed. 'So, sometimes Graham *is* worth more to you dead than alive.'

'Yes. And, despite my continual protestations, he never has the decency to stop breathing for an extended period. In fact, during our last production, *Killing Me Hardly*, he embarked upon a sneezing fit five minutes after being strangled. It shattered the illusion for the seven people in the audience. But, thankfully, the five pensioners who travel in from Lower Goosing—'

'The nicely dressed old girls who attend every show, wear posh perfume, laugh in all the right places and stay to buy the cast and crew a round of drinks afterwards?'

'Yes, those five troublemakers. They had already nodded off because the air conditioning wasn't working, so news of Graham's faux pas thankfully stayed within Upper Goosing.' She twisted her mouth. 'Graham always takes the old girls up on their post-performance-drink offer and orders a bottle of what can only be described as "foreign lager".'

Pattie winced. 'Oh, I am sorry. I didn't know that. I thought he was a dyed-in-the-wool Goosing Ale man.'

'He should be. I've lost count of the number of times I've told him the Trills' place at the top of village high society is hard-won and easily lost. If word gets round that my husband is a foreign-lager drinker … well, we'll be thrown off the croquet team.'

'How are your mallets by the way? I didn't know woodworm could grow that big.'

Jayne's cheeks flushed. 'Graham is still "sorting it". If he hadn't stored them in his carpenter friend's workshop in the first place, we would never have landed in this holey mess.' She tossed her shoulders. 'Anyway, let's please stop talking about my lesser half. It's giving me worse indigestion than that awful venison vindaloo.'

'I quite enjoyed it.'

Jayne frowned.

'The, erm, evening I meant. The vindaloo was pretty average.'

Jayne's frown intensified.

'Below average.'

Jayne was now frowning above and beyond the call of disapproving duty.

'Let's face it, it was bloody awful.'

Jayne nodded. 'I'm glad you agree with me.'

'I do.' Pattie straightened her stamp display. 'So, poor Jepson won't be appearing in any more of your plays, will he?'

'No, he won't.'

'What's your next production?'

'*Murder at Dress Rehearsal*. It's a one-act play by somebody called Paul Mathews.'

'Never heard of him.'

'Neither had I. But he wrote to me practically begging the Goosing Players to perform his play. I checked out his publicity photo. He's shaven-headed but seems to have good teeth so I gracefully agreed. He was so grateful, he promised to come along to one of our rehearsals.'

'That was nice. Who's in it?'

'Well, after a couple of cameos – and with a lack of thespian availability due to members thoughtlessly booking summer holidays – Jepson had graduated to the lead role.'

'Oh! Have you already started rehearsals?'

'Yes – eight weeks ago. It's been the longest two months of my amateur-dramatic life, Pattie. Lady Peculiar warned me about his chronic stubbornness. And, much as I hate to admit it, the mad old bat was right. That miserable old butler wouldn't take direction. And he thought he was a comedy genius. But onstage that man was only ever funny-strange – never funny-ha-ha.'

'Why didn't you kick him off the production?'

Jayne huffed. 'I did try. But he threatened to create a comedy amateur-dramatics character for his stand-up act and base it on me. I couldn't have that, Pattie.'

'No, you couldn't have that, Jayne.'

'But Jepson's performance isn't something I shall have to worry about now.'

'No, it isn't something you'll have to worry about now, Jayne.'

'And there'll be no butler satirising *me* on the comedy stage.'

'No, our comedy stages will be satirical-butler-free, Jayne.'

'Because Jepson has exited stage left.'

'That's right, Jayne. I mean left, Jayne. I mean—'

'And, as always, the show must go on!'

'It must, Jayne. It must go on. And on and on. And on and on and—'

37

The post-office door swung mercifully open and a short, rosy-cheeked, bespectacled man in his fifties greeted them with a massive smile.

'Good morning, ladies!'

'Graham,' sighed Jayne. 'How many times have I told you? When talking to your long-suffering wife in a room containing three or more people, address me first and then move on to the less important individuals.'

He gritted his teeth. 'Good morning, darling wife.' He ungritted. 'And good morning, dear Pattie.'

'That's better, Graham,' sneered Jayne. 'So, pray tell, is there a reason for your intrusion or have you just mistaken the post office for a supermarket selling bottled foreign lager?'

Graham raised an excited finger. 'I've had an idea about a replacement for poor old Jepson – God rest his soul.'

'Let's not bring God into this, Graham. He's never helped us sell tickets for opening night. Just spit out whatever you've got to say and then leave us to discuss the high-society topics of the day without unwanted male interference.'

'Let's ask that bloke who runs the Getting Away With Murder museum with his missus.'

Jayne tutted. 'If by that ugly colloquialism "missus" you mean "wife", Graham, I assume you are referring to Mr and Mrs Willie?'

'Yeah, the Willies. Herman Willie does loads of roleplay at the museum: serial killers; psychos; husbands who've been pushed over the mental precipice by their overbearing tyrannical spouses, taken matters into their own hands and –'

'Yes, yes, yes,' interrupted Jayne. 'We get the idea. But why would Herman Willie agree to help us? He's never been involved with our drama society before. And I don't remember him or Morticia ever attending one of our shows.'

'I know. But this is how we'll sell it to him. It's a murder-mystery play, right? So him playing the lead role would be good publicity for their museum. Same type of clientele, isn't it? We could advertise the museum in the programme. Ask Dickie

38

Blinder to do a bit in the *Goosing Times* about it, you know. Quid pro quo.'

Jayne bit her lip. 'I suppose it's not a totally stupid idea.'

'Sounds like a great idea to me!' chirped Pattie.

Jayne glared at her.

'I mean, it sounds like quite a good idea, Graham.'

Jayne kept on glaring.

'By "good idea", I meant "not a totally stupid idea".'

Graham winked. 'Don't worry, Pattie, I know *exactly* what you meant.'

Jayne switched her glare to her husband. 'Graham, please! You're flirting!'

Graham made a face. 'I'm what?'

'Flirting! With a woman who's at least five years older than I am!'

'Actually, Jayne,' squeaked Pattie, 'as we went to school together, I think we're both the same—'

'Get out, Graham!' ordered Jayne, pushing him in front of her. 'Pattie, I won't be taking the *Daily Mail* today. Graham has spoiled my plans for a quiet morning with a quality newspaper.'

'But I'm being helpful!' protested Graham, as he was bundled out of the door.

'Erm, bye,' croaked Pattie, as the Trills disappeared from view.

Chapter 7

As Inspector Trump opened the door to Detective Superintendent Euan Block's smart air-conditioned office on the top floor of Upper Goosing police station, his highly tuned detective senses informed him that his boss was not a happy law-enforcement bunny. Block's downturned mouth, crumpled forehead, flushed cheeks, crossed arms, furious eyes and nasal breathing were subtle signs that could easily be missed. A lesser detective – one with duller powers of perception – might not realise what was in store. But Clinton knew alright – he was about to receive a dressing down from his boss for not following police protocol at Peculiar Manor last night. And he would handle his latest transgression as he always did when facing authority in times of trouble. He would be as evasive as possible, pile on the excuses, deny as much as he could without being fired, and try and change the subject wherever possible.

Clinton flopped into a red leather swivel chair opposite Block's desk. 'Beautiful piece of seating paraphernalia, superintendent. Did you choose the colour yourself? Cerise, is it? Or more burgundy? It's difficult to tell under the strobe lighting.'

'Don't play your games with me, Trump. Just listen to my questions and answer them without getting on my nerves even more than you have already.'

'I'm sorry to hear you're having problems with your nerves, sir. Perhaps you should see a doctor? But don't try and book an appointment with Dr Black. He was battered to death with a candlestick in Brokenshire Central Library yesterday. Terrible business.' He swivelled the chair nonchalantly. 'Delayed my passage to Peculiar Manor, which meant I was rather pushed for time when I arrived.'

'Is that your excuse for not examining the corpse?'

'The Major gave me a full description of Jepson's body, as it was found, which was good enough for me.'

Block tutted. 'And what if the Major killed him, eh?'

'Oh, I very much doubt that.'

'Based on what evidence?'

'The Major doesn't have the organisational skills to commit a murder.'

The superintendent appeared at risk of spontaneously combusting. 'He was in the army for forty years! He's killed more people than I've had lukewarm cups of coffee at the Tourist Trap café. You underestimate an ex-military man at your peril, Trump.'

'My father was a military man.' Clinton swivelled some more. 'There's an extraordinary story behind how he enlisted, actually. It all began back in 1977 during the Queen's Silver Jubilee. He was running a pub at the time and one of the Buckingham Palace guardsmen left his bearskin in the ladies' lavatories and—'

'Stop waffling, Trump!' shouted Block. 'You always waffle when I'm trying to get some sense out of you.' His shoulders slumped. 'I don't know why I'm even trying. I can't remember the last time I heard you say anything remotely sensible.'

'If you'll allow me to return to the subject of the Major, we can talk sense. Because my gut instinct informs me the old warhorse isn't involved in any way.'

'Your gut?' grumbled Block.

'Yes. And Lady Peculiar assures me she had nothing to do with Jepson's death. A woman of her social standing would never lie to a police detective – it's simply not the done thing. So, we can scratch at least two names off our list of possible suspects. And that, in my book, is solid detective work.'

'It's solid something.' Block took a deep breath. 'Now, I'm still waiting for the official scenes of crime report, but our guy told me he found nothing on or around the body. No fingerprints, no fibres, no hair, no nothing.'

'Your final "no" in that sentence was extraneous, sir.'

'Button it!' blasted Block, before taking a few seconds to compose himself. 'I'm also waiting on the autopsy to confirm the details of how Jepson died. I'm ninety-nine per cent certain foul play is involved. But we can't go public about it being a murder until a report confirming he was forcibly drowned is on my desk.'

Clinton patted his stomach. 'My gut has already confirmed it as murder, sir. I told Lady Peculiar and her curry ladies as much, last night.'

The superintendent bared his canines. 'You did *what*?'

'When you have a gift as big as mine, sir, you simply have to share it.'

'Stop loving yourself and open your ears, Trump! This investigation is going to be about cold hard police work – done the proper way. And not by processing everything through your guts.'

'Absolutely. You can rely on me. I'm the man for the job. Now, is that everything?'

Block's lip curled. 'This is your last chance to show me you're a detective worthy of the job title.'

'And I shall grab it more firmly than I've ever grabbed a last chance before.' He swivelled triumphantly. 'Rest assured, the *Goosing Times* will very soon be reporting that Inspector Trump has solved the murder.'

Block half smiled. 'Reporting that Inspector Trump *and* his deputy, Detective Constable Troy Dinkel, have solved the murder.'

Clinton's guts rumbled in fear. 'Dinkel? You're not putting him on the case?'

'Yes, I am. It's the highest-profile crime in Brokenshire this year. The tourist-trade vultures might revel in this village's reputation as the murder capital of Europe but I don't. It needs to be solved quickly. And two heads are better than one. Especially when one of those heads is yours.'

Clinton was lost for words, as the superintendent pressed a buzzer on his desk.

'Send in DC Dinkel.'

A few seconds later, a fresh-faced twenty-something in a crisp grey suit and dark-blue tie strode into the room.

'Morning, superintendent.' He nodded at Clinton. 'Detective inspector.'

Clinton still wasn't speaking.

Block chuckled. 'You've stopped your waffling I see, Trump. I'll have to pair you two up more often.' He gestured to another red leather swivel chair next to his desk. 'Sit down, Dinkel. I want to hear your thoughts on what we'll assume is a murder.'

Clinton glared at his junior colleague as he took his seat but remained silent.

'Thank you for the opportunity, superintendent. Now, first thing that came to mind was this death bears a striking resemblance to one in a book written by our resident author, Agatha Twisty. It's one of her lesser-known murder-mystery novels – *Murder in an Odd Manor*.'

'As you know, Dinkel, I'm a big fan of the murder-mystery genre. But I haven't read that particular tome. Enlighten us.'

'To cut a long story short, sir, it's set in an idyllic English village – not dissimilar to Upper Goosing – and a murder takes place one August evening at Odd Manor. The long-serving butler is murdered in the kitchens during a big dinner party for all the well-to-do ladies of the village. If you don't mind me adding in a spoiler, sir—'

'Not at all. Very kind of you to forewarn me, Dinkel. I'll be noting that in your yearly appraisal.'

It was Clinton's turn to look as if he was about to spontaneously combust.

Dinkel grinned. 'Thank you, sir. Well, Lady Odd planned it, and her male friend the Colonel did the deed while everyone was tucking into the main course.'

The superintendent glared at Clinton. 'What about the detective in this tale, Dinkel – how did he shape up?'

'There were two actually, sir. One detective constable who knew what he was doing, and his detective inspector who was a bit of a blunderer. The inspector allowed a serious of obvious clues to pass by unnoticed, didn't follow protocol, and almost let the murderer slip through his fingers. It was only thanks to his inexperienced deputy that the murderous plot was uncovered and Lady Odd and the Colonel were arrested and charged.' He glanced at Clinton. 'The senior detective took all the credit, of course.'

'Quite right, too!' snapped Clinton, finally regaining the power of speech.

'Shut up and listen, Trump,' barked the superintendent. 'Carry on, Dinkel.'

'It got me thinking, sir. The Major is a massive Agatha Twisty fan – he and I attend the same book club and he's read every one of her novels a dozen times. He was first on the scene. He chucked the body in a freezer without asking anyone – almost as if he was trying to destroy evidence or something. And, from what I've heard, Lady Peculiar wasn't Jepson's biggest fan.'

Clinton crossed his arms. 'Why would her ladyship and the Major stage a murder in a way that could point the finger of suspicion at them?'

Dinkel continued. 'That's just it! Everyone will think it's too obvious and discount them. Plus, mirroring a scene from one of Twisty's novels could implicate any of her readers – pretty much everyone in the village reads her books.'

'I don't,' grumbled Clinton.

Block snorted. 'That doesn't surprise me in the least, Trump. You should try brushing up on great detectives – fictional and non-fictional. You might learn something.' He turned to Dinkel. 'I like your thinking, constable. And I see where you're going with the Lady Peculiar and Major theory. But my sixth sense is kicking in now and it tells me they aren't the murdering type.'

'Your sixth sense?' muttered Clinton, sounding highly unimpressed.

'Yes. And you, Trump, might crack more cases if you paid a bit more attention to what's left of your five senses.' He faced Dinkel again. 'But our discussion about Lady Peculiar has jogged my memory. Her gardener, Cripps, is an ex-con.'

'Oh, yes,' replied the constable. 'I was coming to that, sir. I did a bit of research this morning. Cripps has done time for quite a few things. Not murder. But some pretty vicious assaults. And, on another day, some of those assaults could have ended up with someone being killed.'

'Excellent work, constable. I can see you're going to go far.' He switched his attention to the inspector. 'And you, Trump, I hope you'll go far, too.'

Clinton beamed with a satisfaction Cheshire cats would struggle to emulate. 'Thank you, sir.'

'As far away from here as possible – once this is over.'

Clinton's smile vanished.

'Now, I want both of you detectives to go and speak to that Cripps fellow before he legs it. And get a concrete statement from him.'

'Does it really require the both of us, sir?' whined Clinton. 'Dinkel's just about capable of performing the task himself. I could concentrate on the cerebral side of things.'

'Yes, it does require both of you. Cripps is a nasty piece of work. He's got a temper shorter than a dwarf tying his shoelaces. If that ex-con turns violent, Trump, I want you to deal with him.'

'Why me, sir?'

'One – you're the senior detective. Two – you've got a thicker skull.'

Dinkel stifled a laugh.

Block stood up. 'Right, stop cluttering up my office and move your derrières!'

Chapter 8

Lady Peculiar was in her drawing room sipping Earl Grey – accompanied by a slice of Sorrento lemon and dash of manuka honey – with her usual devotion to tea-drinking decorum. She savoured the refreshing burst of bergamot on her tongue and perused the face of the seventeenth-century grandfather clock in the far corner. It was 9.50 am. Her gardener should be here any minute.

She had taken two more delicate sips when the stout, bearded figure of Cripps bustled into the room. He was dressed in his dark-green work overalls and heavy black boots.

'Morning, your ladyship,' he growled in his gravelly rural accent. 'You wanted to see me?'

'Yes, one did. Please make yourself comfortable.'

The gardener planted himself in a nearby armchair and glanced up at the face of the grandfather clock.

'Don't worry. This won't take long, Cripps.'

'Good, because I've got to rake the orchard. And that job's an absolute killer.'

Lady Peculiar coughed daintily. 'It is with the greatest of sadness that one has to inform you that Jepson passed away last night, during my curry evening.'

Cripps sniffed. 'I heard already.'

'Oh. Well … bad news always travels fast in Upper Goosing.'

'And good news,' huffed Cripps. 'Because I never liked the miserable old coot. And, if we're being honest with each other, neither did you, your ladyship.'

Lady Peculiar carefully placed her bone-china cup on the arm of her tea throne. 'Jepson served this manor for many years, Cripps, so we shan't speak ill of the dead. We shall arrange his funeral, afford him the customary eulogy – offering only generous words in his memory – and not speak of the pig-headed, irascible, cold-hearted, professional troublemaker everyone at the manor knew only too well.'

Cripps twisted his mouth. 'I never understand all this tiptoeing around when someone's snuffed it. Tell it how it is, that's what I say. It's not like they can sue you for slander. Stand up at the funeral and say "I never liked him. Good riddance to bad butlering rubbish. Anyone in this church could do a better job than him with one hand tied behind their back."'

Lady Peculiar smiled politely. 'An interesting sentiment. But, as in many areas of life, honesty may not be the best policy here – for reasons of social etiquette *and* criminal investigation. You see, the detective who was here believes Jepson was murdered.'

'Which detective was that?'

'Detective Inspector Clinton Trump.'

Cripps rolled his eyes. 'I wouldn't listen to anything that old fraud Trump tells you. What comes out of his mouth is usually only fit to feed my roses.'

'On that point, we'll have to disagree. One has a lot of admiration for the detective inspector, as do other many other highly respected members of the community from lower down the social ladder.'

'People round here need to open their eyes. Trump is like one of them peacocks. He's all strut, tail and feathers, with a brain the size of a walnut. He hasn't got me fooled. That peacock's time will come. Just like it did for Jepson.'

Lady Peculiar drank more tea and pondered his response. 'Moving on from peacocks, one knows you would never return to a life of excessively violent and, in some cases, sadistically vengeful, crime, Cripps. But do you have an alibi for last night? Because the police will want to account for the whereabouts of all the staff at the time of Jepson's death.' She sipped again. 'Especially those with a criminal record as impressive as yours.'

Cripps stroked his beard. 'I was home alone. Usually go to my reformed-prisoners' gardening club on Tuesday nights. But my sciatica was playing me up something rotten, so I gave it a swerve.'

'Sciatica? You never mentioned you were a fellow sufferer.'

'Unlike some dearly departed butlers I could mention, I didn't like to grumble.'

'What medication have you been prescribed for it?'

'I haven't been to see any doctors. I don't trust them. Last one I saw, I put *him* in hospital.'

'Oh.' She finished her tea and leant forward. 'One wouldn't make this offer for all of one's staff. In fact, one would only make it for you – Peculiar Manor's most faithful and trusted employee. And, as of yesterday evening, its longest-serving.'

'What offer, your ladyship?'

She took a deep breath. 'If you require an alibi, just let one know.'

Cripps' eyebrows dipped. 'You're offering to provide me with a false alibi?'

'Correct. One has a couple of exceptional acquaintances who owe one favours. And they would be delighted to provide the police with a statement that you were spending Tuesday evening with them. You'll be scratched off any list of suspects and avoid a lot of bother at police stations and being the subject of village gossip. The manor will also benefit, as it will stop you being diverted from your gardening duties. And the orchard is in desperate need of attention.'

His eyebrows bounced back up. 'I appreciate the offer. But I don't want to exploit your kindness any more than I've done already during my five years here. You gave me a job when nobody else in this village would. And that was, and always will be, all I ever ask from you, your ladyship.'

'Oh, come now. It was nothing out of the ordinary, Cripps. The estate urgently needed the services of a gardener after the last one was murdered in cold blood by one of the maids – such a tragedy, because no one has ever been able to turn sheets like she did. You were available, possessed the necessary skills, and were happy to accept the terms of employment.'

'I hear what you're saying, your ladyship. But if I need an alibi, I'm perfectly capable of finding one myself. So, with respect, it's a "no" from me.'

Their conversation was interrupted by the drawing-room door swinging open. Standing in the doorway were Inspector Trump and Constable Dinkel.

'Morning, your ladyship!' tooted Clinton, with a swish of his bouffant.

'And good morning to you, detectives.'

Clinton tossed his head. 'Your maid let us in. Apologies for the lack of notice but this is simply a routine call to speak to you, the Major and the members of your staff who haven't been drowned in mango chutney.' He spied Cripps. 'Just the man – the first name on our list!'

'Should one stay here?' asked Lady Peculiar, exchanging a glance with Cripps. 'Or make oneself disappear?'

Constable Dinkel nodded. 'We'd appreciate it if you left the three of us alone, your ladyship. We'll speak with you later.'

Lady Peculiar bowed her head, lifted herself from her tea throne, waved regally and departed.

Cripps glared at both policemen as they sat down on a sofa.

'So, tell me, how are things in the manor gardens, Mr Cripps?' asked the inspector in a cheery tone.

'Pretty rosy,' sneered the gardener.

'Greenfly been a problem this summer?'

Cripps stared at Clinton. 'Same old pests come round here every year.'

'What about vine weevil? Little devils have moved into my allotment. This year's tomato crop is going to be terribly disappointing compared to the bumper yields of 2016 and 2017.'

Cripps didn't appear too distraught by this news.

'Looks like I shall have to top up my cherry-tomato supplies at the village mini-mart. And you know the prices they charge. It's criminal, really.' Clinton heaved a sigh. 'It wouldn't surprise me if the owners deliberately introduced the little blighters into the allotments to restrict supply and drive up the price. I may have a word with the superintendent when I return to the office. See if we can launch a covert investigation.' He waved a finger. 'Police work isn't all about catching murderers. Sometimes it's about bringing down the price of tomatoes.'

The constable intervened. 'Mr Cripps, we want to discuss your whereabouts last—'

'Let your senior officer speak first, Dinkel,' interrupted Clinton. 'The youth of today,' he muttered in Cripps' direction, shaking his head. 'No respect for authority. It's sad.'

Cripps flicked a sympathetic glance in Dinkel's direction.

'Now, Cripps,' continued the inspector, 'you're an old hand at this interview game. We'll dispense with the good-cop–bad-cop routine because we're all busy men, with important jobs to do – mine being far and away the most important, it goes without saying. So, I shall come straight to the point. There's been a murder.'

The constable nudged him. 'It's not one hundred per cent confirmed yet that it is a—'

Clinton nudged back. 'Ignore my colleague, Mr Cripps. He's not very au fait with genius-detective protocol.' He blinked twice. 'Where was I? Oh, yes. There's been a murder.'

'Has that been one hundred per cent confirmed?' asked Cripps, with a sarcastic sneer.

'What? Oh, erm, no. Not one hundred per cent. But it won't be long now. And my gut has already confirmed it, so let's not dwell on that particular point for too long, lest we become distracted from the matter in hand.'

'And what's that, Mr Detective Inspector?'

'As I was saying – there's been a murder.'

The grandfather clock chimed ten so loudly that everyone had to wait for it to play out its timely reminder. While it did so, Clinton checked his hair was as magnificently springy as it should be at this time of the morning – failing to notice when the chimes had ended.

The gardener huffed. 'I haven't got all day to watch you preening yourself.'

'I know you haven't, Mr Cripps,' chirped Clinton. 'Be with you in a second.' He whispered to his colleague. 'I forgot to mention, I'm meeting a contact for elevenses. And I won't need you with me.' He turned back to Cripps. 'So, what were we discussing?'

Dinkel answered. 'There's been a murder. Though it hasn't been one hundred per cent confirmed yet.'

Clinton's jowls tensed. 'Are you deliberately trying to annoy me, constable?'

'No, inspector. It's just—'

'Because South East England's greatest detective is starting to feel more than a tad annoyed.'

'Sorry, sir, but I wasn't—'

'And when I start to feel annoyed I start to lose my thread.'

'Do you, sir? I can't say I've ever noticed you—'

'And when I start to lose my thread, I start to … um, well, you know.' He searched for a word that wasn't coming to mind. 'I start to, erm …'

'Waffle, sir?'

'Please, constable! Never describe me as a waffler. I never waffle. Ever. Waffling isn't something I've ever practised. My investigations are waffle-free. And I never work with wafflers. So, if you want to stay the right side of me, you'll refrain from waffling in my presence.'

Constable Dinkel clamped his mouth shut and nodded.

'That's better. Now, Mr Cripps …' He took a deep breath. '… there's been a murder.'

Cripps cracked his massive knuckles. 'Let me save you the bother of coming up with your clever questions. I wasn't anywhere near this manor last night. You ask anyone at that meal. Check the statements. My name won't be mentioned.'

Clinton smoothed his bouffant. 'We haven't actually taken any statements yet.' He turned to Dinkel. 'My junior colleague here will be picking up all the mundane, day-to-day investigative work. I shall be leading on the brilliant brainwork, high-level hypothesising and, ultimately, superb solving of this case to the relief and eternal gratitude of everyone. Possibly including Her Majesty the Queen.' He clutched his tie knot. 'There may even be a knighthood in it for me.'

'Yeah, whatever. But when you speak to them curry-club ladies, you'll see I'm telling the truth. I finished at six, got home by seven, and was tucked up in bed by ten.'

'Can anyone confirm that?' asked the inspector.

The gardener's lips rippled. 'Maybe. Memory's a bit hazy – had a couple of whiskies before I hit the sack. Think I might have had a visitor. Or popped round to borrow a whisky glass from a friend. Or rung my dear old mum for an extended chit-chat. You know the kinda thing.'

'The kind of thing that, once you've agreed a story with someone, can be used as a false alibi?' suggested Constable Dinkel.

The inspector waved an admonishing finger. 'Dinkel – how discourteous! This man has given up his time to take my questions and all you can do is throw around unsubstantiated insinuations. Well, I shall be having words with the superintendent about this!'

'No need to get your truncheon in a twist, Trump. The kid's got a right to ask questions like that. You could learn something from him. Because, so far, all you've done is squawk at me like a demented parrot that there's been a murder when, from what the kid says, it's not even definite yet.'

Clinton stood up. 'There has been a murder – I'd stake my professional reputation on it.'

'That's not saying much!' spluttered Cripps.

'What's that supposed to mean?' asked the inspector, sounding mortally offended. 'I'm South East England's greatest detective.'

'Says who?' scoffed the gardener.

'Says me. And, erm, Constable Dinkel.' He nudged his colleague. 'Say it, Dinkel.'

'You're South East England's greatest detective, sir.'

Cripps glared at the inspector. 'Before today, I only ever heard you saying it, Trump. Again and again and again.'

'Then you're not moving in the right circles. Too much time spent talking to your plants, perhaps. A little more human contact wouldn't go amiss. The intelligent variety, of course – the Upper, not Lower, Goosing set.'

Cripps' shoulders hunched. 'You think you're so clever, don't you?'

'Yes, I do, actually,' replied Clinton with the utmost sincerity. 'I obtained a lower-second-class honours degree in Advanced Golfing Studies from Brokenshire University. I would have got an upper second but I misread "Tuesday" for "Thursday" on the exam noticeboard and turned up two days late for my driving test. But what's that got to do with anything?'

The gardener shook his head for five seconds. 'You're nothing but a pumped-up peacock, Trump.'

'Is that intended as an insult?' asked the inspector. 'Because I'm rather fond of peacocks. I used to pretend I was one as a child, using nothing more than a pair of mother's oriental fans, a feather boa and my navy-blue pyjamas.'

'You wanna play peacock, we can play peacock. I'll be the pea. You can be the ...' Cripps checked himself. 'Well, you work it out, detective genius.'

Dinkel stifled a snort.

'Work what out?' enquired Clinton, though he received no reply. 'What do I have to work out?'

Cripps chuckled. 'South East England's greatest detective, eh?'

'What is it, Dinkel? What have I missed?'

The constable's cheeks twitched with suppressed laughter. 'Erm ... nothing ... sir.'

'I'm almost tempted to return to a life of crime,' cackled Cripps. 'Peacock poaching, perhaps? Or maybe just pea poaching, as I'm a gardener. Might give you more of a chance of catching me.'

Dinkel's eyes bulged with non-tittering effort.

The inspector's cheeks flushed. 'I've no idea what you're snickering about, Mr Cripps, but my gut instinct tells me I am being insulted. And I don't intend to stand around being slighted any longer.' Clinton hoisted up the constable. 'Come on, Dinkel, look lively – we're finished with Mr Cripps!'

'Are we?' asked Dinkel. 'Already?'

'Yes! And before you ask, I'm one hundred per cent certain of it!'

Chapter 9

After abandoning Constable Dinkel at Peculiar Manor – leaving him to take formal statements from Lady Peculiar, the Major and the surviving staff then catch a bus back to the police station on his own – Inspector Trump hopped in the sportiest unmarked police car in the Upper Goosing police fleet and headed for the Tourist Trap café for elevenses with Ms Savage, the butcher's widow.

His café date was already there – fifteen minutes early. But it was always sensible to arrive in good time for elevenses when dining out. Every English country lady knew that.

Josephine Savage had nabbed the square table in the corner – the one with the best view of the village green – just before four American tourists had charged into the establishment, thundering the floorboards with their colossal casual footwear and demanding 'the best seat in the house'. The waitress had nodded obediently and guided them to the second-best seat in the house – the one with a pleasant view of the well-watered golf course and the meandering River Sticks which neatly bordered it.

Josephine was just beginning to wonder why anyone would want to thrash a ball around such beautiful greenery for hours, instead of just enjoying the scenery, when a tall dark figure came into view on the other side of the café. The individual was sporting a white baseball cap and the type of tasteless sweater popularised by golfers – a ghastly deep-red garment splattered with white and dark-blue diamonds. Her mind wandered as the person approached her table. Why were golfers immune from the carefully constructed norms of English country fashion? Indeed, any country's fashion? And what went through golfers' minds when they admired themselves in the mirror, preparing for eighteen holes of expletive-peppered ball-bashing? It must be a similar phenomenon to that whereby otherwise respectable men over seventy suddenly started wearing inappropriately short athletics trunks around the village when the temperature hit twenty-five degrees Celsius. Come to think of it, most of those elderly perpetrators were regulars on the Goosing golf circuit. Yes, there was definitely something very peculiar about golfers. Still, at least you could spot them from twenty metres in a crowd and avoid when necessary – which was almost always.

She jolted out of her golfing reverie and peered at the unexpected visitor who was now only a couple of metres away. She'd assumed it was a man approaching her table – perhaps one searching for a victim to hold hostage for ten minutes and regale with stories of birdies, bunkers and bad luck over a cup of tea. But when the person removed their baseball cap, Josephine recognised the female face. It was Svetlana – the Russian who'd been sitting two places along from her at dinner last night. Thankfully, the huge woman who ran the local Weight Losers' club had been seated between them and acted as a physical and conversational barrier. Svetlana possessed the most humourless character in Upper Goosing – and anyone who'd ever spent an evening with the pub darts team knew what a serious accusation that was.

'You wait for someone, huh?' sneered Svetlana in an accent heavier than a bronze statue of Lenin.

'Yes,' croaked Josephine, sensing a Russian interrogation was imminent.

Svetlana almost smiled. 'I know who you meeting.'

'You do?'

'You have rendezvous with Trump.' She tapped her right ear. 'I hear you make secret arrangement. My ears like satellite dish.'

Josephine took a sharp breath. 'There's nothing secret about it. This is a public place.'

'Conversation will be public?'

'No. It will be private.'

The Russian nodded. 'Of course it will, Miss Master's-in-Advanced-Criminology. You will have what you English call "cosy little chat" with inspector who investigate murder. And that strange behaviour. In Russia, we not allow police officer to drink tea and eat cream cake with suspect.'

Josephine's response caught in her throat for a second. 'What do you mean "suspect"?'

'I saw you leave dining room last night. You near door. Easy for you to go to kitchen, kill butler and come back.'

Josephine tried to remain as calm as possible. 'How could I do that when I never left the room?' She gulped for air. 'I didn't murder Jepson!'

'That what you say.'

'And it's the truth!'

'When Lady Peculiar give talk about history of poppadom, and everyone focus on her, Svetlana see you sneak out.'

Ms Savage's tone hardened. 'Whoever you saw leave, Svetlana, it wasn't me.'

The Russian put both hands on her hips. 'Svetlana see you.'

'I don't know what you were drinking last night, but I can only assume you smuggled in some cheap Moscow vodka and the resulting hangover has affected your memory. Because I *didn't* leave that room until the inspector and I departed for the kitchens.'

The Russian's eyes still burnt with suspicion. 'Maybe I wait for inspector and give him statement, huh? Or speak with my boyfriend.'

'What's your boyfriend got to do with this?'

'He editor of local newspaper. Sometimes journalist know more than police. This happen often in Russia.'

'Yes. And it rarely ends well for the journalist.'

Svetlana inhaled through her nose. 'You mean, like it not "end well" for your butcher husband?'

Josephine's nose twitched. 'What's that supposed to mean?'

'In Russia, when someone fall in mincing machine, they usually have … helping hand.'

'In case you hadn't noticed, this isn't Russia.'

'No. It England. And it much less fun here. Especially if you marry woman whose husbands all have strange accident.'

Josephine's face lost its remaining colour. 'I don't know what you're talking about.'

'You have different husbands. But same result. Before butcher, there baker. Before baker … candlestick maker.'

'My first husband manufactured sustainably sourced ornamental scented-candle holders, actually. There's a big difference.'

'Yes. They three times price. But difference not matter to first husband after "accident" with hundred gallon of liquid metal.'

Josephine swallowed hard. 'He overbalanced on his step ladder.'

'Easy to do, huh? And your second husband – buried alive in own cake mixture when attempt to cook world's largest Victoria sponge go wrong.'

'I kept telling him the mixture wasn't thin enough,' squeaked Josephine. 'But he wouldn't listen!'

Svetlana's eyes narrowed. 'I can see you work *real* hard for your Master's in Advanced Criminology.'

They were interrupted by the sound of Inspector Trump bowling through the door.

'Morning, ladies and gentlemen!' He flashed a knee-crippling smile at the lady behind the serving area. 'Mrs Trap! What a wonderful surprise to see our favourite café owner back so soon after her near-fatal dose of salmonella. We were all thrilled you pulled through – because nobody glazes a tartlet like you do, my dear!'

Mrs Trap stopped stuffing one of her own cream horns into her mouth, wiped both hands on her dirty pinny, and spluttered in her distinctive rural drawl. 'It'll take more than a contaminated batch of chocolate eclairs to send me six feet under!'

'I'm elated to hear it!' piped Clinton, as he glided to the cake display. 'Now, I do hope there's a honey-glazed fruit tartlet available for this ravenous detective!'

Mrs Trap retrieved a glob of cream from her lips and sucked it off her finger. 'Let's see what I got for your sweet tooth.'

'It's not just one sweet tooth, Mrs Trap – it's a whole set of them!'

The owner giggled, along with the other village ladies in the café, as Clinton mock-bowed to his adoring audience.

Svetlana scowled at the inspector and then turned to Josephine. 'Take my advice, *Ms* Savage. Don't spend too much time with Trump.' She grinned in a way a James Bond villain might do while stroking a white pussycat. 'You never know what detective dig up from your past.'

Svetlana turned and marched out of the café, leaving a shaken and stirred Josephine to contemplate her next move.

A minute later, the inspector arrived with two plates – each bearing a fruit tartlet.

'Good morning, Ms Savage.'

'Hello, inspector,' she replied flatly.

'Tea's still brewing. I always prefer a four-bag pot. They normally only triple bag here. And it's only two for the tourists – one if they're being particularly loud and obnoxious. But Mrs Trap and I have a special four-bag arrangement.' He checked nobody could overhear. 'Just don't let anyone else know about it, or it could jeopardise my whole tea-drinking operation.'

'I won't,' mumbled Josephine.

'You don't mind if I bagsy the strawberry tartlet, do you? It was the last one and they're my absolute favourite.' Clinton sat down and passed her a plate. 'I managed to salvage you a peach one.'

'Thank you.'

'Our American friends over there are polishing off their peach tartlets with gusto, so I'm sure your more refined English palate will find it agreeable.'

She pushed her plate away. 'Actually, I'm not feeling at all peckish.'

'No? Then you won't mind if I help you out.' He grabbed her peach tartlet. 'What a team we are. The two cake-a-teers – all for one, and one for all!' He took a large bite and smacked his lips. 'Hmm. Tastes more pear than peach. Perhaps Mrs Trap misread the label on the cans? Easy mistake to make. She mixed up the cocoa and curry powder last week and the resulting Black Forest gateau could have blown a small child's head off. I'm not sure we'll see the German coach party who bought it ever again. I just hope they made it back to Dresden.'

Josephine wasn't listening.

'Anyway, enough of curried cakes. We have a curried murder to focus on. And before I consume any more strawberry, peach or pear tartlets, I want to say that I'm looking forward tremendously to tapping into your criminal expertise over four-bag tea.'

'Actually, I've been giving it some further thought, and I'm not sure it would be appropriate for me to become involved in your investigation, inspector.'

Clinton froze, his strawberry tartlet about to enter his mouth. 'Why ever not? I have to solve the Jepson murder by the end of the week so I can focus my energy one hundred per cent on retaining my golfing crown!' He lowered his voice. 'There's a rather snazzy jumper in the members' shop that I'm planning to buy with the prize money. Bright green and turquoise checks with splashes of earthy brown in the shape of bunny rabbits.' He bit into his strawberry tartlet. 'So, if you want to see yours truly parading up the high street in all his sartorial and sporting glory, you'll lend a helping hand.'

Josephine shuddered at those last two words. 'You must have other detectives assisting you.'

Clinton nibbled his tartlet. 'Only that wet-behind-the-ears deputy of mine – Dinkel. He's about as much use as a baseball cap in a hailstorm.'

'But isn't a baseball cap rather useful in a hailstorm?'

'Not if you refuse to wear baseball caps, as I do.'

She fiddled with her jacket buttons. 'I'm sorry for leading you up the advanced-criminology garden path, inspector, but I don't feel I can help you.'

Mrs Trap arrived with a large pot of tea.

'Here we are, my lovelies! One very special pot of tea for a very special detective sergeant.'

'I'm a detective inspector, actually, Mrs Trap.'

The café owner cackled and nudged Josephine's shoulder. 'Ooh! He's a detective inspector, actually! I shall have to remember not to make that mistake again. Else he'll have me off in handcuffs down that police station and put me under one of them interrogations of his.'

Clinton and Josephine smiled politely.

Mrs Trap dumped the pot on the table, spilling a large pool of tea. 'I bet you're a sight to see when you're all fired up in that interrogation room.'

'Erm, thank you, Mrs Trap,' replied Clinton, mopping up the spillage with a napkin.

The café owner clunked two teacups onto the table. 'But you policemen know how to keep your emotions under control. Unlike some people I could mention.' She puckered her lips. 'I won't name names due to client confidentiality and all that data-protection rubbish. But I'll tell you which country she's from – Russia. And her name rhymes with "wet banana".'

Josephine jerked back her chair and stood up. 'I'm sorry, but I have to be somewhere else.' She turned to Clinton. 'I'm sure you'll be able to manage on your own.'

Before Clinton could protest, Mrs Trap was ruffling his hair and making him lose his train of thought.

'Oh, don't worry about my little detective sergeant here, Ms Savage.'

'I'm a detective inspector, Mrs Trap.'

She patted him on the head. 'I know that. I'm just …' She tickled his chin. '… playing with you.'

'Goodbye, inspector. Farewell, Mrs Trap.' And Josephine scurried outside without another word.

The café owner surveyed her clientele. 'We're not too busy at the mo'. And my husband is out back if anyone wants serving. So maybe you and me could share this four-bag pot of tea?'

Clinton was staring at the exit. 'Sorry, what was that?'

'We can finish up this tea. And I can tell you all about that Russian customer of mine who's always making a right royal scene in my café.' She sniffed messily. 'It's not good for business. Half the tourists are Americans. And they don't want to see a crackpot Russian losing her rag about the thickness of my meat-pie crusts – or the cream in my cream horns – while they're shoving overpriced cake down their gullets.'

'I imagine not,' sighed Clinton.

'Wherever she can find fault she does. Didn't even buy anything when she came in just now – harassed poor Ms Savage before you arrived then she went on her way. I'm telling you, the next pot of tea she orders in here'll have no teabags in it.' She cleared her throat noisily. 'I don't know what I've done to her – apart from overcharge her a couple of times when she first arrived in the village because she wasn't too familiar with the banknotes and I thought she was a tourist.'

'She's still settling in to village life, I expect,' replied Clinton, checking his watch.

'She's had six months to settle. And she still don't trust my kettle. That tells me she's a wrong 'un.'

Clinton crossed his fingers under the table – hopefully this diatribe would end soon and he could be on his way.

'It's like she's on some kind of mission to put us out of business. This café has been a cornerstone of village life for years.' She poured the tea. 'Well, it wasn't always called the Tourist Trap. And it wasn't always a café – I think it was a public lavatory back in the seventies and a high-class brothel in the sixties. And the building's been rebuilt at least three times. But it's always been here in one form or another.' She picked up a cup and slurped. 'Like the sign says in the window, this café is a site of historical snacking interest and that's important – because it means we can charge twice as much for a cheese and pickle sandwich than anywhere else in the village.' She crashed her cup on the table. 'So, that Russian busybody is starting to get on my tartlets, if you know what I mean.'

'I do.'

'Why don't you investigate her, sergeant?'

'Inspector.'

'I know.' She squeezed his cheek. 'Just teasing.'

'One needs grounds to investigate someone, Mrs Trap. And disrespecting your pie crusts in a public place doesn't tick all the necessary boxes.'

'Why don't you charge her with Jepson's murder? That'll keep her out of my café for a while. Give me and the Americans a break from her constant carping.'

'Impossible, I'm afraid.'

'Did you see that?' shouted one of the American tourists. 'Guy just sunk a putt from thirty yards!'

Clinton downed his cup of tea in one gulp and sprang to his feet. 'A superb brew. But duty calls, Mrs Trap. Please donate the rest of the pot to our golf-loving friends from across the Atlantic.'

Her face fell. 'If you're sure.'

Clinton adjusted his bouffant. 'As sure as my golf swing on a hot summer's day.' And he scooted out of the café before he could be ruffled, patted, stroked or squeezed again.

Chapter 10

The Getting Away With Murder museum lay on the southern outskirts of Upper Goosing, not far from its border with Lower Goosing. A popular tourist spot, it was even busier than usual for a Wednesday in August. But two of the visitors pulling up in the car park weren't tourists. They were villagers – Jayne and Graham Trill. And they were a couple on a mission – to find a replacement actor for their group's production of *Murder at Dress Rehearsal*.

Once they had reluctantly paid their fifteen-pound entrance fees, the Trills set about locating the male proprietor – Herman Willie.

Graham gazed up as they walked along a dimly lit semi-circular tunnel. 'This isn't exactly scary – a few backlit black-and-white photos of long-dead murderers that nobody has ever heard of is hardly the stuff of nightmares, is it?'

'This is merely a curtain raiser, Graham. Being an amateur dramatist, I would expect you to know that.'

'Where's all the stuff they advertise on the posters? You know, Upper Goosing's top ten murder weapons, the food hall of death and the plan-your-own-murder family activity centre?'

The main exhibits are further on. That's where Herman usually entertains the tourists.'

'Are you sure?'

'Don't question me, Graham!'

'Pardon me for breathing.'

'Yes. And breathing is one of your more annoying habits – both onstage when playing cadavers and offstage when playing the world's most useless husband.'

He muttered under his breath.

'Did you say something, Graham?'

His scowl suggested he had but wasn't brave enough to repeat it at a higher volume.

'No. I didn't think you did. It must have been a rat squeaking. Now, it's straight on and left.'

They hurried along.

'I've just realised, Jayne – we haven't been here since our honeymoon.'

'Please, Graham, don't remind me of our honeymoon in Upper Goosing. Not that it deserves the name. We were only living in the next village.'

'All you ever talked about when we were courting was Upper Goosing. At that pizzeria on our first date, you told me you always dreamed of escaping Lower Goosing's cheap restaurants for the overpriced eateries of this place. We did – and you're still not happy.'

Jayne glared at him. 'Who could be happy when they're married to a serial whinger?'

Graham tutted. 'Better a serial whinger than a serial killer, eh?'

'I'm beginning to wonder if the latter would be preferable. At least you'd get out from under my feet every once in a while.'

'Yeah. And if I got caught, I'd get a minimum thirty-year break from your nagging.'

'Graham, please! How many times do I have to correct you? It's not nagging – it's constructive criticism.'

'Let's be honest, it's destructive criticism. Last time you gave me a compliment, Tony Blair was prime minister.'

'That recently?' She tossed her head. 'I am surprised.'

They continued in familiar marital silence for another minute until they reached the first exhibition room – the food hall of death.

Graham stopped and pointed at a well-dressed mannequin who was face down in a silver bowl filled with a lumpy yellow liquid. 'Here, that looks like custard.' He chuckled. 'What a way to go, eh?'

Jayne spun round. 'Graham, we are not here to enjoy ourselves!'

'No, we never are.' He read out the sign in front of the mannequin. 'The trifle murderer's first victim was drowned in egg custard. The killer dispatched his next victims with sponge fingers soaked in poisoned wine, strychnine-coated jelly, assorted fruit sprinkled with deadly nightshade, and pound-shop whipped cream that was six months past its use-by date.'

'Trifling talk is your speciality. Can we move on?'

Graham didn't budge. 'Face down in a bowl of custard – sounds similar to how poor old Jepson snuffed it.'

'Not really. That theatrically challenged butler was drowned in mango chutney.'

'Mango chutney, custard – when it's shooting up your nose, slurping down your windpipe and slopping into your lungs, it's more or less the same thing.' He thought for a second. 'I wonder if Jepson's murderer was inspired by this creepy old place.'

'You're being melodramatic.'

'Maybe so. But I won't be touching your mother's sponge fingers for a while. Anyway, how do you know Jepson was drowned in mango chutney?'

'The inspector mentioned it. Now, I don't want to hear any more nonsense about food-related deaths, Graham. We have a Willie to find.'

They started moving forward again and soon entered the *Life After Death* exhibition – a replica of the local mortuary.

After battling past some German tourists whose rucksacks were obstructing the interactive autopsy display, the Trills located Herman Willie – lying on a concrete slab and wearing nothing but a pair of underpants.

Jayne leant over him. 'Mr Willie!' No response. 'I say, Mr Willie!' Still deadly silence. 'I know you're working, but I would appreciate a quick word with you.'

Herman didn't move. In fact, it wasn't obvious he was even breathing.

'You see that?' continued Jayne, glancing at Graham. 'Now there's a man who plays a cadaver to perfection.' She pulled out a hand mirror from her bag and placed it over Herman's mouth. 'Not a droplet of condensation. Superb diaphragm control. Something you can only dream of, Graham.'

'Perhaps you'd prefer it if I really did die onstage next time. Then you'll finally stop moaning at me.'

Jayne's eyebrows zipped up. 'Not a bad idea.'

'I hope you're not serious!'

She half smiled. 'Of course not. It's not practical. It would only work for opening night. We'd need at least two understudies for the Friday and Saturday performances. And we simply don't have the bodies.'

Graham turned his back on his wife and took over the corpse interrogation. 'I'm really sorry, Herman. But the reason we're here is we need a replacement for Jepson for our next play. It's a murder mystery – you know, one of those silly ones with loads of comedy characters who are always bickering – and we were wondering if you fancied treading the boards. It'd be good publicity for this place.'

Herman continued to rest in peace.

Graham wasn't giving up on communicating with the dead just yet. 'With one cast member already bumped off, there'll be tons of interest – and a stand-in who runs a murder museum is the icing on the killer cake. And it gets better – if the police fail to solve Jepson's murder, you'll be able to set up a new getting away with murder exhibit. You can use some of our scenery and props for it. Really bring it to life.'

'You could call it *Murder in a Peculiar Manor*,' suggested Jayne.

'Or *A Very Funny Murder Mystery*, because Jepson was a stand-up comedian in his spare time, wasn't he?'

Jayne sniffed. 'Mine was a cleverer suggestion, Graham.'

'No need to be too clever when it comes to murder.'

'I think you'll find you have to be *extremely* clever to get away with murder. A level of intelligence far beyond your reach. But comfortably within mine.'

'Murdered before, have you?'

Jayne bit her lip. 'No, I haven't. But I'm sorely tempted right now.'

'You hear that, Herman? My own wife is threatening to do me in. If the police find me face down in a bowl of Cocoa Pops tomorrow morning, make sure they dust my back for her palm prints.'

'Very droll,' sneered Jayne.

They both stared down at the body. It didn't rise from the dead.

Then Graham spotted Morticia Willie circulating among the tourists in her black Victorian mourning hat and gown. 'Hey, Morty! Come over here and help us, will you?'

Herman's wife shimmied in acknowledgement, widened her huge eyes and swished her jet-black hair. Then she hovered across the floor, curtsied extravagantly and greeted them in a suitably theatrical accent.

'Warmest felicitations, Mr and Mrs Trill! How wonderful to see you returning to the museum after your glorious honeymoon trip here in 1999.'

'Yes,' snuffled Jayne. 'It feels rather like I'm returning to the scene of a crime.'

Morticia chortled. 'Ever the wit, Mrs Trill – ever the wit! Yes, nearly twenty years have passed since then. Can you believe it? I certainly can't. So much has happened in that time. So many changes. So many tourists. So many unsolved murders. And that's how we like it at the Getting Away With Murder museum. Unsolved murder is our business – without it we *go out* of business!'

'It's splendid to be back,' replied Jayne, with as much warmth as she could muster with honeymoon memories still bobbing around in her brain. 'We were trying to reanimate your husband.'

'That won't be possible, I'm afraid. He's imbibed one of my homemade sleeping elixirs. He won't be back in the land of the living until eventide.'

'That's unfortunate,' sighed Jayne.

Graham jabbed a finger at Herman. 'We wanted him to join the cast of our next murder mystery.'

'Jepson has left us in the lurch,' added Jayne. 'But Herman could spring to our amateur-dramatic rescue.' She stared down. 'Once he's back with us.'

Morticia pressed her palms together. 'Unfortunately, Herman is fully booked up. He will be with us as a corpse until the autumn. After that, he's taking a short break before returning as a live exhibit – the trifle murderer: you may have already seen the display about him?'

'Yeah, we did, Morty. I was wondering whether his custard victim might have been the inspiration for Jepson's killer.'

Morticia raised a finger. 'Now there's a murderous thought! Wouldn't it be delightful if it had done? Our museum – nurturing and inspiring the murderers of the future!'

Graham nudged Jayne. 'I'm *definitely* never touching your mother's sponge fingers again.'

'Where was I?' asked Morticia, immediately answering her own question. 'Oh, yes. Herman's schedule. After his trifle adventures, he'll be back to the cadavering nine-to-five when we launch our *Dead Body Beautiful* exhibition in the winter.'

Jayne's face crumpled. 'So he's unavailable?'

'Yes, my dears. But feel free to pop in any time you want to see Herman and update him on your drama activities. He may look as dead as a decapitated doornail, but my husband can hear everything. And your updates will make a nice change from tourists making unkind comments about his hands being large enough to throttle an elephant.'

Jayne forced a smile. 'Thank you. But amateur dramatics in Upper Goosing is fast and furious. There's very little time to even apply the brakes, never mind stick one's head out of the window and speak to those snoozing in the slow lane. Because—'

'That reminds me,' interrupted Graham. 'I forgot to pay and display in the car park.'

Jayne appeared grateful to hear this news. 'Then we had better bid you farewell and return to our vehicle, Mrs Willie.'

Morticia's voice deepened. 'Before you returning honeymooners do depart this world of ours, I was wondering if you knew anything about the police's investigation into Jepson's death – specifically, if any suspects have been identified?'

'All a bit too early for that, Morty,' whispered Graham. 'Trump's on the case.'

'That's wonderful news, Mr Trill. Because, if I may offer a personal opinion in the strictest of confidence, Mr Trump isn't the sharpest tool in the box.'

'No, Morty. In fact, I don't even think he's *in* the box.'

Morticia nodded. 'I would have to agree with you. And much as I admire Mr Trump's self-belief and enthusiasm, his methods are somewhat unorthodox. So I expect this case to end up colder than a cadaver in an Icelandic mortuary.' She stroked her husband's naked leg. 'An unsolved murder at Peculiar Manor offers up all sorts of possibilities for our museum. And it's not like solving Jepson's murder is going to bring him back, is it?'

'Let's hope not,' sniffed Jayne.

Morticia tittered. 'Such a wit, Mrs Trill – such a wit!'

Chapter 11

Inspector Trump was in his minimalist, glass-walled office in Upper Goosing police station recuperating from a substantial canteen lunch by swivelling idly in his executive chair with the consummate ease of a seasoned desk-professional. Having indulged in a double portion of shepherd's pie and a generous slice of apple crumble, he was now fully engaged in flicking through the latest copy of *Detection Monthly*.

'The nonsense these journalists come up with! It beggars belief – it really does.' He shook his head and read a headline.

TOP TEN TIPS FOR CRACKING MURDERS WHEN THERE'S NO BODY

'What a waste of newsprint. Just find the body, for goodness sake! No need for psychologists, psychiatrists or psychics.' He gazed through the glass wall at Constable Dinkel. 'Or, indeed, sidekicks. They only get under your feet.' He turned back to the magazine. 'It's all twaddle. Just get out there and keep your eyes peeled for someone lying on the floor who hasn't breathed for a while, and your nostrils open for a bad whiff. A corpse will soon turn up.' He tossed the magazine onto the empty desk in front of him. 'These journalists should be reporting on real cases that have been superbly solved by gifted sleuths such as myself. Not dreaming up better ways of solving murders when they've probably never seen a man battered to death with a stale baguette or a woman throttled with her own hair extensions.'

A knock on the door interrupted his thoughts. He could see through the glass that the interrupter was Dinkel – the shadow he wouldn't shift until the Jepson case was solved. Or shelved.

71

Though he would only contemplate suggesting the latter if it was seriously threatening to shorten his lunch breaks.

He sat back, folded his arms and followed his own personal protocol for first-time door knocks from junior staff – he completely ignored it. If it was important, the annoying little constable could knock again.

After fifteen seconds of promising silence, Dinkel knocked louder and longer.

Clinton swivelled ninety degrees, clenched his arms tighter to his chest, and assessed the strength of the knock. In his opinion, it was on the border between important and not important. Yes, it was definitely in that no-man's land where communications could break down between senior office-based staff – or 'officers' as he preferred to call them – and juniors in the open-plan front line – the easily replaceable and expendable 'soldiers'. Employing such a half-hearted knock was a classic error committed by younger members of today's detection army. When he was a new recruit, he knew precisely when to tap tentatively and when to knock firmly on an officer's door. Sometimes a soldier was obliged to push forward – such as when he was bearing an urgent report from the front line – even if his officer was on the retreat – after battling with a long lunch, for example. It was up to modern soldiers to make those kinds of split-second judgements for themselves. And Clinton's stomach was currently doing battle with his colossal luncheon. So this young soldier would do well to return to barracks and avoid jeopardising this officer's vital digestive operations.

Dinkel knocked so loudly it couldn't be ignored.

'Come in!' barked Clinton in a voice so unwelcoming a parade-ground sergeant major would have hesitated to advance any further.

The constable entered the office and shut the door. 'I'm back from the manor, sir.'

'Really? And there was me thinking your identical twin brother had joined the force and decided to interrupt my lunch break.'

'But it's a quarter past two, sir. All lunch breaks have to be taken between the hours of midday and two o'clock. It says so in the rule book.'

'Don't quote rules at me, Dinkel, or I'll send you back into the information-technology wilderness out there and ask you to put whatever it is you want to say in an email – Times New Roman; fourteen point; double spaced; strictly one space after a full-stop; no slang, euphemisms or American spellings on pain of instant dismissal; and triple-checked for grammatical errors.'

Dinkel pulled up a swivel chair and sat down. 'I've taken six statements, sir.'

'Congratulations. I'll have a mango-chutney cake with half a dozen candles sent to your home address. Now, tell me what was in those statements.'

'Well, there's not much to tell, sir. To summarise briefly —'

'Very briefly.'

'Yes. Lady Peculiar claims she was in the dining room all evening. The Major told me nothing new – apart from the best way to navigate an enemy minefield.'

'What's that, out of interest?'

'You send the infantrymen out in front of you to clear a path, sir. Officers go last.'

'Sounds eminently sensible to me. Let's hope, for your sake, that this investigation doesn't drag us into any minefields.'

Dinkel consulted some notes. 'The maid just took the message from the Major to her ladyship after the body was found. The other three staff do various odd jobs around the place and they weren't working on Tuesday evening.'

The inspector uncrossed his arms. 'So, in terms of statements, we're firing blanks?'

'Yes, sir. Though we didn't take a formal statement from Cripps the gardener, did we?'

'There was nothing stopping you from taking one, while you were at the manor.'

'But you ordered me out of the drawing room after you had that chat about greenfly and vine weevils with him.'

'That's correct, Dinkel. But I didn't forbid you from going back into that drawing room, did I? Or from seeking out Cripps once more after I'd left on urgent elevenses business.'

'No, sir. But I just assumed you didn't want me to take a formal statement from him.'

Clinton held a finger aloft. 'Assumption is the enemy of deduction, constable!'

The constable shuffled in his chair. 'Actually, it was more presumption than assumption, sir.'

The inspector faltered for a second. 'What?'

'My decision not to take a statement from Cripps was more of a presumption than an assumption.'

Clinton checked in his desk drawer for something to fiddle with, but found only a box of staples. 'What are you trying to say?'

'Presumptions are based on probability, sir. And, from your actions back at the manor – when you said you were a hundred per cent certain you wanted us to leave and dragged me out the door and along the corridor so fast my shoes were skidding on the marble – I would suggest it was fair for me to presume that, in all probability, you didn't want us to obtain a formal statement from Cripps.'

Clinton double-checked his drawer. Nothing had materialised to ease the loneliness of his box of staples and offer him greater fiddling opportunities.

'And don't forget,' continued Dinkel, 'the superintendent wanted you to lead on the Cripps side of things.'

In an act of desperation, Clinton began fiddling with the box of staples. 'I'm fully aware of the orders that were given to me, constable.'

'So, what are you going to tell Superintendent Block when he comes in here in five minutes and asks you? Because I just saw him grabbing a mega-jumbo espresso at the executive coffee machine, and he only ever does that when he's coming to see you.'

'Correction. You mean what are *you* going to tell the superintendent. As your commanding officer, I put you in charge of statements.'

Dinkel sat up straight. 'I'll tell him what happened in the drawing room with Cripps, sir. He can decide who disobeyed orders.'

It wasn't often that soldiers outmanoeuvred officers, but this was one of those rare occasions. 'Alright, Dinkel.' He shoved the box of staples back in the drawer and slammed it shut. 'I have a suggestion that will spare us both a court martial.'

'What's that, sir – going AWOL?'

'No. A game of crazy golf.'

The constable didn't reply.

'Did you hear me, Dinkel?'

'I think so, sir.' The constable paused. 'Crazy golf.'

'That's right – crazy golf.'

Dinkel tried to get his head round the idea. 'Do you mean we should play a normal game of golf in an unhinged manner?'

'Sorry, I don't follow you.'

'I mean, do you want to go around Goosing golf course pretending we're a pair of lunatics – smashing saplings with our putters, aiming tee shots at squirrels and running over members' big toes in our golf buggies?'

'No. In any case, there are no squirrels. The Major shot them all.'

'So, you mean actual crazy golf – that kids play?'

'Not just juveniles. Many upstanding adult members of the village community often enjoy a round or two at Royal Crazy Golf.'

'Such as?'

'Myself. And countless others who no doubt play when I'm out solving murders.' The inspector sprang up. 'Let's get to it! We have eighteen of the most fiendish concrete putting greens to navigate. I still haven't made par on that seventh hole. I can never get past Prince Charles' ears in under five shots.'

Dinkel got up. 'You want us to go right now, sir?'

'Yes! We don't want Block to corner us in here. We need to retreat, escape our enemy's expected advance, and plan our next move.'

The constable's forehead wrinkled. 'Couldn't we just go back to the manor and take a statement from Cripps? He'll be there until six o'clock.'

Clinton shook his head. 'That's *exactly* what Cripps will be expecting us to do.'

'It's certainly what the superintendent would be expecting us to do, sir, if he knew we hadn't taken Cripps' statement already.'

'Maybe so, constable.' Clinton hurried to the door. 'But there is another good reason for this trip.'

'And what's that?'

'I'm in desperate need of some putting practice before Saturday's tournament. Now, quick march out of headquarters!'

Chapter 12

Dickie Blinder, long-time editor of the *Goosing Times*, was wedged into his battered white leather seat, staring out of his office window and admiring the birds on the feeders he'd installed to provide him with much needed entertainment – and occasional inspiration – when major news events were thin on the ground in this corner of Brokenshire. And they generally were in August. It was the silly season, when barging to the front of a bus queue, allowing your garden hedge to overgrow or riding your bicycle on the pavement could put you on the front page of your village newspaper.

He thought back to last year, when he'd resorted to a front-page story about the dwindling local blue-tit population based on nothing more than his own personal office-chair observations. No readers had written to the letters page to challenge its flimsy assertions, shaky science or sparse evidence. Probably because nobody had bothered to read past the first couple of paragraphs.

A blackbird launched into a melody that reminded him of Chopin's funeral march. Not unusual in Upper Goosing, given the number of birds' nests under the eaves of Saint Crippen's church roof. However, there would be no need to dream up any 'Bye-Bye from a Blackbird!' headlines this week. The impossible had happened. While even local murderers usually took a holiday in August – which, if you thought about it, was only reasonable because they needed a break like everyone else – there had been a suspicious death – almost certainly a murder – at Peculiar Manor. Exactly the kind of story the *Goosing Times* needed to boost readership and sell more advertising.

The office door flew open and the towering figure of Fenella Cocky, Dickie's chief reporter, lolloped into the room like a giraffe with a bus to catch.

'The police are keeping schtum on the Peculiar Manor death for now,' she moaned.

Dickie turned his chair to face her. 'You spoke to their press officer?'

'Yes. She's almost as useless as the detective in charge of the case.' She shook her head. 'Trump gives idiots a bad name.'

'Come, come, Fenella! No more of that unpleasant talk, please.'

'Just because you're bosom buddies with the cocksure clown doesn't make it any less true.'

'Truth is relative, my dear. Doubly so in journalism. Triply so when you're in the editor's office. Now, can I suggest you attempt to make contact with my detective chum yourself?'

'I've already tried.' She poked out her bright pink tongue. 'His office number is unavailable.'

'Probably unplugged it, knowing Clinton.'

'And he never carries a work mobile phone.'

'No. He's a very wise man, if you ask me. Smartphones have ruined this country. Not only are people obtaining their news from the internet using them, they seem unable to cross a road, traverse the pavement, sip a cappuccino or consume a meal without consulting them for vital updates on whether their selfie has another "like" or whatever it's called.' He scrutinised his mobile phone's screen. 'Six text messages from my mother: first one asking what I've eaten for lunch; second checking if I received her first message; third asking if I'm ignoring her; fourth asking where I am and who I'm with; fifth enquiring about the successful delivery of the first four texts; and number six – the pièce de résistance – is the first five texts copied and pasted into one message with the sign-off "I'm busy now, son. Don't message me!"' He sighed and put the phone away. 'This is the way the world will end. Not with a bang but a giant text message.'

'Before it does end, I need to get official confirmation that the Jepson case is a murder investigation. The press officer was about as much use on that point as a … well, as a press officer.'

'They're probably waiting on the autopsy report.'

'But Trump told the curry ladies Jepson was murdered.'

'That will have been his gut instincts commandeering his vocal cords. Happens a lot.'

She rolled her eyes. 'Okay. Let's stop talking about the detective, assume it is a murder and talk about suspects. I've got a couple in mind.'

'Who are they?'

'First up, Lady Peculiar. She's a strange old bird. Shoots anything with four legs, wings, or a "Vote Labour" sticker. She could have arranged Jepson's murder because he was so useless. Apparently, he couldn't tell a tureen from a chamber pot.'

'Why not just fire him?'

'He must have had something on her.'

'That's rather a quantum leap you've taken there, Fenella.'

'You forget I've got the longest legs in regional journalism.'

Dickie gazed up at the skinny, six-feet-four-inch reporter. 'That is true.'

'The second name in the frame is Ronald Cripps. He's a violent ex-crim who works as a gardener at Peculiar Manor and will have rubbed shoulders with Jepson for years.' She made a strange mewing sound. 'Cripps and I have crossed paths at several vegetable shows. Last month, my marrows were mysteriously vandalised the night before Goosing Big Veg. Cripps' marrows won first prize. And he wasn't afraid to gloat about it afterwards.'

'Don't let gargantuan vegetables cloud your judgement, Fenella. Cripps is a reformed character. He's now an upstanding member of the community and hasn't so much as returned a library book late since he joined the manor staff five years ago.' He tapped his desk. 'He's also a regular reader of our esteemed organ, so let's not risk reducing our circulation by one by pointing fingers where fingers shouldn't be pointed.'

'I'm the best reporter you've got, Dickie, and you know it. Let me follow my hunches and I promise I'll get you a front-page story.'

'I prefer facts to hunches.'

'I'll give you facts. And I'll do my best to dig them out before the police have made anything public. Knowing the local force, they'll stay tight-lipped until the end of the week.'

'Yes. They do tend to be a bit slow out of the blocks when it comes to informing the media.'

'Exactly. We'll be crossing the finishing line while they're still tying their shoe laces.'

A gang of sparrows mobbed one of Dickie's bird feeders. 'I don't know, Fenella. It's a tricky one.'

She nodded at the window. 'Imagine that bird feeder is my story and our readers are the sparrows. They'll be flocking to it from all over Upper Goosing. And when the nuts are gone, we just refill. We've got the capacity to print extra copies of the newspaper if we need to. The managing director will be happier than a seagull with a bag of chips.'

Her editor hinted at a smile. 'Nice analogy.'

Fenella's eyes focused on Dickie like a hawk. 'So can this story fly?'

Dickie admired the sparrows. Then he nodded. 'Yes, Fenella. Fly away!'

Chapter 13

Inspector Trump was one hundred per cent focused on the job in hand – attempting to safely navigate his golden golf ball through a miniature version of Windsor Castle without crashing into its ramparts or bouncing off the tiny mechanical replica of the Queen which was moving from side to side in front of it.

'Am I aiming straight, Dinkel?' asked Clinton, steadying his red, white and blue putter.

'As far as I can see, sir.'

'And how far is that?'

'What, sir?'

'How far is it that you can see? Because if you suffer from any form of myopia, you're of no use to me.'

'I've got twenty–twenty vision according to my optician.'

'Is it the one next to the North Korean deli on the high street?'

'Yes, sir – Eye for an Eye. Chap with an eyepatch runs it.'

'Don't trust him. He told me I need to wear reading glasses because of my advancing years.'

'Oh. And you don't really need glasses, you mean?'

'No. I do need glasses for reading. What I meant was, he could have put it rather more delicately. He used the phrase "when you get to our age". And he celebrated his fiftieth birthday in the spring. I'm still forty-nine for another six months. There's no comparison.'

The constable maintained a discreet silence.

'That optician has been in business in the village for years now,' continued Clinton, still eyeballing the tiny replica castle as Her Majesty zipped back and forth. 'You'd have thought he would've learnt that brutal honesty isn't welcome in close-knit communities.'

Dinkel shuffled his feet. 'If I can be brutally honest with you for a moment, sir, I'm not sure playing crazy golf is the best use of police resources. Especially since the superintendent messaged me forty-five minutes ago to say the autopsy has confirmed the amount of mango chutney in Jepson's lungs is consistent with forcible drowning and, therefore, murder.'

'I already knew he was murdered,' grumbled Clinton, adjusting his putting stance.

'But still, if we're spotted at Royal Crazy Golf by a member of the public, word might get back to the superintendent.'

'You worry too much, Dinkel. Now, stop fretting about our superiors and start concentrating on helping me make par on the eleventh hole. After that disaster at the sixth with the corgi's tail, I can't afford any more slipups.'

Before Clinton could make his putt, a middle-aged American tourist appeared, decked in an 'It's Murder in Upper Goosing' T-shirt, baggy beach shorts, and tennis shoes.

'Hey, fellas! You two on a royal walkabout or something? Coz you're moving slower than a prince's bride on her wedding day at Westminster Abbey!'

'We're not too slow,' muttered Clinton, without glancing back. 'You're too fast.'

'I like my movies fast and furious. But when I play crazy golf fast I don't wanna make nobody furious. So, sorry if I upset you guys. I was just kidding around.'

Clinton grunted and practised his putting swing.

The American offered Dinkel a hand. 'Name's Randolph Frickelburg the Third.'

The constable shook his hand. 'Good afternoon, Mr Frickelburg. I'm Troy Dinkel.'

'Get in the hole!' whooped Randolph, startling Clinton as he hit his ball towards Windsor Castle. It flew along the concrete, smacked the Queen slap-bang in the face, and rolled slowly back to where it had started. A posh female voice played from a speaker on the front of the castle: 'One is not amused with that shot.'

'Oh, for king's sake!' shouted Clinton. 'You'd have thought with all the public money we give that family, they would at least have the decency to allow taxpayers such as myself access to their mini royal residences.'

The American grinned. 'I love your accents! You fellas from England, huh?'

'Yes, we are,' confirmed Dinkel.

'You on vacation?'

'No, we live here.'

The tourist nodded unsurely. 'Okay. It's just crazy golf is a touristy kinda thing for a couple of guys to do. You know, even if you got time to kill on a Wednesday afternoon.'

Dinkel laughed. 'You'll always have time to kill in Upper Goosing.'

The tourist's face went blank.

'Sorry, that was just my little joke. We have a lot of murders here so, you know, you always have time to *kill*.'

The American exploded back into life. 'I getcha, Troy my boy!' He staccato-sniggered. 'I love your British sense of humour! I don't always understand what the hell you Brits are going on about – but I love it! Even more than I love crazy golf.' He patted his putter. 'I never play in the States. Only when I come over to England.' He adjusted his 'Make Britain Great Again' baseball cap. 'There's something quaintly English about crazy golf. You know, like roasted lamb, apple sauce, Yorkshire desserts and that sage-and-onion stuff.'

Clinton spun round. 'Firstly, it's roast beef, Yorkshire puddings and stuffing. Secondly, we eat pork with apple sauce, lamb with mint sauce and, for future reference, turkey with cranberry sauce – though nobody who's alive today seems to know why. Anything goes with chicken – although I'd recommend light seasoning and no more. Thirdly, some of us quaint Englishmen take our crazy golf extremely seriously. So, if you wouldn't mind—'

'Oh, you want me to join you? Sure thing, buddy!' He muscled between them. 'So what d'you guys do round here when you're not banging golf balls against Her Majesty, huh?'

'Mr Trump and I are detectives,' replied Dinkel, a second before Clinton nudged him in the ribs. He turned and engaged in an impromptu whispering conference with his boss. 'What's the matter, sir?'

'You've let the detection cat out of the bag now, constable – word could get back to the superintendent that Trump and Dinkel were here instead of solving a murder.'

'I know. That's what I said two minutes ago. But you told me to stop fretting.'

'No, I didn't.'

'Yes, you did, sir.'

'Dinkel, I most certainly did not tell you that fretting was off the agenda.'

'You most certainly did, sir.'

'I didn't, Dinkel.'

'I hate to contradict a superior officer, but that was the clear message you communicated to me, sir.'

'Really? Well, here's another message – it's your word against mine.'

'Sir, but I specifically said—'

'Officer's word versus a soldier's? No contest. Victory is mine. Accept defeat gracefully.'

'Everything okay?' asked the American, adjusting his cap.

Clinton stood tall. 'Sorry, we shall have to leave you.'

'Something I said, huh?'

'No, it wasn't, Mr Rolf Fragglerock, or whatever your name is.'

'It's Randolph Frickelburg. And that ain't no Russian alias, if that's what you're thinking.'

The inspector furrowed his forehead. 'Why ever would I think that?'

'Let me explain, guys. See, I'm ex-CIA.'

Clinton's forehead furrowed further. 'What's XCIA? Some sort of international cross-country-running association?'

Dinkel coughed. 'I think he means he worked for the Central Intelligence Agency, sir.'

The American penny dropped. 'Oh, the CIA! Why didn't you say so, Mr Frockelburg?'

'I thought I did. And it's Frickelburg.'

'Ah. American English, you see. Stick to British English and you'll never go wrong.'

'Okay. So, like I was saying, I'm ex-CIA. I still got a contact works there. And I always get them to check out where I'm visiting on vacation. Just to see if I need to avoid any places – you know what I mean?'

Clinton nodded. 'I understand. And I suggest you steer well clear of the Eye for an Eye opticians.'

The tourist ignored the interruption. 'This contact tells me there's some low-level intel about a Russian spy in the area.'

'In Upper Goosing?' asked Dinkel.

Clinton tutted. 'Don't be so stupid, constable. It'll be Lower Goosing, if anywhere. Foreign operatives will be attracted to the seedier side of Goosing: the vintage bed and breakfasts, cheap restaurants, modern cafés, fish-and-chip shops, classic British pubs, big-name retailers and easy-access car parks.'

'Matter of fact, guys, it was Upper Goosing and —'

'Of course!' interrupted Clinton. 'Always expect the unexpected when it comes to the Russians. I mean, who would have thought they would ever win Eurovision?'

Randolph looked puzzled. 'Eurovision – that another optician I oughta avoid?'

'No, it's a song contest,' replied Clinton. 'You Americans really should brush up on your European culture before you cross the Atlantic. Now, what's all this about a Russian spy, Mr Fruckelburg?'

'Frickelburg. And it's only a five or ten per cent possibility, max. It's based on some encrypted email chatter the CIA ain't got to the bottom of yet and maybe never will. But if it's true, this spy will have probably been deep undercover here for years – maybe even before the Iron Curtain fell.'

'I find that hard to believe,' scoffed Clinton. 'They'd stick out like a thumb that's been hit with a hammer and sickle.'

'Uh-uh. I know how these spies operate. They'll probably have a better English accent than you guys, cut the crusts off their afternoon-tea sandwiches and *always* pour their milk into the teacup last.'

The inspector clicked his tongue. 'Since when did it become obligatory to cut the crusts off all sandwiches? I usually only do it for the cucumber variety.'

Dinkel intervened. 'The Tourist Trap café always cuts the crusts off its wide selection of afternoon-tea sandwiches, sir. And they charge double for the privilege.'

'Basing your conclusions on one piece of afternoon-tea evidence is sloppy sleuthing, Dinkel.'

'I was going to add, "And every other place I've been for afternoon tea in Brokenshire does exactly the same."'

'Do you regularly partake of afternoon tea?' asked Clinton.

'Yes, sir.'

'At the correct hour?'

'Always at four o'clock, sir – on the dot. The time it was originally taken by Anna, seventh Duchess of Bedford, when she first introduced it to this great country of ours in 1840.'

'Did the Duchess trim the crusts off all of her sandwiches, constable?'

'That hasn't been noted in the historical record, as far as I know.'

The inspector beamed with joy. 'Then I win the argument!'

Something buzzed in Dinkel's pocket. He extracted a pager from it and read a message. 'We're wanted back at the station, sir. Superintendent says he's found out some vital information about a person of interest to us.'

'Hey, before you English guys go, I got a question.'

'Please be quick,' sighed the inspector.

'Are you investigating that death at Peculiar Manor last night?'

Clinton expanded his chest. 'That responsibility was naturally bestowed upon me – South East England's greatest detective.'

'You think the Russians could be behind it, guys?'

Clinton shook his head. 'Upper Goosing attracts some of England's finest murderers, Mr Frankenburg.'

'Frickelburg.'

'Whatever. And it's a very competitive market. New entrants from overseas would have a very tough time breaking into it. So I suspect this is a traditional English murderer we're dealing with.'

Dinkel tapped his pager. 'We'd better get moving, sir.'

'Yes. Goodbye, Mr Whatever-your-name-is. Enjoy the rest of your holiday.'

'You mean my vacation?'

'I mean your holiday. We're in England.' And he and Dinkel abandoned their putters and headed for the car.

Chapter 14

After his crazy-golfing encounter with the two English detectives – one of whom seemed a real down-to-earth guy and the other a bit of a smartass – Randolph Frickelburg the Third had developed a thirst for English afternoon tea. And he was pretty sure the Tourist Trap café they'd mentioned wouldn't mind serving it to him a little early. He'd consulted his American guidebook a few minutes ago and it gleefully noted that three tourists had perished there in the last ten years – but they were German, French and Canadian, so there was nothing to worry about. The guide's helpful map showed him the café was half a mile from the crazy golf. With no public transport in sight, he took a few deep breaths, yanked up his socks, retied his shoelaces and marched down the hill to the high street.

Ten minutes later, he was crashing through the café door – already fantasising about the afternoon delights that lay ahead. He breathlessly scanned the dining area for a free table and noticed a lady in her seventies sitting immediately to his right. As she lifted her head, he saw her face and all thoughts of Earl Grey tea and cucumber sandwiches with the crusts trimmed off drained from his mind. His favourite English author – Agatha Twisty – was within touching distance and tucking into a cream horn. For a moment, he considered walking on by and leaving his literary idol to finish her cake in peace. But that moment soon passed. This was too big an opportunity to miss. He composed himself, cleared his throat and launched into a conversation.

'Excuse me, ma'am, but aren't you the world's greatest murder-mystery author, living legend and all-round high-class English lady, Agatha Twisty?'

The impeccably dressed woman peered over her horn-rimmed glasses and smiled. 'That I am. And nobody has paid me such a wonderful compliment in years.'

Randolph took off his cap. 'Would you do me the honour of spending a few minutes in my company, ma'am? Name's Randolph Frickelburg the Third. I'm from Miami. But don't let that put you off. All my vices are legal.'

The novelist flashed him a mischievous smile. 'So are mine … well, most of them.'

'The next tea and cream cake is on me as a thank you for all the murderous pleasure your brilliant writing has given this humble reader over the years.'

'You do have rather a way with words yourself, Mr Frickelburg. And what an intriguing name you have.'

'Born in the States. But I'm a quarter each Polish, German, Russian and English. We don't let world wars get in the way of things in our family.'

Agatha chuckled. 'Please sit down, Mr Frickelburg. I'd be delighted if you would join me.'

Randolph's cheeks nearly burst. 'I'd be even more delighted!' And he parked himself opposite her.

Agatha sipped her tea. 'Frickelburg – sounds like the sort of name I spend hours trying to dream up.'

'Maybe you could name one of your characters after me, ma'am? Just imagine – a murder-mystery novel starring a Randolph Frickelburg the Third. It would be a dream come true for me and all the other Frickelburgs.'

'Are there many of you?'

'Just me, Mrs Frickelburg and the two kids – Crockett and Tubbs. But I left them at home. They don't travel well.' He jabbed a thumb at himself. 'And they need a break from yours truly.'

'I can't see why. You're just the type of strong, vibrant, no-nonsense personality we need around here. Village life can be frightfully dull. Too many people minding their Ps and Qs.'

'Oh, I know all about your queues, ma'am. I spent a good chunk of my vacation in your post office already. As for peas, well … they were served with my traditional beef-and-ale pie in the local pub. I've chewed softer bullets.'

Agatha burst out laughing. 'Superb stuff – hard peas and long queues! If I may, I'll include that mischievous play on words in my next murder-mystery novel.'

'You think people will laugh?'

'So hard, some may risk serious abdominal injury.'

'Way to go! I can say I played a part in a work of literary genius!'

Agatha beamed. 'And a fractured-rib epidemic.' She noticed Mrs Trap bustling up to the table. 'Leave this woman to me, Randolph. She's a pain in the posterior.'

'Sure. You're the English etiquette expert!'

Mrs Trap was wearing a dirty apron and a jumbo-sized smirk. 'I see you got yourself a toy boy, Aggie. Then again, most men are toy boys when you get to your age!'

Agatha half smiled. 'I'm surprised you're such an expert on toy boys, Mrs Trap. How old is your husband?'

'Fifty-seven – same age as me.'

'The same age as Jepson the butler.'

'Was he fifty-seven? Looked much older – more your age. I'd hate to look that old.'

'Well, at least I made it to fifty-eight. Let's hope you and Mr Trap see another birthday.' She stabbed a fork into her cream horn. 'You never know in Upper Goosing.'

'Yeah.' Mrs Trap wiped her nose in deep thought. 'Last time I saw Jepson, he was buying some anti-ageing cream in the chemist's. Won't need it now, will he?'

'No,' replied Agatha coolly. 'Death is the most effective anti-ageing remedy there is.'

'Funny old fruit, wasn't he? Always bought a small tea, the cheapest biscuits, and used too many paper napkins. He's no great loss.'

'No,' purred Agatha. 'No loss at all.'

'Drowned in mango chutney, I heard, while her ladyship and her curry ladies were stuffing their fat faces with venison vindaloo.'

'So I gather. But I wasn't anywhere near the manor, of course. Dinner parties aren't my thing.'

'No!' shrieked Mrs Trap. 'Killing off the dinner guests is more your thing, isn't it?' Deep thought consumed her again for two seconds. 'Maybe I should add "Peculiar Manor poppadoms" to the menu for the tourists?'

'Excellent idea. Just make sure they're not drowning in mango chutney.'

'I will, your ladyship!' cackled Mrs Trap. 'Right, do you and your toy boy want anything else?'

Randolph joined in. 'Sure! I'm paying the check but it's this English lady's choice.'

'Thank you, Randolph. Two chocolate eclairs and a pot of Earl Grey, please.'

'Coming right up!' squawked Mrs Trap. 'And don't you worry. I guarantee these eclairs will be salmonella-free – or I'll give you your money back.' And she scurried away to the serving counter.

Randolph puffed out his cheeks. 'I think she's what you English call a "character".'

'We English call such people many things. But, as I'm in polite company, I'll stop there.'

The American rubbed his chin. 'What she was saying about the butler – was it true?'

'I believe so.'

'Just – if you don't mind me saying – his death reminds me of what happened in one of your novels.'

'Which one?'

'*Murder in an Odd Manor*. Butler dies during some fancy dinner party at a country pile.'

'Really? I've created so many murderers, suspects, victims – it's all too much for an author's brain to retain.'

91

'Yeah, trust me – I know your stories better than I do the rules of baseball. But this real-life butler getting whacked in a Peculiar Manor – it could be fantastic for your book sales, ma'am. Tourists will love it. Murder-mystery fans will love it. Heck, even Mrs Trap's gonna love it!'

'I'm not convinced she can read.'

'Then she'll learn – just so she can check out the book that everyone's talking about!'

'A tad optimistic.'

'No, believe me – you could make a killing!'

The author's eyes sparkled. 'I already *have* made a killing.'

'Excuse me, ma'am?'

'Made a killing – with my twenty books. Granted, sales have dried up in the last few years but tastes change.'

'You still got the killer touch, ma'am. Bet your books are still selling.' Randolph pulled out a smartphone. 'Let me check out where *Murder in an Odd Manor* is in the charts.' He tapped on his phone for twenty seconds. 'Number 2,241 in the e-book store. That's not too shabby.' He took a sharp breath. 'Oh, my!'

'What's the matter?'

Randolph forced an unconcerned look. 'Nothing, ma'am.'

'No, go on – what is it?'

After a pause, he continued. 'The latest review gives it one star. It's titled "Murderously Awful". I won't read what it says but it's not complimentary.' He tapped the phone's screen. 'And the same person's one-starred stacks of your other books. Can you believe it? Why does the jerk bother reading them all if they don't like them? I just don't understand some people.'

Agatha slammed a hand down on the table and raised her voice. 'I do. They have no talent of their own so seek out those who do and spend their sad, pathetic lives denigrating, defaming and destroying that person's life's work.'

'What was that deceased butler's name again?'

'Maurice Jepson.'

'Oh. Coz the username of the person who left the reviews is Goosing Jeeves.'

'That means nothing to me.'

'Jeeves was P.G. Wodehouse's fictional butler. Maybe that reviewer is a real-life butler. By that, I mean Jepson. Because I doubt there are many other butlers round here.'

'I've no idea who Goosing Jeeves is.' She chortled to herself. 'But I suppose if the spiteful one-star reviews dry up, we'll know it was Jepson.'

Randolph spotted Mrs Trap approaching with the eclairs and tea. 'Yes, ma'am. I suppose we will.'

Chapter 15

Inspector Trump and Constable Dinkel were sitting in Superintendent Block's office, waiting for him to return from the executive coffee machine.

'Leave the talking to me, Dinkel.'

'I normally do, sir.'

'Was that you being impertinent, constable?'

'No, it was me stating a fact, sir.'

'Then please stop stating facts – too many of them annoy me. Preferably, say nothing until we're safely out of this office.'

'What if the superintendent addresses me directly, sir?'

'Then I shall dive in, divert, disrupt and do anything else beginning with a "d" that's necessary to save my detective skin.'

Dinkel's nose wrinkled. 'You mean save *our* skins, sir.'

'I mean save my skin, first and foremost. Save your skin, if absolutely necessary.'

'My skin is absolutely necessary, sir. It stops my internal organs from flopping out.'

'Very droll, constable. Just make sure you keep everything together during this interrogation.'

'I'll do my best.'

'Your best isn't good enough. It isn't even up there with my worst.'

'With the greatest of respect, sir, I've seen your worst. And I'm confident I can significantly improve on it.'

'Is that you being doubly impertinent, constable?'

'No, sir.'

'I'm glad to hear it. We wouldn't want your forthcoming promotion assessment to be jeopardised by impertinence.'

'No, sir.'

'Because nobody likes a smartass, Dinkel.'

'No, sir.'

'Is that all you've got to say for yourself – "No, sir"?'

'No, sir. I mean, yes, sir. I mean, don't worry, sir. Constable Dinkel has formulated a convincing explanation for the missing Cripps statement.'

'Forget your explanation. And stop talking about yourself in the third person. Only detectives of the highest calibre are entitled to do that.'

'Yes, sir.'

'Detective Inspector Clinton Trump – the finest sleuth the Home Counties has ever seen – has this situation completely under control. Sit back. Relax. Act naturally. And everything will run smoother than a Rolls Royce on an ice rink.'

Superintendent Block burst into the room, making Clinton jump two centimetres off his swivel chair, return with a bump and rotate ninety degrees to face the wall.

'You seem a bit twitchy, Trump,' noted the superintendent, putting his mega-jumbo espresso on his desk and sitting down. 'And a twitchy Trump is never a good sign.'

Clinton beamed a professional smile as he reoriented himself. 'Everything is absolutely tickety-boo with this tip-top detective, sir.'

Block glared back. 'I'm ecstatic to hear it.'

Clinton stroked his bouffant. 'I thought you would be.'

The superintendent muttered something under his breath. 'Right. Before I brief you pair on latest developments, what happened with her ladyship's gardener, Trump?'

'Cripps? Oh, nothing much really, sir. Bit of a blind alley.'

'What did he say in his statement?'

'His statement? Well, he spoke to us – making various statements in the process – and we responded to those statements with further statements of our own. There was a general back and forth of statements for a period of time. And, at the conclusion of our game of statement ping-pong, we signed off with the customary end-of-statement goodbyes.'

The superintendent squeezed his coffee cup. 'I meant a formal statement – written down in black and white.'

'Absolutely no need,' scoffed Clinton. 'I know how eco-conscious the chief constable is, sir. It would be a waste of trees to commit it to paper. Excess carbon dioxide would have been produced if further discussion had been entered into. And the ink is better served signing off my outstanding expenses claims.' He nodded at the superintendent's in tray. 'You do have all forty-two of them, don't you, sir?'

'Yes, I do,' grumbled Block. 'And you and I will have a chat some other time about how a round of golf, a sand wedge, a cheese-and-caviar soufflé, two bottles of Chablis and a pair of Tiger Woods 'Get In The Hole!' underpants constitute legitimate police expenses.' He rolled his eyes. 'Now, why wasn't a formal statement taken from that ex-con gardener?'

Clinton ummed and ahhed for five seconds.

'Well, Trump?' snapped Block. 'Answer your superior officer.'

Clinton croaked something unintelligible.

'Last chance. Or I'm opening formal disciplinary proceedings against you.'

The croaks morphed into squeaks.

Dinkel attempted to come to the rescue. 'Cripps said he wasn't at the manor at the time of the murder, sir. And the detailed statements I took from Lady Peculiar, the Major and the maid back that up.'

Block pondered this news. 'Does Cripps have an alibi, constable?'

'Possibly. He was a little vague. He said he went straight home on Tuesday after work and indulged in an alcoholic tipple before bedtime. He also stated that he may, or may not, have spoken with a neighbour or a relative that evening. But soon after, erm, he became, um … threatening.' He shuffled in his seat. 'Just like you said he might, sir.'

Block stared at Trump. 'You'll corroborate all this, I assume?'

'Certainly, sir. If it's what you want to hear and it will put me in the clear.'

Block cocked his ear. 'Sorry, what did you just say?'

'Apologies. I meant once you hear the full story, you'll see it puts me in the clear.'

'Hmm. Continue, constable.'

'Cripps was acting in an extremely aggressive manner, sir. After valiantly attempting to calm him down without success, the inspector took the brave decision to dispense with a formal statement and terminate the interview, thereby avoiding any physical harm to himself or, much more importantly, as he informed me afterwards, myself – a constable he trusts, wants to work with a lot more in the future and will be recommending for promotion to the rank of sergeant at the earliest possible opportunity.'

Clinton flashed a confused glance at Dinkel, but didn't interrupt.

'The other three staff weren't at the manor on Tuesday evening,' continued Dinkel. 'And they rarely fraternised with Jepson, who they said was a bit of a loner. None of them mentioned Cripps at all.'

'What else did the statements from her ladyship, the Major and maid add to the mix?' asked Block.

'Nothing of any use to us, sir.'

'Hmm.' Block slurped his espresso. 'It's your lucky day, Trump. I'm issuing you with an official superintendential pardon for failing to take Cripps' statement.'

'That's rather a longwinded word, sir.'

'Pardon?'

'No, not "pardon". I meant "superintendential".'

'I know what you meant, Trump. And if you ever reach high office – heaven forbid – you'll be able to describe your actions using whatever language you wish. But, until that dark day arrives, you will not question how I choose to describe my pardons. You will be grateful for receiving one and keep your adjectival opinions to yourself.'

'Right you are, sir. Was there anything else? It's just I'm giving another murder-prevention talk at Goosing golf club this evening and I don't want to bring the good name of the force into disrepute by being late for it.'

Block gulped down more coffee. 'How successful are these talks in terms of your audience not being murdered?'

'If you round up to the nearest ten per cent, I have a hundred per cent success rate.'

'So, less than a hundred per cent?'

'Only if you don't round up, sir.'

'Don't try and bamboozle me with statistics, Trump. Just tell me how many people have been murdered after you've availed them of your expert advice. Otherwise, I'll round down your superintendential pardons to the nearest ten, leaving you with zero pardons – and disciplinary proceedings to face.'

'Very well, sir.' The inspector dredged his memory. 'Four of my golf club audience have departed this world. Though one's membership expired the day before he did, so we'll scratch him from the record. Thus, if we're talking members, it's only three.' More dredging. 'One was a caddy, so we won't count him. That leaves us with two. And one of those had an appalling swing, never raked the sand after bunker shots, and trod my ball into the rough on one occasion, so she rather brought untimely death on herself. That leaves just one – the woman who ran the Killer Beats music shop. She never removed those ghastly headphones of hers, so she probably wasn't listening to my words of wisdom. It's sad, but I find a lot of my audience don't pay attention.'

'I'm not bloody surprised,' snorted the superintendent. 'Enough of your golfing nonsense, Trump. It's time to listen to me.' He wolfed down the last of his coffee. 'Cripps and Jepson appear to have shared a desire to become comedians.'

'Cripps, sir?' asked Dinkel. 'He's even more cheerless than Jepson.'

'My thoughts exactly. But, by a huge stroke of luck – the type of random event that only happens in detective drama to move the plot along – this morning, my nephew signed up for something called The Big Titter at a comedy venue called Planet Mirth. And he checked out his rivals. Jepson's name was the first on the list. Cripps was the second.'

Clinton jerked with realisation. 'Oh, that comedy competition? I think the butcher's widow mentioned Jepson had signed up for it.'

The superintendent crossed his arms. 'And you didn't think to mention it to anyone?'

'Well, I'm mentioning it now, sir.'

'After I've already mentioned it to you.'

'After it had been mentioned to me, yes. It's what I call a mentioning chain. You will no doubt mention it to someone else. And they will mention it—'

'On your letter of dismissal, if you don't button it.' Block put his head in his hands and then resumed. 'Dinkel, I want you to focus on that gardener. Do a bit of digging, have a root around and see if he comes up smelling of roses or compost.'

'Of course, sir. I'll leave no stone unturned, rake through the facts, and get my hands dirty if I have to.'

'I'm blooming happy to hear it. Right, off you toddle down the garden path. I want a quick tête-à-tête with the tête sitting next to you.'

'Is it about my expenses?' asked Clinton hopefully.

'No,' grunted Block, nodding at the door. 'Shut it on your way out, Dinkel.'

The constable left the room as the superintendent scrunched up his coffee cup and tossed it in the bin. 'I am concerned, inspector.'

'About Dinkel? I don't blame you, sir. Admittedly, he can talk the talk when necessary, but he's very green.' He chuckled softly. 'I expect that's why you asked him to focus on the gardener.'

'No. I did that because he has a tendency to listen to what I say and actually do what I ask him.' He looked up at the ceiling, sighed, and returned his gaze to Clinton. 'Do you know what,

Trump? If Jepson's death was a storyline in one of Agatha Twisty's novels, rather than a real-life mango-chutney drowning, her detective inspector would already be halfway to solving the crime.'

'Oh, I am halfway – most definitely.'

'How do you work that out?'

'Well, we've one half of the jigsaw puzzle already in place – the victim. The other half is the murderer.'

'If only solving murders was as easy as a two-piece jigsaw. When you're investigating, it's more like a ten-thousand-piece puzzle of a clear blue sky.'

'All the pieces will be clicked together by the end of Friday, sir. I promise you that.'

'Which Friday are you talking about?' huffed Block. 'Because I retire in five years.'

'This Friday, sir. The Goosing Golf Open is on Saturday. And I can't risk any work-related interruptions or distractions.'

Block smacked his lips. 'Our Lower Goosing colleagues have already arrested and obtained a full confession from the Monopoly Murderer – less than twenty-four hours after Dr Black was found battered to death with a candlestick in the library.'

'Oh, who's the killer?'

'Some posh professor with a plum in his mouth. A borrowing dispute over the last copy of *Fifty Shades of Grey* turned nasty. And the Monopoly Murderer will be going straight to jail without passing "Go". That means the pressure's on us to solve the Peculiar Manor murder.'

'Do we have a nickname for our killer, sir? Because I'm a dab hand at that sort of thing.'

'No, we don't. I want you concentrating on progressing this case rather than dreaming up fancy names.'

'The Curry Killer, perhaps?'

'Are you listening to me?'

'No, too obvious. How about the Peculiar Predator?'

'You're not listening to me.'

'Jack the Pickler?'

The superintendent leapt from his seat. 'Shut up about nicknames! Just solve this murder by Friday or you'll be spending the whole weekend with psychologists, psychiatrists and psychics trying to find out who bumped off that butler!'

Clinton's body stiffened. 'But ... the golf tournament. I'm the reigning champion – attempting to make it a record four wins on the trot.'

'I don't care if you've won the Nobel prize for detection for the last ten years! No result by Friday and you'll be working from dawn till dusk this Saturday and Sunday – and every weekend after that – until we make some progress on this case!'

'I'm fairly sure there isn't a Nobel prize for detection, sir. Though, if there were, I share your confidence in my ability to dominate the award for a decade. Probably more.'

'Put a sock in it and listen!' yelled the superintendent. He took a deep breath and composed himself. 'One last thing to be aware of, before I boot your backside out that door. That chief reporter from the *Goosing Times* has already been harassing our press officer about the case.'

'The Cocky woman?'

'Yes. Cocky by name, even cockier by nature. We know how she operates – she'll be sniffing round, grilling anyone who knew or spoke to Jepson recently and putting two and two together and making twenty-two.'

'I can handle her, sir.'

'Make sure you do. Because her charm, smooth-talking and false flattery has fooled more than one of my officers into spilling his investigative beans. So, if you come into contact with Fenella Cocky, stonewall her and say as little as possible.'

'You can rely on me.'

The superintendent bit his lip. 'Yes, I can usually rely on you – to put your size elevens in it. Last time you investigated a murder, you ended up being quoted about ongoing investigations on the front page of the *Goosing Times*.'

'Small misunderstanding over what "off the record" and "on the record" meant, sir. I'm better informed now.'

'I don't want any on- or off-the-record chats, Trump, because your tongue has a habit of slipping at precisely the wrong moment.'

'You have no worries on that score, sir.' Clinton tapped his face. 'My tongue is firmly in cheek.'

'And not for the first time.' Block jabbed his finger at the door. 'Now, hop it. Before I change my mind about that superintendential pardon.'

The inspector obeyed the order and was on his way to the non-executive coffee machine when a passing secretary shoved a piece of paper into his hand. He studied it and saw it was a typed note:

DI Trump – Message from Jayne Trill. Wants to discuss a murder urgently. Meet her on the village green at half past four this afternoon. She'll be sitting on the Ted Penny memorial bench.

Clinton sighed. He'd been hoping to clock off a little early so he could go home to freshen up and feed the cats before heading for the golf club. But, still raw from his superintendent's almost completely unjustified verbal assault on his professional character, meeting with Jayne Trill wasn't an appointment he could postpone – she might just be in possession of valuable information about Jepson's murder.

He checked his watch. It was four o'clock. Not even time for a well-deserved coffee and doughnut on police expenses. The village green was a short walk away, so he decided to head there now – if Mrs Trill was already waiting, he could make an earlier-than-expected escape.

Chapter 16

As Clinton had suspected, drama queen Jayne Trill was already reclining on the Ted Penny memorial bench when he arrived at the deserted village green. He didn't recognise her immediately because, for some reason, she was wearing dark sunglasses, a flamboyant straw hat sporting several coloured feathers, and a bright pink puffer jacket.

He reminded himself that this meeting needed to be as brief as possible. That wasn't always easy with Jayne. Firstly, she loved the sound of her own voice almost as much offstage as onstage. Secondly, she'd attempted on more than one occasion to flirt with him at the Goosing Players' after-show parties. And she hadn't been too subtle about it.

Jayne didn't seem to notice him approaching, so he made his way to the bench and sat down next to her – making sure there was a reasonable no-man's-land between them. 'It's me, Mrs Trill – Clinton Trump. Upper Goosing's premier policeman.'

She whipped off her glasses. 'Oh, inspector! How rude of me. I can hardly see a thing through these.'

'Then why are you wearing them?'

'In case we're spotted together.' She giggled girlishly. 'I don't want word getting back to my husband that I'm having dangerous liaisons with handsome police inspectors.'

'There's nothing dangerous about it, Mrs Trill. We're sitting on a park bench in broad daylight.'

Jayne patted the wooden seat. 'Try telling that to old Ted Penny.'

'Two quite different scenarios. Ted was on this bench on midsummer's day, commenting on the world going by, when an unsavoury group of druids took issue with his observations on their choice of summer attire and attacked him with his own

103

rolled-up newspaper. As the autopsy report noted, if that evening's copy of the *Goosing Times* had been of normal thickness, and not included a feature entitled "365 things you didn't know about the summer solstice", the old chap would have most certainly survived. Terrible business.'

'But don't you think there's something strangely exciting about sitting on a wooden bench where a dastardly deed was once committed?'

'Dastardly deeds are committed by local youths on this bench every night. And I prefer not to think about them.'

'Ha-hah! Well, there's no need to worry, inspector. I haven't brought a rolled-up newspaper with me.' She coughed three times. 'But I imagine you'll be commenting kindly on *my* choice of summer attire.'

The inspector frowned. 'I wasn't planning to. I'm in rather a hurry.'

She waggled her cheeks. 'Such a busy bee. And so am I. I'm shooting off to rehearsals shortly and this is my costume. I'm playing the chairwoman of the local amateur-dramatics group.' She edged a little closer. 'She's a real busybody who sticks her nose into everything, flirts outrageously with the detective inspector, and thinks the world revolves around her silly little drama club.'

'It must be a very challenging role for you, Mrs Trill. But let's turn our attention to the murder you wanted to discuss – Jepson's I assume.'

'Oh, no, no, no. Jepson is history. Already a distant memory to those unfortunate enough to have known him. I'm talking about the future.'

'I'm afraid this detective genius doesn't quite follow.'

'Our next theatrical production – *Murder at Dress Rehearsal*.'

'I still don't follow.'

'Jepson was starring in it. He was playing a character called Clinton Starr.' She edged even closer. 'And I want you, Clinton, to be the new star. You'll light up that stage like a controlled explosion in a community centre. Captivate our audience to the point where they'll only fall asleep ten minutes before the end. And bring an energy and style that we've been sadly lacking since Ted Penny junior was shot dead onstage after he upset the prompt by fluffing his lines too often.'

'And what happens to this Clinton Starr character?'

'He's murdered onstage when someone swaps real bullets for blanks.' She placed a hand on his arm. 'It's not how I would've done it – too obvious.' She stared into the detective's eyes. 'How does one get away with murder, inspector?'

'You should ask my superintendent. He's been getting away with murder for years.'

Jayne screeched with laughter. 'You and Superintendent Block really don't see eye to eye, do you?'

'That's putting it mildly.'

Her voice dropped three octaves. 'Would you like Jayne to … put him right?'

'In what way?'

'Don't ask questions. Just know that I can scratch your back …' She breathed in through her nose. '… if you scratch mine.'

'My back is rather sensitive, Mrs Trill – especially around my left scapula – so I'm not sure it would appreciate your digital intervention.'

'A gentle massage, then.' She rubbed his shoulder. 'I do hope you'll … come on board.'

Clinton shrugged off her attention. 'Thanks for the offer, Mrs Trill. But an actor's life isn't for me.'

'Acting wasn't for Jepson, but he still accepted the role.'

'And look where he is now.'

'In a far better place – from my point of view. And I can only hope for the sake of the rest of the dearly departed that there is no amateur drama in the afterlife.'

'You weren't on the best of terms, I take it?'

'No. He was an abysmal actor. If he hadn't died in those kitchens he would have died onstage several times a night. So he should be thankful he only died once.'

105

'Every murderous cloud has a silver lining. Now, if you have nothing more to tell me about Jepson, I shall be on my way.'

Jayne's eyes twinkled. 'Oh, there is something.'

'What's that?'

She checked none of the local wildlife were listening. 'Being at the very top of the Upper Goosing social ladder, I'm not the type to gossip. But I do believe Jepson ...' She double-checked the squirrels weren't earwigging. '... was seeing a lady.'

'Lady Peculiar, you mean? That's hardly news. Working and living at the manor, he would see her almost every day.'

'No, inspector.' She leant into him, so her hot breath was on his neck. 'I mean in the romantic sense.'

Clinton thought hard for ten seconds. 'He had a girlfriend?'

'I'm not sure if it was that serious. But he was fiddling with his phone during the last couple of rehearsals in a way I've seen leading men do when they're communicating with an offstage leading lady. And he was insistent on leaving his final rehearsal fifteen minutes early because he was "meeting someone for a drink".'

'Did he say who?'

'No. But high-society people such as ourselves know to never keep a lady waiting, so it must have been a woman – a love interest, I presume.' Her shoulder touched his. 'Do you have a love interest, inspector?'

Clinton jumped to his feet. 'I have no interest in love, Mrs Trill. I'm far too busy feeding cats, playing golf and solving murders. And, as I have two famished felines at home, and a lecture on murder prevention to deliver at the golf club, I shall bid you farewell.'

And he sprinted to the bus stop as fast as his size eleven shoes could carry him.

Chapter 17

Clouseau the ginger tom was pleasantly surprised when his human came tumbling through the front door a little earlier than his body clock was anticipating.

'Evening, chaps!' boomed the human, bounding in from the hall. 'I expect you're both starving.'

Clouseau waited for the inevitable follow-up, while his one-eyed companion Columbo did his best to track a bluebottle's progress around the flat from the arm of the sofa.

'What do you fancy, eh? Chicken, beef, lamb or rabbit?'

Clouseau meowed in the hope that a fifth – yet-to-be-identified – flavour might be on offer. At the very least, he hoped it wouldn't be beef. He was bored whiskerless of beef. Surely his human had noticed his beef with beef?

'Beef it is! Your favourite, Clouseau!' He pointed a finger at the other cat. 'You'll have to be quicker next time, Columbo.'

Columbo overbalanced as he swung a paw at the fly and toppled to the floor, hitting the carpet with a furry thud.

'Hard lines, Columbo!' laughed the human, zipping to the kitchen.

Clouseau meandered over and checked Columbo was still in fine feline fettle. His flatmate was scratching his ear with an intensity he rarely saw humans reach when their ears were itchy, so there was clearly no harm done. *Inconsiderate human,* Clouseau thought. *He must be rushing off out again.* And his human never brought back anything from these second hunting trips. You'd think he'd learn his evenings were better spent dangling fluffy mice on strings in front of them, catching bluebottles, and re-filling bowls with food. But he didn't.

After dishing up a disappointingly beefy dinner, the human disappeared into his sleeping den. Ten minutes later something unexpected occurred – a giant canary emerged. Clouseau might only be an indoor cat, but he knew an avian opportunity when he saw one. His prey instincts triggered, he launched himself at the canary's highly polished shoes.

'Get off me, you silly cat!' cried the canary. 'It's me – your lord and master!'

Clouseau understood this sentence. But he wasn't aware he had a lord. Or a master. He was, after all, a cat – his own lord and master. So he assumed this talking canary wasn't addressing him and carried on clawing its shoes with renewed vigour, tossing in a few scary hisses for good measure.

'What are you doing, Clouseau?' shrieked the canary. 'Get off me!'

This was odd. The canary knew his name. Maybe he'd been doing some research? This bird was more dangerous than he'd thought. He sunk his teeth into the canary's shoes to teach it a valuable lesson about snooping on house cats.

'It's me!' screamed the canary.

The canary wasn't being specific enough about its identity, so Clouseau ignored its latest plea and started shredding its shoelaces.

'I'm your dad!' squealed the big bird.

Clouseau ceased clawing and started staring as he realised his mistake. This wasn't an oversized canary. It was his human. And, for some reason he would probably never understand, he was covered from head to shiny shoes in canary yellow.

'This is my new golf attire, you reckless pussycat! Designed to dazzle my opponents in every possible way and, in a lecturing environment, stop my audience from nodding off.' Clinton assessed the damage. 'And you've ruined my brand-new yellow leather shoes. They were so shiny I could see my fabulous reflection in them and now they're scratched beyond recognition.'

Clouseau decided the best way to deal with this situation was to slink off and hope everyone else in the room forgot about it before the next mealtime.

'I haven't got time to change,' sighed his human. 'The taxi's outside.' And he headed off on another futile hunting mission.

Chapter 18

The large screen installed at one end of the Goosing golf club members' bar was displaying the ninety-ninth and penultimate slide of Clinton's murder-prevention presentation. His audience had dwindled from forty-something to single figures over the past two and a half hours, but that was par for the course when you were lecturing golfers. They would rather commit alcoholic sacrilege by ordering a G&T with pink gin, bore bar staff with tales of bunkering bravado, or chat about the latest line in Justin Rose knitwear than listen to advice about how to stay alive on and off the golf course. Of those who remained, at least a handful appeared mildly engaged – including that odd Russian woman, Svetlana, whom his best friend Dickie Blinder was dating. He had never witnessed her in sporting action but Dickie had informed him she would be competing on Saturday and he'd heard rumours she was pretty handy with a seven iron. But first-timers never won the trophy. Mainly because old-timers Clinton and Dickie knew this course like the back of their putters. For nine of the last ten years, one of other of them had claimed the crown. The only gap was the time he'd been ill with flu and Dickie had been on holiday somewhere much hotter and less murderous. Therefore, history was on their side. And Clinton was supremely confident of winning this year – as long as he could sneak in a couple of practice rounds and solve the Jepson murder before Friday so he wouldn't be dragged into work over the weekend. Maybe he could spend the day here tomorrow and ask some searching questions of his fellow golfers about Jepson's murder. Clues often emerged from the most unlikely of places. And the golf course was as unlikely as they come. Yes, an all-day-Thursday golfing expedition sounded like a totally reasonable use of police time. And he'd be able to charge it to expenses.

He smoothed down his canary-yellow sweater, clicked a remote control and moved to the final slide. 'In summary, here are the main points to bear in mind when you're out and about in Upper Goosing and don't wish to be murdered.'

'Hurry up, Clinton!' shouted a barman. 'We wanna put *Nick Faldo Explores the Amazon* on the big screen in five minutes. He's tracking down the Yanomami tribe and showing them the best way to tackle a water hazard.'

Neither Nick Faldo nor the Yanomami tribe nor anyone else was going to break Clinton's stride, so he ignored the interruption and addressed what was left of his audience.

'Here are the key tips I want everyone here to take away and remember from this most instructive of lectures, thereby ensuring you aren't throttled, stabbed, drowned, shot or battered to death with your own evening newspaper.'

'Or bored to death by pompous policemen,' grumbled the barman, who was fiddling with his own remote control.

'I heard that!' snapped Clinton. 'And I'm sure you've told enough tedious tales about clogged beer lines to send both Ryder Cup teams to sleep.'

'Yes, let inspector speak,' shouted Svetlana, glaring at the interrupter. 'He help you stay alive. You not listen, maybe you end up dead barman.'

Clinton straightened his canary-yellow tie. 'Thank you, madam.' He checked the ends of his canary-yellow trousers were still covering the worst of his shoe scuffs and continued. 'To stay safe on the streets of Upper Goosing, we recommend the following. Number one – don't annoy the locals. Not all of our murderers are outsiders. We have a healthy tradition of murdering our own in this village. And pushing in front of someone in the post-office queue, spilling their pint at the pub, or walking too slowly in front of them on the high street while fiddling with your smartphone may be a minor misdemeanour in many places, but in Upper Goosing it can have deadly consequences.'

A woman on the front row snored so loudly she woke herself up.

'Number two – avoid drawing attention to yourself. Murderers are, more or less, the same breed as magpies. They're attracted to shiny objects. Dress too brightly and you could be snatched away. Black and white are the best shades to wear – that way, the murderous magpies will see you as one of their own and leave you be.'

'Doesn't look like you're taking your own advice, inspector,' sneered a snub-nosed man in the third row. 'You're more canary than magpie.'

Clinton waited for the sniggers to die down before responding. 'No policemen have ever been murdered in this village. We're far too smart.' He lifted his chin. 'Now, finally, a simple but often overlooked piece of advice. If you don't wish to be murdered in this wonderful village of ours, don't be here in the first place. Move away or – if you're here on holiday – choose an alternative destination.'

'Like the Canary Islands, you mean?' snorted the snub-nosed man.

Before Clinton could cut this canary-obsessed cretin down to size with a devastating put-down that he hadn't thought of yet, a woman called out from the back.

'I can recommend Llandudno. I trained there as a reporter. No chance of being murdered because nobody visits anymore – apart from the seagulls.'

Clinton craned his neck to see the woman's face and, to his surprise, he recognised her. 'Ms Cocky, what a pleasant surprise. I haven't seen you in this fine establishment before. Is it business or pleasure that brings you here?'

'Pleasure, of course. I've heard all about your wonderful murder-prevention lectures, inspector. The bar manager kindly signed me in as a guest and I caught the last hour or so.'

People were streaming out of the bar without having been formally dismissed or offering a thunderous round of applause. But he was intrigued by this journalist's presence so, rather than summoning everyone back for a formal farewell, he clapped his hands, offered a quick 'Thank you, everyone,' and headed towards the back of the room.

Fenella fiddled with one of the shoulder straps of her fairway-green dress. 'Can I buy you a drink, inspector, as my own personal thank-you for such a fabulous lecture?'

Clinton remembered his superintendent's warning about fraternising with Fenella. But this was the golf club. It was neutral territory – the equivalent of an embassy or consulate in a foreign country. He could indulge in a little post-lecture chit-chat. Especially if it involved free drinks and compliments.

'I'd be delighted to accept your offer, Fenella.'

'Will a white-wine spritzer do you?'

'My favourite tipple. You've obviously done your homework.'

'Just a lucky guess. It's mine, too.'

While Fenella attempted to attract the attention of the remote-control-obsessed barman, Svetlana sidled up to Clinton.

'Very interesting lecture, inspector,' she announced in her flat Eastern European voice.

'Thank you, erm, Ms ...'

'Svetlana is fine.'

'Thank you, Svetlana. I appreciated your help at the end.' Curiosity got the better of him. 'Did you play much golf in Russia?'

'I play golf, yes.'

'How much golf?'

'Eighteen hole.'

'No, I meant how often?'

'It always eighteen hole.'

Clinton clenched his teeth. Conversing with a journalist would be child's play compared to this East–West exchange.

'No, I meant how many times did you play in Russia?'

'I not count.'

'Less than ten?'

'Fewer than ten.'

'You've played fewer than ten rounds?'

'No, you say "less than ten". Correct English "fewer than ten".'

'Alright, let's forget English grammar. I want to be frank.'

'Who Frank?'

'Nobody.'

'Frank play golf here?'

'No. I mean, there is someone called Frank who plays golf here – annoying middle-aged chap who's always probing newcomers about their golfing proficiency at the bar – but that's not what I meant.'

'Frank here this evening?'

'No, he isn't. Forget Frank.'

'I not know him. So how I forget him?'

'Frank's not important. What I really want to know is how skilled are you at golf, Svetlana?'

'We have saying in Siberia: "If it Wednesday, don't ask about weather for weekend."'

'And what does that mean?'

'It mean find out on Saturday how good I play golf.'

Clinton sighed. He'd met his golfing match this evening. Hopefully, that wouldn't be the case in three days' time. He checked on Fenella. She was still waiting for the barman – who was intent on locating the Nick Faldo documentary before taking her order – so he continued the conversation. 'Will you be teeing off with Dickie on Saturday?'

'Dickie not play.'

Clinton thought he'd just heard Svetlana saying his best pal wouldn't be competing in Brokenshire's premier golfing event. 'I think you may have misspoken, Svetlana. Dickie most certainly is taking part in the Goosing Golf Open. Only major illness or holiday plans would prevent him.'

'Dickie have problem with leg.'

Clinton frowned. 'I saw him a couple of days ago and he was walking completely freely.'

'He hide it well.'

'That's odd. He never mentioned it to me. And we always share our medical problems, describe the symptoms in intricate detail and agree how brave we are to soldier on regardless. It's a great English tradition dating back centuries.'

'It small problem. I study medicine here in England. I find problem. I tell Dickie, "We not want it become big problem." And he listen to me.'

'Well, I suppose it means I'm a racing certainty to win the tournament.' His chest expanded impressively. 'That means the cross of Saint George will continue to fly from the club flagpole for another year, rather than the Scottish saltire which is hoisted up after Dickie's victories – on the dubious grounds he spent his early years in some godforsaken place north of the border called Dun-something-or-other.' His chest returned to normal proportions. 'But still, I would rather Dickie played. Healthy rivalry at the top of the leaderboard is what gifted sportspeople thrive on. Without it, there's always the risk an outsider could make a challenge.'

Svetlana's shoulders hunched. 'You mean outsider like me – a Russian?'

'I didn't mean you personally. And I wasn't implying that a Russian national winning the tournament would in any way be a problem.' He reflected briefly. 'Although, of course, it might not go down well with some of the locals – they still haven't forgiven that family from Saint Petersburg who allowed their offspring to Cossack dance all over the daffodil displays. And many of us are still rather sore about the Russian president cancelling his visit to the Getting Away With Murder museum on his last trip to the UK so he could officially open one of Lower Goosing's new easy-access car parks because it was funded by some oligarch chum of his.' More reflection. 'Neither would such a triumph be welcomed by the regular golf club members who aren't familiar with the Cyrillic alphabet and don't particularly want to fork out extra money for a bilingual trophy engraver or a Russian flag.' Another second of contemplation. 'And a Russian victory would go down like a lead beefburger with the American tourists who almost single-handedly support our local tourism industry. Americans staying away could ultimately mean job losses, businesses going to the wall, homes being repossessed, marriages collapsing and, if things get really bad, people having to cancel their annual subscriptions to *Country Living*.' He forced a smile. 'Other than that, I don't see any problem at all.'

Fenella returned with two white-wine spritzers. 'Sorry about the delay. That barman was having a lover's tiff with the TV remote.'

As the opening credits of *Nick Faldo Explores the Amazon* flickered onto the big screen, Svetlana held up a hand in farewell. 'Good to talk, inspector. See you Saturday.'

'Most definitely, Svetlana. Goodbye.'

And the Russian darted out of sight behind a fat man in a ghastly sweater.

'Even here, in the deepest, darkest corners of the Amazon rainforest,' drawled the documentary's Californian narrator, 'it's hard to believe there are human beings who are so isolated they've never heard of Tiger Woods, Ernie Els or, indeed, Nick Faldo. People who've never held a dimpled ball in their hands, who wouldn't know a sand wedge from an eight iron, and who have never experienced the joy of sinking a sixty-yard putt from the edge of the green to save par. This is all about to change, as Nick Faldo … explores the Amazon.'

'Fenella, rather than subject ourselves to a documentary not narrated by Cameron Diaz, shall we retire to the terrace?'

'What a wonderful idea.' Her tall frame shimmied and she handed him his drink. 'You lead the way, inspector.'

After a couple of rights and lefts, they were standing on an impressive first-floor terrace overlooking the eighteenth green while the sun dipped beneath the distant horizon.

'The sunset is wonderful tonight,' sighed Fenella. 'Almost as radiant as you are, inspector. Canary yellow suits you better than the birds.'

'I like to think so.' He looked down. 'Though scuffed shoes weren't part of the plan.'

'We're all a little scuffed.' Her eyes widened. 'But some of us buff up better than others.' She moaned softly with contentment. 'The sunset illuminates Peculiar Manor so magnificently. Butlers may be drowned in their own mango chutney, but that's of no consequence to the planets and the stars. They still put on a show whatever the occasion.'

Clinton sipped his spritzer. 'Eloquently put, Fenella.' He raised his glass. 'Cheers, my dear!'

'And cheers to you, South East England's greatest detective.'

Clinton chuckled. 'That's normally my line. But I won't object to you stealing it.'

She mock-gasped. 'Don't let Jayne Trill hear you say that. If she had her way, line stealing would be punishable by death.'

'Hmm. Enduring one of her productions is what I call a near-death experience.'

They laughed, composed themselves and sipped their spritzers in perfect harmony.

'Actually, inspector, Jayne Trill accosted me earlier today. She was asking what I knew about the Jepson murder investigation. I told her I'm not working on that story, Dickie's leading. Then she asked me if I had any theories about who the perpetrator was.'

'What did you say?'

'I said at least we know the butler didn't do it.'

More harmonious laughter.

'Oh, Fenella! For a journalist, you really are surprisingly inoffensive.'

'And for a police detective, you're surprisingly candid. Although I expect you won't tell me anything about the Jepson case. And good for you. Never trust a journalist, I say – even if they're not *remotely* interested in the case you're investigating.'

'Discretion is my middle name.' He downed his spritzer and winked. 'But who ever uses their middle name. Care for another?'

'I haven't finished this one yet.'

'Then down it while I'm at the bar, Fenella. Because I'm buying us two more. Tipsiness on a weekday evening wasn't a crime the last time I checked the statute books.'

Fenella waited until Clinton was out of sight then chucked the contents of her glass over the balcony. She hadn't planned on them both getting tipsy – only on Clinton having one too many. And his inability to handle more than three drinks was legendary. Another half hour or so of small talk and spritzers and he would be in loose-tongue territory.

Within forty minutes, Clinton had almost finished spritzer number four. Fenella was holding what was nominally her fourth drink, but most of the contents of her previous three glasses had disappeared onto the golf course below. Now the detective was swaying gently and waffling even more than usual, it shouldn't take long to extract the information she needed.

'So, tell me, inspector, off the record, who do you think bumped off that belligerent butler?'

'I'm afraid I'm under orders not to speak on or off the record to members of the press.'

Fenella rested a long arm on the terrace wall. 'Oh, don't be a spoilsport. I've been banished to school fêtes and sports reports for August. Dickie cherry-picks all the good stuff – he's still very hands on.'

'Yes. Just a shame he won't have his hands on any golf clubs this weekend. He's pulled out of the tournament.'

'Ah. That means you're the hot favourite and I'll have to write a superlative-studded story about you when you celebrate your inevitable win.'

Clinton cocked his head. 'Really? How many words would you write?'

'As many as you like – if you satisfy my curiosity about the Jepson case.'

'I thought you weren't remotely interested in it, Fenella?'

'In terms of writing a story, no. But I have a bet with one of my newsroom juniors about who the killer is. And I'm interested in finding out if I'm onto a winner. If I am, I may increase the bet.'

'What's your guess?' asked Clinton, with a playful twizzle of his wine glass.

'Cripps the gardener. Ex-con, history of violent crime, short temper, knows Peculiar Manor inside out.'

Clinton deployed his best enigmatic smile. 'Have you ever considered joining the police force?'

'So, I'm on the right lines?'

'On the record, I couldn't possibly comment. Off the record – yes, you are. Cripps is most definitely our prime suspect.'

'What about motive?'

He felt his stomach gurgle. 'Cripps and Jepson were rivals in comedy, apparently.'

'What do you mean?'

'They'd both signed up for something called The Big Titter – a stand-up comedy competition. There's rather a substantial prize on offer and their names were first on the registration list.' He rubbed his stomach in an effort to ease the rumbling. 'The Major found a joke book next to Jepson's body when he discovered the corpse in the kitchens, face down in a bowl of mango chutney. The joke book was Jepson's own creation and pages had been ripped out. We're still searching for them.'

'A joke book? Are you sure that's what it was?'

'As certain as I am of my own brilliance. I saw it as clear as day.' He hiccupped. 'Much clearer than I'm seeing now.' He groaned in abdominal distress. 'I knew I shouldn't have sampled the complimentary peanuts at the bar.' And he lurched to the terrace wall, leant over it, made a disturbing noise and threw up – much to the annoyance of the greenkeeper directly below him.

Once he'd composed himself, croaked an apology to the soggy greenkeeper and wiped his mouth with a napkin, he turned to apologise to Fenella. But she was nowhere to be seen. Maybe she was ordering more drinks? He staggered back to the bar and checked the faces. Hers wasn't one of them. After five minutes of waiting in vain for her to emerge from the ladies' loos, he concluded that the fourth spritzer must have been too much for her and she'd decided to call a taxi and head home. He should get back to base, too. Tomorrow would be a big day – he would be playing thirty-six holes of golf on expenses. And, hopefully, solving a murder.

Chapter 19

Clinton always had odd dreams after he'd ventured beyond three white-wine spritzers. And tonight's dream was a strong contender for the oddest of the lot.

He found himself standing in a sun-soaked orchard, dressed in his canary-yellow ensemble complete with scuffed leather shoes. He scouted around and noticed the fallen leaves were substantially larger, grass blades taller and thicker, and morning dewdrops somehow plumper than usual. A passing stag beetle must have been overdoing it down the gym – and possibly using steroids – because it was the broadest, beefiest beetle he'd ever seen. Seconds later, a butterfly the size of a light aircraft glided by on the breeze while ants as large as dachshunds scurried past. Either the world had undergone a growth spurt or he'd somehow shrunk from over six feet tall to six inches small. He cowered as a mole raised a mountain of earth nearby and concluded that, unless this was some quintessentially English version of Jurassic Park without the ghastly dinosaurs or screaming Americans, he'd almost certainly shrunk.

As Clinton shielded his eyes from the enormous sun dominating the patch of sky within his field of view, he spied a cat leering down at him from the branches of a nearby apple tree. Their eyes met and he scrutinised its feline features. He'd never seen a cat sporting an unimpressed scowl but there was a first time for everything. The sulky creature reminded him of someone. But it wasn't a starving Clouseau or Columbo. Or even that neighbour's cat who sometimes hopped in the lift, got off at the wrong floor and couldn't work out why Clinton wouldn't open the door to his persistent meows. Whose was this familiar visage?

The cat answered his question by hissing loudly, baring its yellow teeth, and speaking in the gruff voice of Superintendent Block.

'Listen up, Trump, you bird-brained little tweeter. I'm fed up with you prancing on your perch and preening yourself while looking in the mirror and asking "Who's a pretty boy, then?" It's time to spread your wings and start pecking for answers.' The cat's paw swatted the air. 'I want the suspects in the Jepson case singing like canaries by the end of the week or, mark my purrs, there'll be feathers flying further than an Arctic tern.' He swished his tail. 'And polish those boots – you look like something the cat's dragged in!'

Clinton was preparing to respond to this series of second-rate puns with a first-rate witty riposte – once he'd managed to formulate one – when he was unexpectedly scooped up by a giant left hand.

'You poor little darling,' warbled a female voice he hoped wasn't Jayne Trill's. She stroked his hair with her right index finger. 'Such a beautiful creature – so well defined, so delicate and so in need of love.' She kissed his head with her mammoth lips. 'Say hello to your new mummy.'

He declined to say hello for risk of encouraging any more colossal-lipped attention.

'And such a stroke of luck!' she chirruped. 'We need a canary for our Christmas pantomime – *Puss in Killer Heels*. I'm playing the lead role – Miss Pushy-Puss – and the canary and I form a strong bond. And when I say strong bond, I mean superglue pales into adhesive insignificance in comparison.'

It was definitely Jayne Trill. He wasn't sure if miniaturised humans mistaken for canaries swore or tweeted or performed a combination of both. But, whatever they did, he was sorely tempted to do it.

Jayne kissed his head again, pulled both hands to her chest and closed them. 'You're safe with Pushy-Puss now.'

Completely encased between Jayne's huge hands and her silk-draped sternum, Clinton felt her start walking. He sat down on her sweaty palm and began to see ghostly shapes forming in the murky dankness of her grasp.

'This woman is getting away with murder!' howled one wispy ghoul, who sounded a lot like the eccentric old boy who ran a local museum that focused on just that. 'It's a very funny murder mystery!' hooted the same ghoul, who appeared to be really enjoying his role.

A bowl of mango chutney entered stage right and exited stage left.

'Pity poor Graham!' wailed a female voice which could easily have been the first ghoul's wife. 'For he is married to a murderer! A cold-hearted killer! She murders actors. She murders actresses. And she murders the roles she plays, too!'

Clinton nodded at that last observation – and, taking this as approval, three more ghostly apparitions took the opportunity to float into view and echo, 'Pity poor Graham, for he is married to a murderer!' as an unrequested encore.

The bowl of mango chutney entered stage left and exited stage right.

Ghoulish laughter was followed by a cackle so over the top, even a James Bond villain would baulk at delivering it. The cackle sounded three more times, as if stuck in a loop.

Then a bright yellow spotlight flashed on, lighting up a gaggle of ghouls who seemed somewhat surprised at being illuminated. After five seconds of embarrassed silence, they were plunged into darkness again while an offstage voice wailed, 'Sorry, guys and ghouls! Pressed the wrong button!'

The bowl of mango chutney entered stage left but changed its mind a second later, rushed back off, re-emerged stage right and exited, slightly unsurely, stage left.

There was a pause – as if all the ghouls had forgotten whose turn it was to spook – followed by nervous coughing and confused muttering. Then a shimmering pair of red curtains closed in front of Clinton. Ten seconds later, the first ghoul appeared from behind the curtains and apologised for the break in the performance, saying their leading spirit had suddenly been summoned by a medium and they didn't have an understudy. So they would have to end the show here and patrons could obtain a refund if they showed their ticket stub to the headless phantom in the box office.

Clinton woke with a panicked jolt. It took a second to realise where he was. But the fuzzy figures of Clouseau and Columbo at the end of the bed told him he was at home and not clutched in the sweaty palm of Miss Pushy-Puss.

He propped himself up on his pillow and tried to make sense of the dream. He occasionally gained inspiration from his brain's night-time meanderings, but tonight's curious adventures offered nothing of any value. Whoever drowned Jepson in his own mango chutney was a professional killer. Or at least someone well-versed in Indian cookery. Jayne Trill was neither – she played murderers onstage but wasn't a convincing killer even then, and her mushroom korma wasn't worthy of the name.

He repositioned his pillow and drifted back to sleep.

Chapter 20

It was five to eight on Thursday morning. Fenella Cocky was already at her cluttered, coffee-stained desk in the *Goosing Times* newsroom, thrashing away on her laptop as if attempting a Guinness world record for creating the most bullet points in a thirty-minute period. Totally oblivious to the only other person in the newsroom – a middle-aged man cleaning the floor with a buffing machine – she was planning her big story about the murder at Peculiar Manor. Or should that be the peculiar murder at the manor? Or the murder in a peculiar manner? She would have to dream up a headline worthy of such a bizarre story. Her editor always demanded them. And he didn't trust sub-editors to do the job – it was up to Fenella and her fellow journalists.

Another couple of minutes of urgent tip-tapping and the bullets were ready to be loaded up and fired off. She pushed back her chair, puffed out her cheeks and admired her handiwork on the smeary screen. There was a little hyperbole here, the odd assumption there and one or two things she'd completely made up – but nothing her editor would mind or readers care about. After all, news these days was entertainment. And this story was going to be one hell of a rollercoaster ride – if she could persuade Dickie to run with it.

Right on cue, the man himself appeared next to her. 'You're in early. I hope that's not your resignation letter you're working on because I don't accept bullets. You'll have to type it out in full.'

'Ha, bloody ha,' she replied drily. 'No. It's the key points for this evening's front-page story about Jepson's murder. Cripps is the police's prime suspect.'

'Oh yes? And where did you get that from? Because it wasn't from the press officer I left messages for three times yesterday. She didn't call back.'

'I got it straight from the donkey's mouth – Clinton Trump.'

'When?'

'Last night, at one of his tedious golf club lectures. The old fool fell for the first bit of flattery that fluttered his way. After four white-wine spritzers, he was completely sozzled and offered me something off the record.'

'That's not enough for a story.'

'There's more. Jepson was in possession of a joke book. It was found by his body. And pages had been torn out.'

'Go on.'

'Apparently Jepson and Cripps were scheduled to square up against each other at The Big Titter comedy contest.'

'Oh, that. My girlfriend told me about it. She said there's a big prize on offer – some gigs or something.'

'Exactly. A possible motive for murder if Cripps wanted away from the manor and Jepson stood in his way.'

Dickie considered this conclusion. 'Even assuming that Cripps and Jepson would be two of the hot favourites to win a stand-up comedy competition, why would Cripps want away? He's settled at Peculiar Manor. And an ex-con comedian isn't going to go very far.'

Fenella took a sharp breath and cursed her lack of comedic knowledge. There must be a way out of this comedy cul-de-sac. But none of her bullet points were helping her.

Then the cleaner interrupted. 'I hope you don't mind, sir and madam. But I couldn't help overhearing. And I might be able to help.'

'You were listening to our private conversation?' snapped Dickie.

'No. You were talking at normal volume within my cleaning zone. My buffing machine employs some of smartest noise-dampening technology you'll see this side of the River Sticks. I could hear you as clear as a bell.'

Dickie squared his shoulders. 'Listen to me. Anything you hear within these four walls is not to be communicated to anyone outside of them. And if we need your help, we'll ask for—'

Fenella made her own interruption. 'Don't be an early morning grouch, Dickie. Listen to what this hardworking man has to say.'

Dickie pouted in a way that didn't completely discount the cleaner continuing.

The cleaner switched off his machine. 'I was just going to point out – as someone who's done a bit of time in his youth – that a jailbird stand-up comedian would have some terrific tales to tell of life behind the prison walls.'

'I find that hard to believe,' grunted Dickie, folding his arms.

'Unless you've served time at Her Majesty's pleasure, you're not going to know what goes on behind triple-locked doors. And, while they can take away your freedom, they can never take away your sense of humour.'

'Yes,' snorted Dickie. 'But the person you overheard us discussing isn't a cheery comedy character.'

'Comedy characters don't need to be likeable, sir. They just need to be amusing. Look at Mr Burns from *The Simpsons*. Nasty piece of work – but there's guaranteed titters every time he appears.' He turned to Fenella. 'I mean, I bet you've worked with a few, madam – you know, people who can make you laugh at all the madness from underneath their continually grumpy exterior.'

Fenella tried not to catch Dickie's eye. 'Yes, of course I have. Dozens of them.'

'There you go, then. I'd better buff off before my boss catches me nattering. And she's a grouch with no sense of humour.' He winked and laughed. 'Hope I was of some service to you, sir and madam.'

Fenella smiled with satisfaction. 'Yes, you were. Thank you so much.' As the cleaner switched on his machine and departed, she pressed her palms together. 'So, Dickie, shall we run with it?'

'I'm not sure. Clinton's comments were off the record, you say?'

'Technically, yes. But he was so drunk he won't remember. Even if he does, it's his word against mine. I can put him on the record to give it more credibility.'

'I'd hate to land a good friend in trouble with his superiors. But you're right – it would certainly beef up the story for our local detective genius to be quoted by name.'

'Great. That's what I'll do.'

'Wait a moment.' Dickie bit a fingernail. 'There's another avenue we haven't explored.'

'What's that?'

'My girlfriend – who attended the deadly dinner party – mentioned last night that Josephine Savage disappeared during the evening. For long enough to pop to the kitchens, drown a butler in his own mango chutney and pop back again.' He stopped nail nibbling. 'And when Svetlana confronted her about it, she became very defensive.'

'Has your girlfriend given a statement to the police?'

'Not yet.'

'Then it's not relevant. Our story is about who the police consider the prime suspect at this moment in time. That's why we need to run it in this evening's edition. If the prime-suspect situation changes it'll give us another story. You'll get two stories for the price of one. Maybe more.'

Dickie poked his cheek with his tongue. 'But thinking about it again, Cripps' motive – it seems weak.'

'He's an ex-con. He's snapped in the past. He's caused major injury to more than one person. And the police are focusing on the joke-book angle, so that's enough to go with.' She pointed at her laptop screen. 'I was going to speculate that there were staff tensions at the manor to spice it all up – quote a made-up source – and run through Cripps' criminal convictions. Once you throw all that into the mix, you've got a front-page story.'

Dickie stretched his arms over his head. 'One last thing to consider, Fenella. As you know, I dabble in amateur drama. And I've been thinking … In our recent rehearsals, Jayne Trill was none too complimentary about Jepson's acting. She's always rather harsh in her criticism but I've never seen her so vicious or as animated as she was when that butler disappeared out the door. My sixth sense tells me there's a chance she could be involved. A slim one – but a chance, nonetheless.'

'Have the police identified her as a suspect?'

'I have no idea. Did Clinton mention anything to you?'

'He only mentioned Cripps. Nobody else. We can forget about Jayne Trill for now.' Fenella took a deep breath. 'Can I write this front-page splash or not?'

Dickie grabbed a stress ball from her desk and squeezed it. 'Yes. But, as per usual, you'll need to come up with a killer headline. And I want to hear it now to avoid any last-minute fretting. Come on, what have you got?'

'Erm, "Suspect Identified Following Murder in a Peculiar Manor"?'

'Don't like it. Too wordy. Try again.'

Fenella glanced around to see if the cleaner might still be within helping distance. But he was already in the corridor. '"Butler Murder – Did the Gardener Do It"?'

'Even weaker. You've barely persuaded me of the merits of this story, so if you haven't got a catchy headline, we'll leave it for now. The story can live to fight another —'

Out of nowhere, it came to her. '"Manor Men in Mango Murder Mystery"!'

Dickie's eyes nearly popped out of their sockets. 'Now *that* is a headline!'

Chapter 21

At Upper Goosing police station, the day had idled by like any other Thursday. But what hadn't idled by was Detective Inspector Clinton Trump. Nobody had seen him since he'd popped into the office at ten o'clock to retrieve one of his golf-club warmers – which he'd been using as a tea cosy – and loudly informed anyone within earshot that he was about to embark on not one but two rounds of intensive investigation at an external location and was not to be disturbed. Not that anyone would be able to disturb him – he hadn't said where he was going, he never carried a mobile phone and he'd left his pager on his office desk so 'vital police work' wouldn't be interrupted.

Just after four o'clock, Constable Dinkel was loitering in the notoriously treacherous no-man's land between the executive coffee machine and the non-executive coffee machine, wondering if any senior officers would notice him grabbing an executive mega-jumbo espresso, when he was collared by Superintendent Block.

'Any news for me on the Jepson case, Dinkel?'

The constable edged away from the executive coffee machine. 'Yes, sir. I returned to Peculiar Manor and managed to snatch a quick word with Cripps before he disappeared up one of his apple trees.'

'And?'

'He says he was press-ganged into signing up for that Big Titter comedy contest by Jepson.'

'How do you mean?'

'Well, apparently, there have to be a certain number of people registered for the event to take place and there wasn't much interest when registration opened. So Jepson persuaded

Cripps to put his name down. Jepson paid the hundred-pound entrance fee for both of them.'

'A hundred pounds? You're joking me.'

'Competitive countryside comedy is no laughing matter, sir. If there's a substantial prize, contestants often have to stump up big money. And Cripps claimed there was one payment of two hundred pounds from Jepson's credit card and that we can check it, if we like. Cripps told me he had no intention of showing up for The Big Titter. He hates comedy, he says. He once shared a cell with a sociopathic, narcissistic clown and he still bears the mental scars.'

'Sharing an office building with Trump, I know the feeling. But check the card payment, just in case.'

'I already did, sir. Cripps is telling the truth. And I double-checked with the woman who's running the competition and she remembers two men fitting Jepson and Cripps' description coming in and signing up together. She said the snooty chap seemed to be in charge and his grumpy friend was just doing what he was told.'

'Did you find out anything else of interest about that ex-con gardener?'

'Not a sausage, sir.'

'What about his alibi for Tuesday evening?'

'He said he's working on it.'

'Alibi or no alibi, Cripps is out of the frame, as far as I'm concerned – there's not a shred of evidence against him.'

'Right you are, sir.'

Block held up a document. 'In other news, we got the official scenes of crime report through. It confirms there were no signs of forced entry at the manor. And nothing was taken – not even a poppadom.' He lowered the piece of paper. 'That doesn't exactly narrow the field of suspects down. But at least we can be pretty certain the killer wasn't an opportunistic thief who was caught in the act by Jepson.'

The superintendent started walking towards his office and Dinkel obediently followed. 'Sir, we haven't taken statements from everyone who was at the dinner party yet. Would you like me to get onto it?'

'You might as well,' sighed the superintendent. 'Though I doubt they'll stretch much further than descriptions of Lady Peculiar's venison vindaloo, crispy poppadoms or overpriced tableware.'

They passed Inspector Trump's office. 'Have you seen the inspector at all today, Dinkel?'

'Only when he popped in this morning to say he's doing some investigating off-site.'

'Where, exactly?'

'He didn't specify.'

'No, Trump rarely specifies. He specialises in not specifying. And he won't have his phone or pager with him, I'll bet.'

'You'd be winning that wager, superintendent.'

'I'm not a betting man. I took a big enough gamble when I took Trump onto my team. And I've been regretting it ever since.' The superintendent stopped and turned to face Dinkel, who halted next to him. 'If only solving murders was a straightforward as an Agatha Twisty novel, eh, constable?'

'Yes, sir. Twisty's detectives are almost always deductive masterminds.'

'Of the highest calibre. Imagine you and I were characters in one of her murder mysteries – legendary superintendent Euan Block and his dependable detective constable Troy Dinkel – we'd probably be on chapter twenty-something by now, already have identified at least three key suspects, and be well on our way to whittling them down to one by a process of keen-eyed logical deduction. Instead, you and I are careering around in clueless circles, dashing off at detective tangents and ending up in evidential impasses.' He huffed in annoyance. 'Readers wouldn't swallow that kind of non-linear narrative nonsense. I don't see why I should either.'

'I totally agree, sir.'

They continued walking.

'I can't for the life of me think where Trump's gone today. Can you, constable?'

Dinkel pondered. 'Some secret interrogation facility?'

'In Upper Goosing? Where do you suggest that would be? Hidden under the cricket pitch? Round the back of the school bike sheds? Or behind a false wall in the public lavatories?'

Dinkel paused for a moment. 'Maybe he's on the golf course, sir.'

'Don't be ridiculous, constable. Not even Trump would be stupid enough to spend an entire day on the golf course when there's important work to be done.' They'd reached the superintendent's office. 'That will be all, Dinkel.'

'One last thing, sir, if I may.'

'Make it quick. I've got Trump's expenses claims to go through. And I've run out of ibuprofen.'

'I've just had a thought. I know you said Cripps is in the clear for now. And I remember you told us your sixth sense was telling you that Lady Peculiar and the Major weren't the murdering type. But what if her ladyship and Cripps were working together? He owes her everything. And she's well aware of his violent past.'

'Hardly Bonnie and Clyde are they, constable?'

Dinkel lowered his head. 'It was just an idea, sir. We've got so little else to go on.'

'Why would her ladyship and her gardener be partners in crime?'

'That's for us to find out, sir.'

The superintendent's phone bleeped. He quickly read his new message.

'Contact from the detective inspector, sir?'

'No, no. It's just an acquaintance of mine who often bends my ear about matters criminal. Bit of an amateur sleuth – you know the type.'

'Anyone I know?'

'I don't believe so. I was grumbling about the length of the queue in the post office one day when we struck up a conversation and the individual in question expressed a real interest in criminal investigation.' He tutted loudly. 'More so than some detective inspectors I could mention.'

'Who is it, if you don't mind me asking?'

'I never reveal my contacts, constable.'

'Ah. Of course. Schoolboy error.'

'To be honest, I regret passing my phone number on to them because they're a bit of a time-waster. You know the sort of thing – every time someone's daffodils are decapitated, the letter "L" is stolen from the village clock sign, or there's been a garden-gnome-napping, they want to know what we're doing about it.' He sighed the sigh of a man for whom retirement couldn't come soon enough. 'But this contact did come up with one half-decent suggestion. Telling Trump he'd be working the weekend if he didn't solve this case by Friday.'

'Ah, because of the golf tournament on Saturday.'

'Yes – golf. How hitting a ball around a park with a stick became a sport is anyone's guess. But Trump's obsessed with it. And if the prospect of working the weekend doesn't motivate him, nothing will.' He smacked his lips. 'I only hope he's using today wisely and not dropping all his detection eggs into Friday's basket. Because if that case isn't solved by midnight tomorrow, he's coming into this office for the whole weekend if I have to drive him here myself in a golf buggy and chase him into the building with a three iron.'

'Going back to what I was suggesting, sir, I'll maybe pop over to the manor again tomorrow and speak with Lady P.'

'You do that, constable. Arrange a cup of tea and a chat with her ladyship. Nothing formal – see if you can tease something out of the old girl while she's overdosing on Earl Grey.'

'Will do, sir.'

'And, on second thoughts, don't worry about running round getting statements from all the curry ladies for the moment. Your time will be better spent at the manor.'

'Yes, sir.'

'And if you see Trump, tell him I want to know where he's been today and what he's been up to. And if I'm not happy, he'll be docked three days' annual leave.'

'I'll do that as well – if I can track him down.'

'Very good, constable. I can always rely on you.' He flashed a microsecond smile. 'One final thing.'

'What's that, sir?'

'If you solve this case, I'll grant you a month's access to the executive coffee machine.'

'Only a month? I was thinking more like six months.'

'You drive a hard bargain, Dinkel. Let's say three months for now. I may increase it, depending on your performance.'

Constable Dinkel grinned. 'Yes, sir!'

Chapter 22

Clinton Trump was not a happy chappie. He'd struggled to a hugely disappointing fifteen-over-par eighty-seven on his first eighteen holes at Goosing golf club in a round that was birdie-free apart from a jackdaw who'd stalked him for the first nine holes. He'd finally got rid of the creature by tossing a crab-paste sandwich in its general direction and sprinting to the tenth tee. His lucky luminous-orange golf ball, which had been with him since he began his run of three straight Goosing Golf Open victories, disappeared into the River Sticks following a horribly sliced tee shot at the twelfth. And only at the sixteenth hole did he realise he'd left his sand wedge back on the ninth – a mistake which saw a twenty-minute trudge to fetch it eventually rewarded with a bunker shot so uncharacteristically awful for a man of his outstanding golfing abilities that he decided it probably never happened and chose not to count it for the purposes of his scorecard.

But, so far, the golfing gods were looking down on his second round more kindly – possibly because he'd taken off his golfing cap and they could now see who they were dealing with. He'd made improved scores on the first five holes – even managing a birdie on the second – when he spotted the Major up ahead on the sixth tee. Clinton rattled his throat in frustration. Everyone knew the Major could make a round of golf last longer than a North Korean military parade.

'Good afternoon, Major!' called Clinton, in as friendly a tone as golfers can manage when being held up by a serial slowcoach.

'Ah, inspector, jolly good to see you, old boy! What do you say we tackle the remainder of this golfing assault course together?' The Major casually swung his driver at his ball, completely missed and rotated one hundred and eighty degrees. 'Blast! Better have another tot of whisky to steady the old trigger fingers.' He whipped out a hip flask and took a generous swig. 'That's more like it! Where were we? Ah, yes – I was enlisting you to the fighting cause!'

'Due to time constraints, I'm operating alone today, Major. And as you haven't taken your tee shot yet, I shall play through, if that's alright with you.'

'Play through? But I've already addressed the ball.'

'I know, Major, but—'

'Regulation 34, paragraph 6, clause 3, subsection ii) clearly states that members who have addressed the ball shall not be overtaken by other members.'

'Technically, yes, but—'

'A "technical yes" is a "yes" in my military manual.'

Realising the longer this debate dragged on, the greater the delay, Clinton waved a white glove in surrender, and allowed the Major to tee off.

After two more swing-and-misses, the Major finally thwacked his ball in a wonderfully straight drive that landed slap-bang in the middle of the fairway and proceeded like a mini bouncing bomb for fifty more metres before settling in the perfect position for an attacking shot to the green. It was so impressive, Nick Faldo would have been applauding – if he hadn't been stuck up the Amazon teaching the Yanomami tribe the best way to tackle a water hazard.

'What a belter, eh?' crowed the Major. 'Worth waiting for in the end!'

A somewhat surprised Clinton acknowledged the sporting feat with a weak smile.

The Major thrust his driver in his golf bag, abandoned his clubs and stomped over. 'Looking forward to the big G-Day push on Saturday, old boy?'

'Of course,' replied Clinton, checking the time on his wristwatch.

'Heard old Dickie Blinder won't be reporting for duty.'

'No, he's out of action.'

'Shame. I was looking forward to crossing seven irons with Dickie. We always do battle together.' He puffed out his chest. 'Suppose I shall have to call up one of the reserves.' His bushy eyebrows lifted. 'That means you, Trump.'

Clinton blinked twice. 'Me, Major?'

'Yes, you, soldier.' He snorted with laughter. 'And that's an order!'

'Actually, I prefer to play alone in competitions.'

'The lone sniper, eh? Well, I've been thrashing my balls in this rough for nearly half a century and I've never entered the battleground without backup. I shall need someone to hold the flag aloft when I'm gunning for victory on the greens, to cover my tracks in the bunkers, and help me navigate the minefield of the out-of-bounds rule. And that military honour will fall to you, Trump!'

'I'm not sure it's a good idea for me to pair up with anyone, Major.' He rubbed his heel. 'I have a bone spur in my foot that means I'm not available for active golf-pairing service. Better I play at my own pace.'

'If you're not fit for active duty, soldier, then, like Dickie Blinder, you shouldn't be enlisting.'

Clinton adopted his TV doctor's voice. 'My bone spur is a recurrent medical problem that comes and goes but requires no medical intervention. Therefore, it isn't serious and I'm not currently experiencing any difficulties. But I don't wish to risk aggravating it by doing something I wouldn't normally do. Therefore, the wisest course of action is playing solo on Saturday.'

'Sounds a lot of fuss about nothing to me.' The Major wrinkled his nose. 'As this club's newly appointed competition secretary, it's my decision who plays with whom. And bone spur or no bone spur, you're being conscripted to go into battle with me, Trump.'

'But—'

'No buts. This is world-war golf. And I take no prisoners.' He slapped his thigh. 'My preferred strategy is to hunker down in the clubroom trenches, consume substantial breakfast rations, smoke a pouch of tobacco to fortify myself and advance onto the battlefield after a fighting-man's lunch.'

Clinton caressed his stubble. 'But, with the utmost respect, Major, you've finished last in the previous six tournaments.'

The Major thumped a hand to his chest. 'If there's one thing I learnt at officer academy, it's just because you've tried something half a dozen times and suffered massive losses that's absolutely no reason not to stand your ground, push on and do *exactly* the same thing again.'

Clinton frowned. 'Actually, I prefer to skip breakfast and be first on the tee, Major. Set the standard and put the pressure on early. It's worked for me for the last three years.'

'That's all well and good. But never be predictable in a theatre of war. The enemy will be expecting you to mount a dawn attack. They'll be surprised when you bring up the rear with me – with two solid meals inside you and a few tots of whisky to steady your elbow.'

Clinton lost the power of speech as the all-day horror of the Major's master plan shook his whole golfing being.

'Excellent – we're agreed! I shall advance up the fairway in an orderly fashion and attempt to hit the target green with my next shot. After this hole, I shall allow you to play through.' He guffawed so loudly it scared off a pigeon. 'It'll give me the chance to do a bit of reconnaissance on your swing from behind enemy lines!' He laughed even louder than before – scaring off three more pigeons – and marched off to collect his golf bag and find his ball.

Before Clinton could take the golfing gods' names in vain, a heavy hand slapped on his right shoulder and was followed by a deafening 'Hey, buddy!' in his ear. He spun round to see the American tourist he'd encountered at Royal Crazy Golf yesterday.

'Oh, it's you, Rudolph,' muttered Clinton.

'It's Randolph. And what a coincidence – bumping into you on the golf course again. Only it isn't half as crazy this time!'

Clinton glanced at the retreating figure of the Major. 'I'm not so sure about that.'

'Never been on a real golf course before. Thought "What the heck, I'm on vacation!" and the sweet lady in reception signed me in as a guest.'

Clinton quarter-smiled. 'How very hospitable of her.'

He held up a three wood. 'Can't get the hang of these big boys, though.'

'The drivers?'

'Yeah. Maybe it's because you guys drive on the left and we drive on the right!'

'How amusing,' sighed Clinton.

'Think I might putt my way round this hole, buddy. Can't do much worse than the last one. Stopped counting after thirty hits. Or maybe you can give me a bit of coaching – show me how to hold this stick?'

'It's a club, not a stick.'

'I'm a quarter Polish and that's what my uncle from Warsaw calls it – a stick.'

'But we're not in Poland.'

The American laughed. 'You're right there, buddy!' He stopped mid-chuckle. 'Hey, talking of Eastern Europe, found any Russian spies yet?'

Clinton pouted. 'If you're referring to the five-to-ten-per-cent-possibility spy you mentioned yesterday, then the answer is no. Because they're almost certainly a figment of your former employer's imagination.'

'Spoke to my CIA contact last night. It's a twenty-five to thirty per cent chance now.'

'Why the upgrade?'

'More encrypted email chatter or something. My guy can't give me details.'

The inspector suddenly remembered he was nominally here to do some investigating, so he asked the first question that came into his head. 'As an ex-CIA man, have you noticed anything suspicious in the village since you arrived?'

'Suspicious? Can't say I have.'

'Anyone acting strangely?'

Randolph grinned. 'To us Americans, all you Brits act strange, buddy!'

'The feeling's mutual. But has anything out of the ordinary happened?'

A light bulb seemed to go on in the American's brain. 'Hey, yeah – I met Agatha Twisty in the Tourist Trap café yesterday! We had a great talk.'

'Did you discuss the Jepson murder?'

'Yeah. I mentioned the similarities between it and one of her novels.'

'Yes, yes. I know about that. Pure coincidence.'

'That's what I thought. But then I checked out some online reviews of her books. Someone called Goosing Jeeves has been bad-mouthing them and rating them one star. She got real heated.' He shook his head. 'Never seen an old lady all riled up like that.'

'Writers often overreact when they receive bad reviews. Books are their babies. One-star critics are the equivalent of social services. If you'll pardon the pun, I wouldn't read anything into it.'

'I guess you're right, buddy. Though I was kinda surprised she hadn't seen the reviews before.'

'Authors are busy people. Not as busy as brilliant detectives. But still rather busy.'

'Sure. You got any idea who Goosing Jeeves is? I thought it might be Jepson.'

'It could be. But Goosing Jeeves could be anyone. We've all read Wodehouse round here. It's practically a requirement if you want to buy a house in this village.'

'If you say so.' He chewed his lip. 'You know, when I mentioned those reviews, Twisty had a certain look in her eye. I seen it before in men and women who've killed.'

'Agatha Twisty has killed – countless times in the pages of her novels. So, she probably slips into murderous character for a short while when confronted by negative feedback. Then she reverts back to the harmless old lady we all know.' Clinton put on his golfing glove. 'And if you're insinuating that she may have killed Jepson, a woman of her age couldn't overpower a man of his stature.'

'You say that. But, theoretically speaking, if she had already read the reviews and discovered Jepson was behind them, she could've planned his murder and hired someone else to kill him.' He moved nearer to Clinton. 'That novel she wrote – *Murder in an Odd Manor* – could've inspired her to bump off Jepson in the kitchens during a dinner party. And nobody would suspect Twisty because people would say no novelist would be crazy enough to turn their fiction into a reality. It would look too suspicious. But she would *know* that – she's a real clever lady.'

'I don't think even Agatha Twisty would get away with such a fanciful storyline.'

'Just a suggestion, buddy.'

Clinton nodded in thanks and picked up his golf bag. 'The Major's on the green. Time for me to tee off.'

The American yanked his golf bag onto his shoulder. 'Are you and me pairing up for the rest of this not-so-crazy golf course or what?'

'I suppose so,' mumbled Clinton.

Chapter 23

Jayne Trill was tucking into a pre-rehearsal lemon meringue pie in the Tourist Trap café while husband Graham waited outside in the car with the evening paper, a bag of cheese and onion crisps and a can of non-alcoholic Pilsner.

As the drama queen savoured her fifth forkful, and wondered if she might treat herself to a second portion and start rehearsals a little later than scheduled, Pattie from the post office rushed in – eyes wild and limbs flailing.

'Have you seen this?' panted Pattie, holding up that evening's edition of the *Goosing Times*.

'Pattie, please. Can't you see? I'm lemon-meringuing.'

'But the headline.'

Jayne didn't read it. 'Never interrupt a lady of good standing when she's lemon-meringuing, Pattie.'

'A lady of good standing?'

'Yes.'

'But you're sitting down.'

Jayne dropped her fork. 'Oh, give it here!' She snatched the paper. 'What's so important that it can't wait until after—' She stopped mid-whinge. '"Manor Men in Mango Murder Mystery". Oh my!' A smile spread across her face as she read a little more. 'This is a turn-up for the books.'

'Looks like that grumpy old gardener bumped off the even grumpier butler. Maybe Cripps wanted the grumpy-old-codger crown all to himself, eh, Jayne?'

'Don't be flippant, Pattie.'

Pattie bowed her head. 'Sorry, Jayne. I won't be flippant again.'

'Although, as it's Jepson and Cripps we're talking about, I take that back. You can be flippant.'

'Can I?'

'Yes, you can.'

'Right.' Pattie paused. 'I can't think of anything else flippant to say, Jayne.' She paused again. 'How about – whoever killed Jepson did the world a ruddy big favour and I hope they lock up Cripps for the rest of his life – even if he didn't do it – because they're two peas in a po-faced pod.'

Jayne's smile was so big, it could probably be seen from Lower Goosing. 'That's the kind of flippancy I *love* to hear.'

Pattie peered at the paper. 'I haven't read past the first paragraph. I was too excited. What does it say?'

Jayne lowered her reading glasses from her forehead. 'It says Detective Inspector Clinton Trump has confirmed to our chief reporter, Fenella Cocky, that ex-con Ronald Cripps – currently employed as the Peculiar Manor gardener and a man with a violent past – is the number one suspect in the murder of Maurice Jepson. Blah, blah, blah – an unnamed source has confirmed a long-running feud between the two manor employees. Differences over pay and conditions. Blah, blah, blah. Things may have come to a head when both men were due to battle it out at next month's Big Titter comedy contest.' She scanned further ahead. 'What else? Ah. A joke book found near Jepson's body was missing several pages and police are trying to locate them as a matter of urgency.' She folded the newspaper and placed it on her lap. 'I'll finish it at home.'

'Hasn't Graham bought a copy?'

'He has. But his grubby fingers will have smudged the print. And it'll be covered in cheese-and-onion-crisp crumbs and splattered with foreign lager. I shall require my own non-Graham-soiled copy.'

'But I just paid fifty pence for that.'

'Why? You sell them in your post office, don't you?'

'We closed early today – I did a stocktake at my commemorative-stamp storage facility this afternoon – so I'll get my delivery tomorrow. That's why I had to buy the newspaper from one of those automatic dispensers outside the Bad Tidings funeral parlour.'

'Very well. If fifty pence is so important to you.' And Jayne lifted her purse from her handbag and began rummaging.

Neither of them had noticed the huddled, bearded figure in the corner who was wearing dark-green overalls, heavy black boots and a woollen hat that covered three quarters of his face. The well-built man slammed a mug of tea on his table, rose to his feet – shedding a small cloud of dirt in the process – and clomped towards them.

Jayne spotted him mid-rummage. 'I'm afraid I don't have any spare change,' she sneered, wafting a hand in the man's direction. 'If you're after handfuls of dirty coins, try my husband. He's parked fifty metres away by the general household rubbish bin – the avocado-coloured one.'

Pattie whispered softly. 'You mean the green bin?'

'No. I mean avocado, Pattie. We don't do common colours in Upper Goosing. Here our rainbows are scarlet, tangerine, lemon, avocado, cobalt—'

'Give it a rest, the pair of you!' barked the man. 'And give me that bloody newspaper!'

Jayne recoiled. 'And why would I do that? I've just paid fifty pence for it.'

'Actually, I paid fifty pence for it, Jayne. You haven't paid me back yet.'

'All in good time, Pattie.'

'What kind of timeframe are we looking at, Jayne?'

'The near future.'

'How near is near, Jayne? Next ten seconds, sixty seconds, five minutes? Only I need the fifty pence for the biscuit machine. My blood sugar is low.' Her face contorted. 'I could commit cold-blooded murder for a caramel crunch.'

'Do you two hens ever stop clucking?' growled the man.

'Don't be so rude,' sniffed Jayne. 'And if we're hens, I know what that makes you.'

The man whipped off his hat to reveal himself. It was Cripps. 'It makes me a murderer, apparently.' He snatched the paper from Jayne. 'That jumped-up know-nothing Trump is gonna pay for this. You mark my words.'

Stunned into silence, the women watched the furious gardener scan the article and mutter a series of words so colourful they hadn't been heard since a coach party of Irish priests discovered the café didn't serve alcohol. Then he rolled up the newspaper and stomped out the door with it.

'Why is he in such a huff?' asked Pattie, sitting down.

Jayne tutted. 'Why do you think?'

'I've no idea. Maybe someone trod on his giant pumpkin and he needs the newspaper to help mop up all the juice?'

Jayne tutted again. 'It's because he overheard my summary of that front-page story which more or less accuses him of murder, and your flippant comments about wanting him to be locked up for the rest of his life irrespective of whether he's committed the crime or not. It was very foolish of you, Pattie.'

'But you smiled at that comment.' She thought back. 'You smiled quite a lot. You know – like a murderer might smile when someone's talking about an innocent man going to prison for a murder *they* actually committed.'

'You're overdramatising.'

'Am I?' Pattie's lip twisted. 'Is that a good thing? Because the actors in your productions under-dramatise. Quite a lot.'

Jayne completed her tutting hat trick. 'Really, Pattie, sometimes I wonder why I allow you into the outer regions of my social circle. Your flippancy will be the death of you.'

'Am I still being flippant, Jayne?'

'I hope you are, since you've just compared my Hollywood smile to a killer's.'

'Oh, y-y-yeah,' stuttered Pattie. 'I was. Of course I was. I was being flippant.' She hesitated. 'But you don't want me to be flippant any more, Jayne?'

'No.'

'Because you did say I could be flippant not that long ago.'

146

'I was being flippant about being flippant!' snorted Jayne. 'I didn't mean for you to be continually flippant.'

'No?' Pattie scratched her head. 'This flippancy game is a lot flipping harder than you'd flipping well think.'

Graham Trill poked his head round the door. 'Everything alright, ladies?'

Jayne groaned. 'It was until you stuck your big nose through the door.' She wagged a reproachful finger at her approaching husband. 'What have I told you, Graham? Tea is a time for man and wife to relax away from each other – me in the delightful surroundings of this picturesque café, and you in the car by the avocado waste bin.'

Graham snuffled. 'It's not avocado. It's green. I keep telling you – the only things that are avocado-coloured round here are avocados. Though the ones in this café aren't even the colour of avocados sometimes. More like asparagus. And sometimes they taste like asparagus.'

Jayne pressed two fingers to her forehead. 'I can feel a migraine coming on.'

'Are you being flippant, Graham?' asked Pattie.

He smirked and winked. 'Me flippant, Pattie? Never in a million years.'

'Oh. I just wondered.'

'Please explain the reason for your intrusion, Graham. I'm still lemon-meringuing and we shall be late for rehearsals if there are any more interruptions.'

'Alright, alright. Keep your feathered hat on.' He ignored his wife's glare and faced Pattie. 'I popped in because I saw Cripps coming out of the café in a right old strop.' He nodded towards the door. 'I left the evening paper in the car. But Cripps is splashed all over the front page. The police reckon he drowned that butler.'

Pattie lowered her voice. 'We know – we read the story – and we think Cripps did it, don't we, Jayne?'

'Undoubtedly. Why else would he be so rude to me?'

147

'Maybe you were being rude to him?' suggested Graham. 'Anyway, he looked like a man who was on the warpath.'

'What do you think Cripps is going to do, Graham?' asked Pattie.

'He'll probably want to speak to Detective Inspector Trump, seeing as he's the one quoted in the story. And I doubt Cripps is going to offer him a guided tour of his allotment.'

Jayne smiled her killer's smile. 'Yes. Things are going to get *very* interesting in this murderous little village of ours.'

Chapter 24

It was Friday morning. And before arriving at Upper Goosing police station on this momentous day – the day when he would snare Jepson's killer, be hailed a local hero and almost certainly be nominated for a knighthood – Detective Inspector Clinton Trump popped to the post office to grab the latest copy of the *Goosing Times*. Keeping abreast of village affairs was normally a pleasure. But it was strictly business this morning. Perhaps there might be a subtle clue in one of the news stories? Reports about someone who'd been bothering butlers, a photo of a local dignitary opening a school fête with telltale traces of mango chutney on their collar, or a classified advert selling pages ripped from a joke book. When it came to local papers, they were a potential treasure trove for the keen-eyed detective. Admittedly, over the last twenty years, this one had yet to provide anything of the slightest use in solving his cases but, as his school headmistress had told him on many occasions, that's the thing about potential: sometimes it's never achieved but you've got to completely ignore the lessons of the past and jolly well keep trying.

As he waited behind the woman with the five Chihuahuas, who always took an age to select which boiled sweets she would be sucking today, he spotted a pile of *Goosing Times* sitting on the counter and read the headline:

MANOR MEN IN MANGO MURDER MYSTERY

That was rather a coincidence. He decided to run through the possible explanations. It didn't take long. There was only one. Someone had blabbed to the media. He groaned inwardly. Who could it be? Superintendent Block never spoke to the press. It must be Dinkel's loose tongue that was to blame. Clinton would need to read the article ASAP to confirm his suspicions and then deliver some harsh words to his junior about the high levels of discretion required when investigating such a sensitive case.

The woman ahead was still deliberating between aniseed balls and mint humbugs. Desperate times called for desperate measures, he told himself. So he did something he'd never done in his life before – he pushed to the front of the queue.

'I'm sorry, madam, but your boiled-sweet selection will have to wait.' He flashed his police ID at her. 'Detective Inspector Clinton Trump is here on vital law-enforcement business.' He glanced up at the sweet jars. 'Though I can recommend the pear drops. There's many a confession been extracted by my good self after sucking on a quarter pound of those.' He scratched his chin. 'One or two of them were false confessions, admittedly, leading to wrongful convictions which were quashed years later after young lives had been wasted serving time for crimes the confessor didn't commit – possibly as a consequence of me sucking too vigorously and sending my blood sugar skyward.' He placed a hand on his chest. 'But I don't blame myself for that. I blame the pear drops. And the person who sold them to me. And, most of all, the criminal justice system.'

The woman's expression suggested she was either stunned into silence or sucking on a boiled sweet – possibly both.

Pattie Quirk dithered between the jars and the counter. 'How can I help, inspector?'

He picked the top copy of the *Goosing Times* from the pile. 'I shall need this and only this.'

'That'll be fifty pence, please.'

'It's for official police business, Ms Quirk.'

'Oh. Pardon me. That'll be fifty pence, please … inspector.'

'I meant I expect it for free.'

'Sorry, I can't do that.'

'What about half price?'

'Only if we're running a special half-price offer.'

'But you're not at the moment?'

'No.'

'Any plans to do so in the next five minutes?'

'None whatsoever.' Pattie reached for one of the sweet jars. 'Though if you buy a pound of pear drops, I could give you a one per cent discount on the sweets.'

'I'll pass on the pear drops. But come along, Ms Quirk, sell the newspaper to me for twenty-five pence. I don't want to break into a pound coin.'

'I could sell you two copies for a pound, if that makes things easier.'

'Alright,' sighed Clinton. 'You win. Though I hope you'll urgently review your newspaper-selling policy because we wouldn't want a murder investigation held up simply because a brilliant detective has less than fifty pence in change in their wallet.' He rummaged in his pockets and yanked out a plastic bag containing copper coins. 'As a protest, I shall pay with my emergency small change rather than my pound coin.' And Clinton proceeded to count out a pile of pennies and twopence pieces, re-count them, knock over the stack as he was about to hand it over, pick up the coins, re-count them twice more, just about avoid knocking them over again … and then hand over the money.

'Thank you, inspector,' chirped Pattie. 'I'm surprised you didn't buy every copy we've got, to be honest.'

'Why would I do that?'

The woman with the five Chihuahuas butted in. 'Because you're the individual who briefed the journalist. I read the article last night and your flimsy deductions were based on very little hard evidence.' She sniffed dismissively. 'I'd be very interested to know what Mr Cripps will have to say about it!'

Clinton stared unsurely at her, kicked away a Chihuahua who was sniffing his shoes, unfolded the *Goosing Times* and started reading.

The woman decided on mint humbugs, declined Pattie's invitation to purchase a set of European Murder Destination of the Year 2015 commemorative postage stamps, bought a packet of cream envelopes, declined Pattie's second invitation to purchase a set of European Murder Destination of the Year 2015 commemorative postage stamps with a one per cent discount, settled her restless Chihuahuas, declined Pattie's third and final invitation to purchase a set of European Murder Destination of the Year 2015 commemorative postage stamps at a one-and-a-half per cent discount, and hastily departed the post office before Clinton had uttered another word. He appeared to be in a different world – possibly one where he hadn't made such an almighty cock-up.

The library-esque silence was broken by the door creaking open. It was the butcher's widow, Josephine Savage. She immediately sensed something was wrong and rushed up to Clinton.

'Is everything alright, inspector?'

'No,' whispered Pattie. 'He's just had to pay full price for a newspaper.'

Clinton stood as motionless as a statue playing hide and seek.

'Has he suffered some kind of seizure, Pattie?'

'I'm not sure. He's been counting out a lot of small-denomination coins. Maybe all that mental arithmetic has frozen his brain?'

Clinton barely seemed to be breathing.

'You don't have any idea why the inspector is in this state, Pattie?'

'No. None at all.' The postmistress gazed down at the newspapers. 'Unless it's something to do with that front-page story about the Jepson murder that says Inspector Trump has blabbed to the media naming Cripps as the prime suspect even though he's not been arrested or formally charged.' She paused. 'Or maybe it's low blood sugar and he needs to suck on a pear drop.'

'I suspect it's the former but let's not take any chances. Fetch me some pear drops.'

Pattie reached for a sweet jar, tipped a couple of pear drops into her palm and handed them to Josephine. 'Here you are.'

'Thanks, Pattie.'

'That will be fourteen pence, please.'

'I'm sorry?'

'I normally sell them by the quarter pound but it works out as six and two thirds pence per drop, roughly. And I've rounded it up to the nearest penny.'

Josephine slapped a twenty-pence-piece on the counter. 'There you are. Keep the change in case we need another one.' And she shoved a pear drop into Clinton's mouth.

After ten seconds of frantic sucking, Clinton was reanimated. 'My goodness, what happened?'

'You read the front page of the *Goosing Times*, inspector,' replied Josephine. 'Pattie says you were quoted in the lead story and named the prime suspect in the Jepson murder enquiry – Cripps the gardener.'

His memories surged back. 'Ah, yes.'

Pattie raised her voice. 'You paid full price for a paper, after you tried to blag it for free – do you remember?'

'Yes, I do.' He swallowed hard. 'I can only hope Cripps hasn't bought a copy.'

Josephine patted Clinton's arm. 'Let's not worry what Lady Peculiar's gardener thinks about it for now.'

'But did he do it?' asked Pattie excitedly.

Clinton was still too dazed to reply, so Josephine took over the deductive reins. 'As someone who holds a Master's in Advanced Criminology, I very much doubt Cripps is the culprit. Killing a work colleague over a comedy competition is about the weakest motive I've ever heard. And anyway, why would a murderer tear out the pages of a joke book and leave the rest behind as evidence? Surely they would just steal the whole book if that's what they wanted?' She shook her head. 'No, as far as I can see, it smacks of a set-up. And Cripps is the perfect stooge thanks to his long list of criminal convictions, easy access to the manor and his bushy beard.'

153

'His bushy beard?' queried Pattie. 'What's that got to do with it?'

'Men with well-grown beards are ten per cent more likely to commit crimes than clean-shaven men. The police will know that.' She faced Clinton. 'Won't you, inspector?'

'Erm. Oh. Yes. Probably. I mean, someone will know it. In accounts, probably. They're very good with numbers.'

'Ooh!' whooped Pattie. 'You've got it all worked out, haven't you, Miss Marple?!'

'I wouldn't say that. I just know Cripps isn't the killer.'

The door crashed open. The hefty bearded man in green overalls and black boots was instantly recognisable as the gardener they'd just been talking about. And, from the expression on his face, it was clear he wasn't here to buy a set of European Murder Destination of the Year 2015 commemorative postage stamps.

Cripps inhaled through his nose for what seemed like five minutes, clenched both fists and lumbered over. 'I knew you'd be in here, Trump!' He grabbed a copy of the *Goosing Times* and held it up. 'Admiring your half-baked handiwork!'

Clinton was sucking his second pear drop and currently unavailable for comment.

Josephine stepped in again. 'The inspector's not feeling at all well, Mr Cripps.'

'Is that so?' He flung the newspaper to the floor. 'Well, he isn't going to be feeling any better when I'm finished with him.'

'No, no!' insisted Josephine. 'He knows you're not the murderer.' She deftly positioned herself between Cripps and Trump. 'I have a Master's in Advanced Criminology and I've advised the inspector that you're not the killer.'

Cripps grunted unsurely. 'Well, you'd be right. I had no reason to bump off Jepson. And all the stuff in that rag about a feud is claptrap.'

Clinton parked his pear drop in his cheek. 'It's fake news. Happens all the time, these days. Made it all up to sell more papers. It's sad.'

The now-not-quite-so-outraged gardener eyed him suspiciously. 'You saying you didn't speak with that Cocky journalist?'

'Of course I spoke with her.' He hauled an honest smile onto his face. 'But it seems she misinterpreted to whom I was referring, misconstrued key facts about the case, misheard a few things, misread my silence for affirmation and drew mistaken conclusions.'

'That's a lot of misses,' growled Cripps.

'Yes. And I hope this explanation helps to avoid …' He glanced at Cripps' fist. '… a lot of hits.'

Pattie beamed a smile that didn't seem at all appropriate for the occasion. 'Mr Cripps, can I get you anything? Every copy of the *Goosing Times* we have in stock? That's about five hundred. The more you buy, the less chance of your name being mud before the day is out. Or how about a quarter of pear drops for the occasion? Or a set of commemorative stamps?'

Cripps bared his teeth. 'All I want is an end to all the gossip and slurs and loose talk about me being responsible for that butler's death. Because you're looking in the wrong place. I'm sixty next year.' He raised his voice. 'And I'm never going back to prison! They wouldn't allow me so much as a packet of seeds and a window box.' Back to normal volume. 'So, just … leave me alone.'

'I will,' replied Clinton. 'Just as long as you leave me alone.' He pointed at his face. 'These finely chiselled features would cost millions to reconstruct. The extensive plastic surgery required to restore their full magnificence would decimate the police budget, restrict funds for frontline policing and risk riots on the streets of Goosing and a total breakdown of law and order as we know it.' He turned his side profile to Josephine. 'Statistics show that tall, blond and handsome detectives solve a lot more crimes.'

'Which statistics are they?' hissed Cripps.

'I've no idea. But I'm sure they're out there somewhere. It stands to reason.'

'In that case, you'll also find statistics showing falsely accused gardeners don't give pretty-boy detective inspectors dragging their names through the mud with no evidence a second chance. So consider the matter closed. But be warned – I won't be so forgiving in the future.' And he turned and stormed out of the post office.

There were a few seconds of silence which Pattie shattered. 'Someone got out of the wrong side of bed, this morning! And he didn't even buy anything. What a cheek! Probably expected a free copy just because he was named as prime suspect.'

Josephine gently shepherded the inspector towards the door. 'Thank you, Pattie. We'll be off now.'

'Don't you want your third pear drop?'

Josephine turned to Clinton. 'Do you need another?'

'No. You suck on it, Pattie. It'll give your vocal chords a well-earned rest.'

'Oh, thanks very much!' And the postmistress reached up for the jar.

'Come on, inspector,' urged Josephine. 'We're going to solve this murder.'

'We? I thought you'd declined my invitation to join forces.'

'Yes. But I've had second thoughts. We can crack this case together.' She paused. 'Well, with the help of someone who knows a lot about murder mysteries.'

'Who's that?'

'Agatha Twisty – she's a good friend of mine. And she's in town.'

'If you think it will help, Ms Savage.'

'I'm certain it will.'

And they waved goodbye to Pattie, declined her offer of a set of commemorative stamps, and left the post office.

Chapter 25

Constable Dinkel's early morning chat with her ladyship over Earl Grey and chocolate digestives in the Peculiar Manor study had proved to be the biggest waste of his time since he'd turned up to the police Christmas party a day early and been forced to return home to change out of his Rudolph the red-nosed policeman costume.

Lady Peculiar was currently powdering her nose and he was running through his notes which, apart from the words 'no', 'none', 'nobody', 'nothing' and 'not that one is aware', consisted of very little more than badly drawn doodles of peacocks and blank space. He didn't even have a copy of last night's evening paper to flick through to fill the temporal void as he'd been running late and hadn't had time to pop to the post office. And he'd mistakenly left his phone and pager in his rucksack which was hanging on the back of his office chair. So here he was, feeling as cut off and useless as a freshly amputated limb.

Her ladyship returned to the room, closed the door, and wandered over to a drinks cabinet by the far wall.

Dinkel pretended to be consulting copious notes. 'So, just to recap, your ladyship, you can't be sure which of your guests left the dining room after seven o'clock and before Jepson was found dead, you didn't see or hear anything suspicious, nobody that you've spoken to who attended the meal saw or heard anything suspicious, nothing is missing from the manor, there's no damage to windows, doors or locks, and no sign of the missing pages from Jepson's joke book.'

'That all sounds correct.' She stopped at the cabinet. 'Can one offer you a tipple, constable? It's a little early but it's been such a trying few days.'

Having been stuck in his armchair for the best part of an hour, Dinkel seized the chance to stretch his legs and wander over to join her. He had no intention of drinking alcohol but a good detective always enjoyed a snoop. 'Mind if I take a peek at what delights your drinks cabinet has to offer, your ladyship?'

'Oh.' Her eyebrows flittered. 'Well ... one doesn't see why not.'

After perusing the whiskies, ports and liqueurs, he spotted a sleek red-and-white bottle. It was two-thirds hidden, but he could see some elaborate foreign lettering on the label. 'What's in that red-and-white bottle hiding away in the back, your ladyship?'

She pointed to another bottle. 'That? Oh, it's just sherry from Eastern Europe. A gift from one's late uncle. One would never drink it.'

'Not that one, your ladyship. The bottle to the right of it.'

She poured whisky into a crystal glass. 'The pink gin?'

'No. Between the pink gin and the Eastern European sherry you'll never be drinking.'

'One can't read the label without spectacles.' She sipped her whisky. 'Will you be drinking anything or are you simply admiring the bottles? One needs to lock the cabinet.'

Sensing Lady Peculiar had something to hide, Dinkel took an executive decision. He carefully reached inside the cabinet and removed the bottle himself. 'This is the one I was talking about, your ladyship.'

Her face fell. 'Ah. The Russian vodka.'

Dinkel examined the label. He couldn't decipher the gold Cyrillic lettering but the beautifully drawn sketch of the Kremlin at sunrise, together with a series of official seals dotted around the bottle, marked it out as something special. 'I've never seen anything like this before, your ladyship. Where did you buy it?'

'One doesn't buy vodka. One is gifted vodka.'

'And can I ask who gave it to you?'

She hesitated. 'It's so long ago, one forgets. Possibly a birthday present from a Russian diplomat friend who was stationed here a few years ago. Hence all the paraphernalia on the bottle. The Russians do like to make a show.' Her hand hovered near the bottle but she didn't grab it. 'One rarely indulges in vodka. One is a wine and whisky woman.'

Dinkel swished the bottle. 'Someone's been drinking it. It's only a third full.'

Lady Peculiar's voice was strained now. 'One doesn't wish to harass you, constable, but do you want a drink or not?'

'I'd better not while I'm on duty, your ladyship.'

At that, she grabbed the bottle. 'As you wish.'

As Dinkel watched Lady Peculiar replace the Russian vodka, he suddenly remembered the American tourist's claim that there might be a Russian spy in Upper Goosing. And that they could look and sound more English than Troy or Inspector Trump.

Sensing that, now he had seen this exclusive bottle of Russian vodka, it was probably safer to be outside the manor than inside, he made his excuses and left.

Chapter 26

After a brief taxi ride courtesy of Cadaver Cabs, the newly formed crime-fighting duo of Savage and Trump were standing on the porch of Agatha Twisty's impressive seventeenth-century ivy-smothered stone cottage in a leafy country lane on the eastern edge of the village waiting for an answer to their rap on the iron knocker.

The temporary mental paralysis Clinton had experienced in the post office had now passed – thanks to a few breaths of country air – and the neurons in his brain were finally firing in the right sequence. With the reassuring expertise – albeit theoretical – of Josephine Savage to aid the investigation, he was confident he could nail the mango-chutney murderer before four o'clock this afternoon, enabling him to knock off early and enjoy a celebratory cream horn in the Tourist Trap café. He might even put in a call to his best friend, Dickie Blinder, so there would be a *Goosing Times* photographer on standby to snap him striking his trademark another-case-solved-by-South-East-England's-greatest-detective pose while tucking into one of the legendary pastries. He'd also request that a reporter be available – one who was inexperienced enough to allow Clinton to dictate some of the article – so there could be a story including the standard Trump superlatives, a half-page quote where he explained he was only doing his job and didn't want any fuss, and a heavy nudge to any royal readers about becoming Sir Clinton Trump of Upper Goosing in the Queen's New Year Honours List.

The front door clunked open and Agatha Twisty's generous smile greeted them. 'You're just in time for a spot of earlier-than-usual elevenses. What I call half-nineses. I always treat myself on a Friday. Do come in.'

160

They accepted the invitation and joined her in a cosy, low-wooden-beamed living room. The walls were tastefully decorated with black-and-white sketches of her most famous characters and a mantelpiece overflowed with beautifully sculpted awards in the shape of quills, inkpots, books and daggers.

A few moments later, Clinton and Josephine were wedged into opposite ends of a big-armed sofa by the marble fireplace, holding exquisite bone-china cups filled to the brim with breakfast tea and balancing plates of assorted sandwiches – crusts neatly trimmed off – on their laps.

'My dear Josephine,' began Agatha. 'You mentioned in our brief telephone conversation that you needed advice about a murder. Are we talking fiction or non-fiction?'

'It's non-fiction,' confirmed her friend. 'Jepson's murder.'

'Ah. That would explain why our detective inspector is accompanying you. And there was me wondering if romance was blossoming.'

Clinton almost choked on his chicken sandwich. 'I'm afraid affairs of the heart must always take a back seat when a man has been drowned in mango chutney. Or, indeed, if a man hasn't been drowned in mango chutney but there is golf to be played. And there generally is golf to be played somewhere.' Agatha and Josephine exchanged a look that Clinton couldn't decipher but he ploughed on. 'I was rather hoping to solve this case by teatime today, Ms Twisty. And Ms Savage suggested you might be able to help me achieve that goal.' He sniffed dramatically. 'Because it seems our prime suspect – Cripps the gardener – isn't as prime as we thought.'

Agatha chortled. 'I often have that problem when buying steak.' She nodded at Josephine. 'No offence to your recently departed husband's butchering skills.' She turned back to Clinton. 'But prime suspects are rarely the culprits in murder mysteries.'

Josephine placed her cup on her plate. 'That's exactly why I thought we should come and chat with you. You've penned so many novels, undertaken so much research on real-life murders – you seem to have an instinctive knowledge for these things.'

'Very generous of you to say so, Josephine.'

As half-nineses boosted his system, memories came zipping back into Clinton's brain. Constable Dinkel and the American tourist had raised suspicions about the novelist. He hadn't planned to confront Twisty – especially not in her home – but now he was sitting opposite her, drinking her breakfast tea and demolishing her sandwiches, it seemed rude not to. First, he'd deal with the novel she'd written. 'You know, Ms Twisty, there are some similarities between one of your novels – *Murder in an Odd Manor* – and Jepson's murder. Not that I think that necessarily means anything. I just thought you should be aware.'

Agatha's eyes widened. 'Oh, don't be so dismissive of its potential meaning, inspector! And before you ask, I'm not about to unveil myself as a killer author who's so desperate to bump up their book sales they've murdered an innocent man in a similar fashion to the method used by the villain of one of their novels.' She nibbled the edge of a sandwich. 'What I mean is, the real killer may have copied elements of my story to divert attention towards me and away from themselves.'

The inspector pondered this. 'Possibly.' Time to mention the negative reviews. 'There's also the minor matter of someone called Goosing Jeeves bad-mouthing your books on the internet. That could have been Jepson.'

'It could.' She twizzled her eyes playfully. 'Or it could have been you, inspector.'

'Me? But I don't read your novels. I'm more into non-fiction. Golfing manuals, golf-course guidebooks, golfer biographies and autobiographies—'

'Sounds fascinating,' interrupted Agatha. 'But let me make one thing clear. I no longer read my books' reviews. I know my literary worth by now. But I understand you don't have to read a book to leave an online review, inspector. Therefore, Goosing Jeeves could be anyone.'

'But it definitely wasn't this detective.' He turned to Josephine. 'It wasn't you, was it?'

'Of course not, inspector. I adore Agatha's novels and I've awarded every one of them five stars. You should read them, inspector. I can recommend one, if you're tempted.'

'No, thank you. I'll only find fault with the detective's methods.' He smiled at the author, now convinced she was an innocent woman. 'No offence, Ms Twisty.'

'None taken, inspector. Moving on to the murder in hand, you're discounting Cripps – but what about his employers?'

The inspector finished his sandwich. 'I've spoken to both Lady Peculiar and the Major and I'm certain neither has anything whatsoever to do with it.'

'How certain?' asked Agatha.

'Her ladyship is a pillar of the community,' replied Clinton. 'I can't see her bumping off her butler – irrespective of his serving skills – because decent ones must be so hard to find. Better the devil you know, and all that. And as for the Major, he's a harmless old soldier who – even if he had a clear motive – would surely dispatch his prey in much cleaner fashion.'

Agatha nodded. 'Sounds reasonable to discount them for now. Is there anyone else who hasn't been grieving Jepson's loss quite as much as might be expected in polite English society?'

Clinton savoured his breakfast tea. 'I wouldn't put her down as the murdering type but Jayne Trill has been acting oddly. She seems cock-a-hoop that Jepson won't be ruining her latest amateur-dramatics production. He was due to play the lead.'

Agatha waved a hand. 'That woman is always acting oddly. And she's lost cast members in similar circumstances before. A long time ago, when I was still treading the boards, I remember her being in an identically ebullient mood when old Ted Penny was battered to death with his own evening newspaper.' She placed her cup on a side table as her memory clicked into gear. 'He was playing an ageing Romeo to her Juliet in a modern-day interpretation of Shakespeare's classic. It was set in a Great Yarmouth old people's home and, in the days before Ted's death, Jayne had made it abundantly clear she'd had more than enough of his coughing fits, cigar-scented kisses and carefree flatulence.'

Clinton nodded in acknowledgement. 'Then let us forget about Jayne Trill.' He rubbed his jaw. 'But that leaves this detective mastermind in the rather unfamiliar predicament of not knowing where to turn his crime-sniffing nose.'

Agatha drummed her fingers on the arm of her chair. 'You may find this a peculiar suggestion. But then we are dealing with a death at Peculiar Manor.' Her eyes twinkled. 'How about engaging the services of a medium? You could contact Jepson and ask him to reveal his murderer.'

'Contact the dead?' scoffed Clinton. 'That's total nonsense!'

Agatha twirled her nose. 'That was my steadfast view before I researched the subject of mediums for my novel – *Murder on the Other Side*. But I was surprised to learn that many police forces in England use them. Some have done so for decades. With very mixed results, admittedly, but there's been a modest success rate. Not necessarily striking gold in terms of the killer's name, but providing little nuggets along the way.' She collected the empty sandwich plates from her guests. 'Please excuse me while I return these to the kitchen. You can give my suggestion some thought while I pop these in the dishwasher.' And she stood up and disappeared through a doorway.

Josephine edged a little closer to Clinton on the sofa. 'It might be worth a gamble.'

'I sincerely doubt it. I'm Clinton Trump – South East England's greatest detective. I would be the first point of call for any spirit with information on one of my cases. And nobody from the afterlife has so much as left a message for me.'

'But you've got to channel their communications, inspector. They might be ...' She shuffled up the sofa a little more. '... trying to make contact with you.'

Clinton frowned. 'I have a work landline, work mobile, personal mobile, work pigeonhole, letterbox at home, work pager and there's a four-foot-high fax machine down the corridor in accounts through which I can be contacted in an absolute emergency. How many channels do they want?'

'Let's open up a new channel – one that's more reliable than fax machines.'

'Most things on this planet are more reliable than fax machines, Ms Savage. You'll need to be more specific.'

'What I mean is, I know a medium here in Brokenshire. Madame Pootin. She lives just a few miles away in Stonedead. She's from Moscow originally and worked with the Russian secret service for several years before she came over here.'

'Hmm. Sounds like a tall tale to generate more business.'

'No, it's true. She showed me a letter of thanks from the last Russian president; she helped him contact all his dead political opponents so he could wish them better luck in the afterlife. There was a signature and an official Kremlin seal – and she still has the bottle of vodka he sent her.'

'I wouldn't drink it, if I were her. Or even open it, for that matter.'

'She hasn't. But listen, inspector. A friend of mine used Madame Pootin to locate a lost will – the spirit of her dead uncle apparently told Madame Pootin where it was.'

'And where was that?'

'In his underpants drawer. In the rear left corner. Sealed in a turquoise, glitter-studded envelope. Secreted in a pair of Cliff Richard *Mistletoe and Wine* boxer shorts.'

Clinton's lower jaw slackened. 'Madame Pootin was that specific?'

'No. She just said the uncle told her it was probably in a drawer somewhere.'

'Oh. Sounds less like speaking with spirits and more stating the blindingly obvious.'

Josephine shuffled further along the sofa so their knees were almost touching. 'Why don't we give it a go?' She took a sharp breath. 'We've got nothing to lose.'

'Apart from her fee. How much is it?'

Josephine flopped back in her seat and sighed. 'I think there's a fifty pound connection charge to the spirit world and it's five pounds per minute after that – possibly more if the person died overseas or you're contacting them during peak hours.'

'That's extortionate. I could call my aunt in Australia for less!'

'Yes, but is she dead, inspector?'

'I've no idea. I haven't phoned her for years.'

She squeezed his hand. 'Let's put our trust in … fate.'

Clinton jerked his hand back. 'Do you mind? I have very sensitive metacarpals.'

Their host returned. 'Have you two super-sleuths come to a decision?'

The crime-fighting duo glanced at each other.

'Well, I'm not psychic,' trumpeted Agatha. 'Have you or haven't you?'

'Yes, we have,' declared Clinton with all the authority of a man who'd made up his mind a lot longer than three seconds ago. 'We shall search for clues to this murder on the other side!'

Chapter 27

Lady Peculiar's gardener was clunking up Gallows Hill in his heavy boots and dark-green overalls with the steely determination of a fifty-nine-year-old ex-con horticulturalist determined to prove his innocence. But Peculiar Manor wasn't his destination – that was three miles in completely the opposite direction. The former prime suspect in the Jepson case had not yet finished his heated Friday morning confrontations. Next stop on the 2018 wrath-of-Ronald-Cripps tour was the offices of the *Goosing Times*. That so-called journalist Fenella Cocky and her editor needed reminding about the difference between facts, speculation and downright balderdash.

He seized his chance to sneak in the front door of the four-storey building behind a dawdling, headphone-wearing, smartphone-gazing man who had the words 'Grab The Goosing Times' on the back of his t-shirt. After navigating the signage maze in reception, Cripps clomped up the stairs to the newspaper's editorial offices on the first floor. There didn't seem to be anybody around, so he rang the buzzer on an intercom pad.

'Yes?' snipped a female voice.

'I'm here to see Fenella Cocky.'

'She's not here.'

'The editor, then.'

'Appointment?'

'Consider this a request for one. And I'm not going nowhere until he sees me.'

The voice sighed. 'It's about what?'

'It's personal.'

'Name?'

'Ronald Cripps. He'll know who I am. Just tell him.'

The voice broke off. After a minute, it returned. 'He's tied up at the moment.'

'Is he, eh?'

'Yes.'

'Well, tell him he'll be even *more* tied up if he don't see me right now.'

'More tied up? How do you mean?'

'Tell him. He'll understand.'

The female voice disappeared for another sixty seconds. When it responded again, it was even snippier. 'He really can't see you today, Mr Cripps. Or any day in the near future. Sorry.'

The intercom crackled and went dead. Then the dawdling employee who'd facilitated his entrance to the building appeared next to him and woozily waved his security pass. The door buzzed open and Cripps saw a chance for a sneaky encore. Nobody seemed to notice as he bustled in behind the demon dawdler to stand on the white-tiled floor of the newsroom.

Before the dawdler could dawdle off, Cripps slapped a hand on his dawdling shoulder and spun him round – almost causing him to drop his smartphone. 'Where's the editor's office, boy?'

'Huh?' came the reply.

'Where is the office of the editor?'

'The toilets? They're straight on, then left and just follow the bleach smell.'

Cripps whipped off the young man's headphones before he could react. 'The editor. Where is he?'

'Hey! Why did you take my headphones?'

'So you can open your bloody ears for a change and listen to a human being who's addressing you without musical accompaniment. Where's his office?'

'Will you give me my headphones back if I tell you?'

'You'll have 'em wrapped round your ears again soon enough – question is, is there gonna be any pain involved?'

'I know what you mean. They can chafe your earlobes after a few hours. I usually dab a bit of moisturiser on mine. But I was in a hurry this morning.'

Cripps' wafer-thin patience was in danger of melting away completely. 'What are you blabbering on about?!'

'Earlobe care – it's essential these days. You've only got two earlobes. They're as important to your head as your feet are to your legs. Not everyone's got earlobes. You should cherish them.' He pointed at Cripps' head. 'I can see you've got a nice pair yourself. Nowhere near as nice as mine, but then you are a lot older than me.'

Cripps clenched his fists and growled, causing a nearby journalist to check the office for escaped lions.

The young man inspected Cripps' overalls. 'You're not wearing a visitor's pass.'

'I passed on the pass.' His eyes were bulging like two pickled onions in a vice. 'Last chance! Editor's office.'

The man pointed to a door thirty metres away. 'That's Dickie Blinder's lair. But he's always tied up. So I wouldn't bother—'

The headphones had already been slung on the floor and Cripps was rushing for the door.

Five seconds later, Dickie Blinder was surprised to see his office door almost fly off its hinges as a man in green overalls shoulder-charged it. Once both the bearded intruder and the door had recovered and steadied themselves, Dickie recognised Ronald Cripps. The editor's girlfriend, Svetlana, who was standing next to him, hardly batted a Siberian eyelid.

Dickie cleared his throat and pushed his chair back from his desk so he wasn't within easy assaulting distance. 'Good morning, Mr Cripps. As my receptionist informed you, I am rather, erm … busy.'

'Busy spreading lies about me!' bellowed Cripps. 'Because I didn't murder no butler, there weren't no festering feud between me and him, and I weren't nowhere near the manor on Tuesday evening. I've just told that dozy inspector as much and he believes me.' His chest inflated. 'So, nobody's gonna be charging me with nothing.'

Dickie checked there were no sharp objects on his desk. 'There were some double negatives in there, but I understand the point you're making.'

'Stuff your double negatives! Your journalist never even spoke to me. If she had, I would've put her right.'

'Yes, well, as you can appreciate, Mr Cripps, we don't necessarily obtain quotes from the prime suspect in a murder case.'

'Are you deaf?! I ain't no prime suspect!'

Svetlana intervened. 'Mr Cripps. You interrupt us. Leave now.'

'You think I'm gonna let some Russian tell me what to do? This isn't Moscow, sweetheart. Now get lost, so me and him can have this out properly – man to man.'

Svetlana glided out from behind the desk. 'This redhead more man than you are.'

Cripps' fiery rage was partly doused. 'You what?'

'You want to fight?' She flicked a glance at her boyfriend. 'I fight for Dickie. He my man.'

'Can't your fella fight for himself?'

Dickie pushed his chair back a little more in answer to this question.

'I don't fight women,' grunted Cripps.

'I do,' growled Svetlana. 'I fight women. I fight men. I fight animal. And you come into office acting like animal. Not man.'

Cripps' rage was flaring up again. 'You calling me an animal?'

Svetlana moved her face to within a centimetre of Cripps' and, with a voice more threatening than any Dickie had ever heard on the golf course, she spat her reply. 'Yes. I calling you animal.'

Cripps emitted the kind of noise that would worry a werewolf.

'You make noise like animal,' observed Svetlana. 'But can you fight like animal?'

The gardener's wild rumblings grew even louder.

'Svetlana think no. As you English say, you "all bark, no bite".'

Cripps bared his teeth. Dickie noted that the canines were particularly well developed and his thoughts immediately turned to a grovelling front-page apology in the next edition. But Svetlana wasn't finished.

'Go back to your garden, English man, or you find Russian wolf in it real soon.'

'Are you threatening me?' fizzled Cripps.

'Yes. It not obvious? I make more obvious.' And, with a speed Dickie had only ever witnessed at international table-tennis tournaments, she grabbed the jumbo stapler from his desk and thrust it to Cripps' jugular. 'Get out now. Or you feel cold steel of office stapler.'

'You're not gonna touch me,' huffed Cripps, his voice betraying a smidgen of uncertainty.

'It's fully loaded,' noted Dickie. 'And I accidentally stapled my thumb with it last Tuesday. It was very painful and I wore a plaster for two days. Quite a big plaster, as it happens. It's a tad tender even now.'

Cripps backed away. 'I've wasted enough time here. I've made my point.' He turned and lumbered to the door, before swearing loudly at both of them and storming out.

Dickie wiped his brow. 'Thank you, darling.'

'No mention it.'

'That's a side of you I haven't seen before.'

'There many men like him in Siberia. Women have to fight like men. We usually win.'

'Well, in Upper Goosing, darling, we prefer to keep fights to an absolute minimum. Our doctors are really only good for coughs, colds, bullet and stab wounds. So, I'm grateful you maintained your composure and it didn't come to blows.' He paused to reclaim his stapler and place it back where it lived. 'I can see why Cripps was so agitated, assuming what he was saying is true. I shall have to speak with Fenella about how we take our coverage forward.'

'Why you not forget this murder? Nobody care about dead butler. It just bad publicity for village.'

'For any other village, yes. But, bizarrely, the more murders we have here, Svetlana, the better the tourist numbers.'

'But he not interesting man. Wait for more interesting man to be murdered. Then do big story.'

'It could be a long wait. There are some crashing bores in this village.'

'You mean like Inspector Trump?'

Dickie waved a finger. 'No, darling. He's my best friend. If he's a bore, then so am I. And that means you're potentially a bore. And you and I don't want to be labelled the most boring couple in Upper Goosing, do we? Because that would be very boring. Boring for me. Boring for you. Boring for our friends. Boring for my family. Boring for your family. And, I've no doubt, boring for many others who aren't friends and family.'

Svetlana shrugged and yawned.

He clasped his hands. 'Now, what non-boring matter was it you wanted to see me about before we were so rudely interrupted?'

'I have something to tell you, Dickie.'

'Go on, Svetlana.'

'I go away Sunday.'

'Day trip somewhere? Salisbury Cathedral, perhaps? I hear it has a rather impressive 123-metre spire. And a very old clock. Lots of Russians come over to see it, apparently.'

'No. My mother sick. My father die five year ago. I not have brother or sister. No uncle or aunt. Only Svetlana can help.'

'What a shame – I was hoping we could put our heads together for the Goosing Arms pub quiz on Sunday evening. This week's special categories are deadly poisons, venomous snakes and Russian presidents. But sacrifice is all part of life. I shall have to quiz alone, if necessary. How long will you be gone?'

'No more than week. She still sick after seven day, I put her in local hospital. I know doctor who help. He real man – not animal.'

'That's good to hear.'

'I need to buy new suitcase, Dickie. I see you later. Be careful with leg.'

'I will, darling.'

And, after a farewell peck on the cheek, she was gone.

Chapter 28

The lift in Madame Pootin's towering apartment block being out of order, the Savage–Trump collective had made it to the seventeenth floor via the stairs.

'My legs are absolutely killing me,' complained Clinton, grinding to a halt on the narrow landing after hauling himself up the last step.

Josephine joined him a moment later, blew out her cheeks and rested a hand on the wall. 'It'll be worth the strain, inspector. I promise.'

Clinton gazed out of the small window next to him. 'I can only assume Madame Pootin lives this high in the clouds because it's closer to the spirit world.'

'Possibly. She's rented this apartment ever since leaving Russia two years ago.'

He bent down and massaged his left calf. 'And why did she leave?'

'How shall I put this diplomatically? People who work for the Russian secret service tend to have a shorter life expectancy than those who don't.'

'So she moved to Upper Goosing – European Murder Destination of the Year 2015?'

'It's still a lot safer than Moscow.'

He massaged his right calf. 'You're sure this woman can contact the dead?'

Josephine paused. 'I haven't told anyone this, inspector, but I trust you implicitly so I'm going to reveal my secret.'

'You're a Russian spy? Because I've been informed by an ex-CIA man that there may be one operating in Upper Goosing. And, apparently, someone as elegant, well-spoken and quintessentially English as your good self would be a prime candidate.' He waggled a finger. 'And let me make it perfectly clear, just because we've shared fruit tartlets and scaled seventeen flights of stairs together, that doesn't mean I won't turn you over to the authorities, if I have to, as soon as we've climbed back down.'

'No, I'm not a Russian spy, inspector. I could never be. You see, beetroot has never agreed with me.'

'Nor me. So we're both in the clear.'

'What I was trying to say is I used Madame Pootin's services to contact my three husbands after their tragic and completely accidental deaths.'

'You did?'

'Yes. To ask them not to discuss the details of their deaths with any mediums employed by the police to extract information from them.'

'And, erm, why would you do that?'

'I simply didn't want my ex-husbands being bothered with searching questions when they should be enjoying themselves in the afterlife.'

Clinton considered this. 'Sounds sensible. And there are three of them over there now, so I imagine they've formed a dead-spouse alliance.' He nodded knowingly. 'They've probably got better things to do than undergo interrogations from busybody detectives.'

'My thoughts exactly.'

'You're a very intelligent woman, Ms Savage. I'm not the marrying kind but if I were, your razor-sharp intellect would definitely single you out for earnest consideration for the position of Mrs Trump – or "First Lady" as I would insist on calling the fortunate female.'

Josephine quivered gently. 'What a very charming thing to say, inspector.'

'Very charming men inevitably say very charming things. I don't even realise I'm being very charming sometimes – not until somebody else's very charming radar picks up my very charming signals.'

She quivered a little more. 'I shall return the very charming compliment by noting what a shame it is that you aren't the marrying type, inspector.'

'Ah. But statistics show marriage increases the chances of being murdered, Ms Savage. Especially around these parts. One minute you're walking down the aisle in Saint Crippen's. A few months later you're being carried back down it by half a dozen pallbearers.'

Josephine shuffled nervously on the spot.

'Oh, I'm not making any insinuations about your late husbands.'

She touched her neck. 'No?'

'Of course not! The fact they were three healthy, strapping men who all met their ends in bizarre circumstances before you'd been married a year is simply a coincidence. Some people die of a heart attack. Others fall from stepladders into a hundred gallons of liquid metal, drown in a giant vat of cake mixture or trip and fall into their own mincing machines. Perfectly everyday accidents that could happen to any of us, if we were manufacturing ornamental scented-candle holders, baking giant Victoria sponges or attempting to create the perfect sausage.' His forehead wrinkled. 'I've lost my thread. What was I saying before that?'

Her tone was flat. 'Marriage leads to murder.'

'Ah, yes. You know, the local vicar always advises against including "till death do us part" in the marriage vows, just in case there's a killer in the congregation who sees it as a personal challenge. Although one modern couple insisted on changing it to "till murder do us part", which I thought was rather ridiculous. But lots of people said it was very clever so I didn't argue.' He sighed. 'No, better to be a carefree bachelor like myself. The simple truth is, the fewer relationships one enters into, the more likely one is to live to a ripe old age.'

She took a step towards him. 'You know what they say, inspector: "Never say never".'

'Oh, I'm always saying "never". And I've never been proved wrong – no one's shown me that saying "never" isn't the right thing to do when "never" needs to be said. Not ever. And I'm not a man who's afraid to recognise he's got it wrong. When that fateful day arrives – when I am wrong about something – I shall admit it.' He grinned. 'But it will never happen.'

Josephine delivered an admiring pout. 'I shall never stop being impressed by your observations on the world, inspector.'

'Me neither.' He stood up straight. 'Right, my calves have recovered enough to proceed. Which flat is it?'

'Number 1711.'

'Righty-ho. Let's get this meeting with a medium over and done with.'

Chapter 29

Lady Peculiar and the Major were enjoying a glass of Russian vodka in the manor's drawing room – the Major in his favourite armchair and her ladyship on a recliner next to the grand piano.

The Major held up his crystal glass. 'Haven't suckled Mother Russia's milk since before the Iron Curtain fell, Edith. Couldn't stand the stuff. Never put a smile on my face – or anyone else's, as far as I can see.' He took a noisy sip. 'But this vodka isn't too bad on the old palate. Throat's a trifle numb but can still feel it. And digestive system is still functioning normally. So, not a bad show overall.' He snorted playfully. 'Who have we got to thank for it?'

She pursed her lips. 'The constable investigating Jepson's murder asked the very same thing. I'm never at my most composed when unfamiliar police officers are firing questions about murdered staff members at me. You'd think I'd be used to it by now, but I'm not. I couldn't remember.'

'Why was he interrogating you about your drinks cabinet?'

'He seemed to think this vodka was significant. I got the distinct feeling he thought I might be working for the Russians. So I fobbed him off and told him it probably came from a diplomatic contact. But I don't have any.'

'Was it a gift from that charmless oligarch who wanted to buy the manor back in 2015 so he could turn it into a seven-star hotel?'

Her ladyship clutched her pearl necklace. 'You clever old stick, Rupert! That's exactly who it was! As if a bottle of vodka was going to make me change my mind.'

The Major harrumphed. 'Those oligarch chaps want a piece of everything, as far as I can see. That easy-access car park in Lower Goosing will be the thin end of the wedge, you mark my words. Still can't believe the Russian president showed up to open the ruddy thing.'

'It is one of the easiest-access car parks in Western Europe, Rupert. Even easier if you have a Russian number plate.'

'How do you mean, old girl?'

'There's a special entrance and exit for Russian vehicles. The technology is remarkable – if nobody told you, you wouldn't even know it was there.'

'Then who told you about it, eh?' He chuckled noisily. 'Are you sure you're not working for the Reds, Edith?'

'Of course not, Rupert. My dinner-party schedule simply wouldn't allow it.'

'I wasn't being serious! Everyone knows your blood has a royal-blue tinge to it. Last person in Upper Goosing I'd expect to betray their country for thirty roubles.'

'I know you were jesting. I was also being light-hearted.' She adjusted her necklace. 'You know, Rupert, there was a ten-page spread in the *Goosing Times* when that car park was opened. It's not often a world leader comes to visit, so the editor really went to town. The coverage referred briefly to the special entrance for Russian vehicles.' She sipped her vodka in the way the Queen might do when she had special visitors. 'The reporting was rather over the top; some might say obsequious. But the editor's female companion is a Russian, I believe, so that probably explains it.'

'A Russian filly? Who would that be?'

'Svetlana something-or-other – the medical student who's forever griping about something and who descended on us last September. She was at the curry evening. And, most surprisingly, she didn't complain about anything.'

'It was a rip-roaring venison vindaloo, that's why. I know that for a fact because I nabbed the portion Jepson was saving for himself.' He patted his stomach. 'Anyway, going back to Russian car parks, I might slap some Cyrillic plates on Jepson's Fiat Uno, toddle into Lower Goosing and treat myself to some free parking.'

'I wouldn't if I were you. We'll probably never see you again.'

'Good point.'

'Apparently, one of the Lower Goosing farmers has sold several hectares of land to the same Russian who built the car park. There are already rumours of a drive-through fast-food outlet.'

'Not one of those infernal drive-in burger restaurants where youngsters in silly hats try to foist French fries on you every time you do a U-turn in their car park?'

'No. I have it on good authority from one of the local councillors that this outlet would sell beef stroganoff, borscht and a variety of cabbage-based snacks.'

'Doesn't exactly fit into the English countryside idyll, does it, Edith?'

'No, Rupert. It doesn't. And it's extremely troubling.'

'Is that why we're polishing off this vodka this evening?'

'Yes. We must do our bit for Queen and country. I shall be stocking up on nothing but British spirits the next time we replenish our alcohol supplies.'

'Hear, hear! I bet you wouldn't find a bottle of vodka in the Buckingham Palace drawing room.'

'I wouldn't know, Rupert, as I've never been invited. But when that inevitable day comes, I shall ask Lizzy if I can check her alcohol inventory. She will, of course, afford me that courtesy – as her fifth cousin four times removed – and I shall report back to you.'

'Jolly good.' He nodded towards the drinks cabinet. 'Just the one bottle of vodka in there, was it?'

'Yes.' She downed the contents of her glass. 'And it will be the last.'

Chapter 30

Clinton and Josephine had located flat 1711. Its door was ajar but there was no medium – or anybody else – in the dimly lit hallway to greet them.

The inspector peered into the gloom. He couldn't see anything.

'Is there anybody there?' called Josephine.

Clinton cocked an ear. 'Have we started spiritual proceedings already?'

Before Josephine could reply, Madame Pootin's head appeared. It was adorned with a hemispherical red hat that could easily have started life as a fruit bowl. She flicked on the hall light and the rest of her body appeared – covered in a faded brown-and-orange floral dress.

Madame Pootin ushered them into the hallway, shut the front door and addressed them in her harsh Russian accent. 'Please come over … to other side.' She disappeared from the hall and her guests followed her into a small bedroom containing a circular table and three chairs.

Clinton and Josephine took their seats and the medium addressed them.

'Before I establish connection, you want tea or coffee?'

'You don't have white wine, by any chance?' asked Clinton.

Madame Pootin frowned. 'No white wine. I only serve spirits.'

'In that case, I'll have a gin and tonic with ice and a slice.'

Madame Pootin's frown didn't waver. 'It was joke.'

'Ah. Very good. You don't serve alcoholic spirits. You serve human spirits.'

'No need explain my joke to me.'

'Our Madame is lightening the mood, Ms Savage! I like it. As I always say, death doesn't have to be serious. The scenes of crime officer and I often pretend that a corpse is one of our superior officers and have a bit of colourful banter with the deceased. I do the voices. I'm very good at voices.' His thoughts wandered. 'Although next-of-kin tend to object if they're at the scene. But, you know, there'll always be spoilsports who don't want to play along. So, you carry on with the jokes, if it gets you in the spirit.' He chuckled. 'Little "spirit" witticism of my own there – that makes it one-all.'

Madame Pootin puckered her lips. 'It not competition. I make joke because it easier to channel spirit of butler if you relax and happy.'

'I'm not sure about that,' mused Clinton. 'Jepson was a rather glum old fruit. It may make more sense if we depress ourselves, toss around a few insults and try to look on the darker side of life. Then we might have more luck connecting with the miserable blighter.'

The Russian's frown was now a grimace. 'Madame Pootin expert. You sit, listen. We contact this dead man.'

'Will do.' Clinton paused. 'What about a liqueur? Tia Maria is one of my favourites. I've no idea if it was one of Jepson's preferred tipples but it wouldn't do any harm to try.'

The medium's grimace was morphing into the kind of expression a tsar might display before ordering an execution.

'Or Baileys? They do a vanilla version now. And, I believe, an orange—'

'I suggest we dispense with drinks,' interrupted Josephine, 'and dive straight in to the spiritual business.'

'Good idea,' mumbled Madame Pootin, before pulling the room's thick red curtains across its single window, closing the door and settling into the remaining chair.

The Russian snapped her eyes shut. 'Full name of man you want me to contact.'

'Maurice Jepson,' confirmed Clinton.

'Middle names?'

'He didn't have any.'

'Hmm. You not tell Madame this when you make appointment.'

'Does that make things more difficult?' asked Clinton. 'If it's going to increase the hundred-pound flat fee I transferred to you on the way here, we shall have to discuss this further.'

'What make harder is man talking when Madame trying to connect with spirit world.'

'Pardon me for trying to clarify costs,' muttered Clinton.

Josephine rested a hand on his arm and closed her eyes. 'Let's empty our minds and concentrate, inspector.'

Clinton tried. But he had white-wine spritzers on the brain now so it wasn't easy. 'I'm sorry, I'm having trouble emptying my thoughts. I have rather a lot of them. Possibly fifteen to twenty times more thoughts than average people like yourselves. Do you have any red wine, Madame Pootin? It doesn't always agree with me – can cause hiccups – but I'm willing to give it a go if it will help put me in the right mood.'

Madame Pootin's eyes flicked open. 'One more word about alcohol, we cancel session. Shut eyes and no open until Madame say.'

Clinton obeyed and listened to the medium's words.

'Spirit world – this Madame Valerie Pootin.' She closed her eyes again. 'Channel for spirit. I open now – for next thirty minute. And I request connection from England.'

'Won't they know you're in England?' asked Clinton, without opening his eyes. 'You know – like the caller ID facility on telephones?' He missed the Russian's scowl and continued listening after she failed to answer his question.

'Madame Pootin calling Maurice no-middle-name Jepson.'

'Just to make clear to any spirits on the line,' interrupted Clinton. '"No-middle-name" isn't his middle name. It would be a very odd middle name if it were. Possibly something parents in Lower Goosing might contemplate for their child, but not those in Upper Goosing. But to get back to my point, Madame is simply stating – in a rather clumsy way, it has to be said, but

English isn't her first language, so we'll forgive her for that – that the dead butler in question does not have a middle—'

'Inspector,' whispered Josephine. 'Maybe we should just listen and let Madame Pootin do the talking.'

'I'm sure they're as capable of listening to me as they are to her.'

'You not medium!' snorted Madame Pootin.

Clinton chuckled. 'I could tell a rather funny joke here about being an extra-large rather than a medium, but I don't want to overstimulate the spirits.'

'Medium like me hear this joke thousand times. Spirits, too. So no more joke or spirits break connection.'

Clinton finally took the hint.

'Madame calling Maurice Jepson. Come in, Maurice Jepson. Are you receiving us? We request audience with you.'

Silence for thirty seconds.

'Are you hearing anything, Madame?' enquired Clinton.

'Only your voice interrupt.' She muttered something in Russian that Clinton assumed must be some sort of incantation. 'Again, I call for Maurice Jepson, butler of Peculiar Manor.'

An even longer silence.

'Madame calling Maurice. There nothing to worry about. We have policeman here. He want to find who kill you.' She took a deep breath and gurgled. 'I have connection.'

'It's definitely him?' asked Clinton.

'Yes, it him. Maurice no-middle-name Jepson on the line.'

'Hello, caller!' piped Clinton. 'Would you mind confirming your identity to Madame Pootin by telling us the name of the comedy competition you entered?'

'Please stop talking. Connection weak.'

'Yes, but it'll only take a second to answer. Then we can confirm you're not just making it all up, Madame.'

Madame inflated herself. 'I professional medium.' She deflated. 'Not con lady.'

'I shall give you the benefit of the doubt for now. And if whoever's on the line answers my question, that doubt will be stripped away.'

'Spirit not in interview. He say what he want to say.'

'So, what's he saying?' asked Josephine.

'Not much because this policeman keep interrupt.' The medium held her breath. 'Wait.' She breathed out. 'He say … he know person who kill him.'

Clinton sighed. 'That's not saying very much. Everybody knows everybody in our village.'

'He also say "Killer probably female. They wear perfume."'

'Probably female?' whined Clinton. 'As in, if she wasn't female, she was male? Because that's not much use to me. And every lady at that curry evening must have been wearing perfume – to drown out the pungent odour of venison vindaloo.'

'I wasn't wearing any perfume,' noted Josephine.

'You're fragrant enough, Ms Savage. But every other lady would've sprayed themselves silly.' He turned to Madame Pootin. 'I hate to rain on your spiritual parade, but even a man of my almost supernatural investigative talents needs more specific information than that to collar a killer.'

'He say something else.' An extended pause. 'Man in room really annoy me. I go now.'

Clinton shook his head. 'Jepson took all that time to tell you that?'

'He say it many, many times. And he use bad words I not mention because lady present.' Her eyes snapped open. 'Maurice no-middle-name Jepson gone. You open eyes now.'

Clinton and Josephine joined her back in the land of the living.

Madame Pootin sat upright. 'That finish of session.'

'Is that it?' squeaked Clinton. 'I was hoping for a name for a hundred pounds. Or, at the very least, a full description of the killer. All I got was a spirit claiming to be Jepson who couldn't answer a simple question and who said he knew his killer, they might be female and have a penchant for perfume. I'm not paying a hundred pounds for that!'

The medium narrowed her eyes. 'We always at mercy of spirits. Connection between our different worlds always weak.' She pushed out her chest. 'And fee *always* non-refundable.'

Clinton glowered. 'It's taxpayers' money that could have been spent on vital frontline assets – a portrait of me for my office, or a chair with heated cushions, or one of those clever contraptions for my desk where the ball-bearings continually knock together.'

'You not happy,' grunted Madame Pootin, 'you speak with my brother.'

'Where's he?'

'Siberia. I not see him since 1997.'

Before Clinton could develop his glower into a grimace, Josephine intervened. 'I have an idea.'

'Will it get my hundred pounds back?' muttered Clinton.

'No. But it might help you find a Russian spy – you mentioned earlier that there could be one operating in the village.'

Clinton tutted. 'There's only a thirty per cent chance of it – at the very most – so I would respectfully suggest it would be a waste of my valuable time to pursue that line of enquiry. Anyway, it wouldn't help me solve Jepson's murder. And doing that so I can play golf on Saturday is my priority – not unmasking a Russian spy who could be a threat to the good name of this village, rural life as we know it in England, and British national security.'

'But imagine if you did uncover a Russian spy, inspector. You'd be the toast of the detective community for years to come. Whether or not you solved the Jepson case wouldn't really matter.' Josephine's eyes widened. 'And it seems such a waste not to tap into Madame Pootin's knowledge of the Russian secret service.'

'What all this?' asked Madame Pootin. 'I not work for them no more.'

'We know that,' replied Josephine in a soft voice. 'But I have a whole collection of photos on my smartphone of Upper Goosing social events and the people attending them. And maybe, Madame, with your knowledge of the Russian secret service, you'll see a face you recognise – or even somebody acting in a suspiciously secret-agent type of way.'

The medium eyed her unsurely. 'It not as easy as you think. Yes, I meet many agents in my ten year working for them. But they not all look like James Bond villain.'

'Madame is right,' sighed Clinton. 'The thought that Russians could infiltrate a tightknit community such as Upper Goosing is fanciful. And if they had, why would they be targeting our village?'

Josephine shrugged. 'I don't know. But if we unmasked them they might tell us.'

Madame Pootin snorted. 'Again, it not like James Bond film. Russian not confess everything at end before they kill you. Russian just kill you.'

Ms Savage rummaged in her pocket for her phone. 'Let me show you a few photos anyway, Madame Pootin. It can't hurt to try.'

'It more work for me,' grumbled the medium.

Josephine extracted a fifty-pound note from her pocket. 'I'll pay an additional fee if you'll spend half an hour checking the faces.'

The medium gazed up at the clock on the wall. 'Next client come in forty-five minute.' She checked the note was genuine. It was. 'Okay, lady. We have deal.'

Clinton groaned and resigned himself to thirty more wasted minutes in this Russian's costly presence.

Josephine began her photo presentation while Clinton sat back, closed his eyes and nodded off to sleep. She started with snaps from a couple of summer fêtes, then followed up with all the major garden vegetable shows, the annual croquet tournament in July, the Brokenshire county show at the start of

August, and the big 'family duck-shoot' in the grounds of Peculiar Manor. But Madame Pootin recognised nobody.

Twenty minutes had passed and Clinton woke up. 'Any joy?' he asked, rubbing his eyes.

Josephine shook her head. 'I'm just trying to locate the photos I took at Tuesday's Peculiar Manor curry evening. I created a separate folder but can't find it.'

'Pictures of Jayne Trill stuffing her face with poppadoms?' scoffed Clinton. 'I doubt she's working for Moscow. She's more into Christmas pantomimes than Chekhov or Tolstoy.'

'Ah, here are my curry-evening photos, Madame Pootin. Anyone you recognise around this table?'

First photo. 'No.' Second photo. 'No.' Third photo. 'This lady make stupid face.'

'That's Jayne Trill.'

'She definitely not Russian. We never make stupid face for camera.'

'I think that's her normal face,' mumbled Clinton.

'What about this woman – Lady Peculiar?' asked Josephine.

Madame peered at the phone screen. 'Face familiar. She look royal.' She stopped to think. 'Could be related to tsar. But I never seen in Russia.'

'She's lived here for more than fifty years, ladies. She's distantly related to the Queen. She's not a spy – never in a million years!'

'Never say never,' growled the medium. 'Any more photo, Ms Savage?'

'I was sitting near these ladies. This is Svetlana. I don't know her surname. She's Russian.'

All the blood seemed to drain from the medium's face. She opened her mouth but managed only a dry croak.

'Are you alright, Madame?' enquired Josephine. 'You look like you've just seen a ghost.'

'Isn't that her job?' huffed Clinton. 'And if she has seen a ghost, I'm not paying fifty pounds for her to connect with it.'

The medium had to force out each word like a piece of fluff from the roof of her mouth. 'I … know … this … lady.'

Josephine glanced at Clinton, who was adjusting his bouffant. 'You mean Svetlana?'

'That … not … real name. Her … real name …'

'With respect,' interrupted Clinton. 'I think this may be Madame trying to justify the additional fifty pounds you rashly handed over, Ms Savage.'

'Please, inspector, let her finish.'

'Real name … Natasha Kalashnikov.'

'Sounds a little too James Bond villain to me,' observed Clinton.

'She top-level … Russian spy. Kalashnikov … assassin.'

Clinton laughed. 'My best friend Dickie is dating a Russian assassin? I think he might have noticed, don't you? The telltale poison-tipped umbrella in the hallway, the fake passport on the mantelpiece, or the silencer between the scissors and the Sellotape in the kitchen drawer.'

'This not … movies. This … deadly serious.' And the medium slumped back in her chair and broke into a cold sweat.

Josephine turned to Clinton. 'I don't think she's faking it.'

'She's convincing, I'll give her that. But so are my cats when I've already fed them dinner, it's slipped my mind and they start meowing at me in the way they do when they're starving hungry.' He tapped his nose. 'So, let's learn a lesson from well-fed felines and not jump to any Kremlin conclusions.'

His crime-fighting companion shuffled closer. 'You know, inspector, Svetlana – or Natasha, or whoever she is – made allegations about me leaving the dining room for an extended period on Tuesday evening. It was just after you and I had returned from the manor kitchens and I'd mentioned I could help you with your investigation because of my Master's in Advanced Criminology.'

'You have Master in Advance Criminology?' asked Madame Pootin, with an almost religious air of reverence.

'Yes.'

'For Russian secret agent, that like crucifix to vampire. They very scared of Master of Advance Criminology.'

Clinton straightened his tie. 'I'd suggest they're more scared of detective geniuses such as myself, Madame Pootin, but I don't have time to sit around arguing that point.' He shifted his gaze to Josephine. 'And, as far as I know, although we haven't taken a statement from Svetlana, she hasn't volunteered any information about you leaving the dining room to the police.'

'Exactly. It was a false allegation. But I didn't want my name dragged through the manor mud, so I withdrew my offer of help to you.' She bowed her head. 'I'm sorry, inspector. It was very cowardly of me.'

'Oh, don't be silly. Who wants to be a hero? Statistics show that cowards have a much greater life expectancy than heroes. That's why I always err on the side of cowardice in tricky situations. And I'm still alive to tell the cowardly tale.'

Madame Pootin wiped her forehead with a handkerchief. 'This Kalashnikov woman very dangerous.'

Josephine stared into Clinton's eyes. 'Do you think she could have killed Jepson, inspector?'

'I very much doubt it. I mean, what possible motive could she have?'

Josephine shrugged. 'She's not married to him. So I have no idea.'

Clinton rubbed his stubble. 'But we have no other real suspects in this case. And, if I'm to display my golf prowess tomorrow, we're running out of time. So, let's make Svetlana the prime suspect, conduct a search of her living quarters, grab a few random possessions for analysis – clothes, notebooks, digital devices and whatnot – and bring her in.' He nodded at Ms Savage. 'You can inform my superintendent of Svetlana's false accusations. Maybe you could embellish your story a little by saying she returned from the ladies lavatories with hands covered in mango chutney – or possibly that you bumped into her in the post office the next day and she made a full confession while under intense pressure from Pattie Quirk to buy a set of

European Murder Destination of the Year 2015 commemorative postage stamps. I can charge her with murder and my weekend will be freed up. What do you think, Ms Savage?'

'That sounds like an excellent plan, inspector.'

'Thank you. I'd call it a genius plan, personally, but each to their own.' He puffed out his chest. 'I'm glad I came up with the idea of asking Madame Pootin to peruse your photos. Not many detectives would have pursued that course of action. But Detective Inspector Clinton Trump – South East England's greatest detective – is a master of the unexpected.'

Josephine paused for a second. 'Yes, it was a brilliant idea. You deserve all the credit.'

'Tremendous! Thank you, Madame Pootin for all your help. If Jepson does get in touch again, tell him he can only contact me directly via the fax machine in accounts. And that's non-negotiable.' He sprung up. 'Now, Ms Savage, we have a Russian spy to track down! And I know just the newspaper editor to help us.'

Chapter 31

After a call to his friend Dickie to establish where they could find Svetlana for a 'quick chat about the events of Tuesday evening', Inspector Trump and his unofficial sidekick were soon heading for the Russian's expensive apartment in the trendy part of Upper Goosing known locally as 'The City' – partly because it was the premier location for city bankers, lawyers and doctors with country properties in the village, and partly because it was the only road in Upper Goosing that boasted a wine bar, bureau de change and a supermarket that sold balsamic vinegar and artichoke hearts.

Their taxi was currently stuck behind a stationary red Porsche with a 'My other car's a Rolls Royce' sticker on the rear windscreen. A shiny lorry transporting several tonnes of avocados was keeping a courteous distance from their rear bumper while a well-dressed Hell's Angel revved up a brand-new Harley Davidson alongside them. But Clinton was oblivious to the top-quality traffic. He was staring longingly out of the window at the golf course: the ninth green was just fifty metres away to the left – beyond the River Sticks.

'That's where I plan to be tomorrow, Ms Savage,' he announced, in a dreamy voice. 'At the Goosing Golf Open. And, once I've arrested Svetlana on suspicion of murder and subsequently charged her, there'll be nothing to stop me playing my best eighteen holes of the year and retaining my crown.'

'Don't you have to check with your superintendent before you bring her into custody, inspector?'

Clinton's golf-course focus didn't falter. 'Technically, yes. But he'll only start bandying around phrases such as "reasonable grounds for suspicion", "unlawful arrest" and "false imprisonment". And that kind of bureaucracy is how murderers slip through the net.'

'And what about a warrant?'

'A what?'

'A search warrant. Don't you need one?'

'If Svetlana invites me in on the basis I'm Dickie's chum, I don't think I will.'

'No? I seem to remember from my studies that a warrant is rather important if you want to rummage round someone's drawers.'

Clinton was still gazing out the window. 'I'll do it discreetly, Ms Savage. She won't even notice. I have very nimble fingers and a photographic memory – particularly when it comes to socks and underwear – meaning everything will be replaced just as it was.'

'But wouldn't a search without a warrant potentially jeopardise the admissibility of anything you find in a court of law?'

'I'm not sure. I never bother with all that tedious legal nonsense. I simply charge murderers and let the great British justice system decide what to do with them.'

'You know best, inspector.'

'I was wondering if I should have that inscribed on my tombstone.'

'You've a good few years left in you, I hope.'

'Oh, decades. I'm forty-nine now. In a few years, I shall have to face up to the fact that I will be approaching middle age and the autumn of my career. But that's a long way off. Plenty of cases to solve before then. And, possibly, a Russian spy to arrest and charge with a murder she almost certainly didn't commit, so I can play golf at the weekend. We shall see.'

The taxi eventually started making progress again. Within fifteen minutes, they were at their destination – Margaret Thatcher Towers. A handsome Armani-suited security guard admitted them after Clinton flashed him his police ID. As the inspector wandered to the lifts, he noted that the ground floor smelt pleasantly of expensive perfume and freshly minted banknotes. And the lift was in perfect working order, spoke the Queen's English, delivered them to the nineteenth floor in ten seconds and was only too delighted to open its doors and thank them for using its service.

'That was a rapid ascent,' noted Josephine, as they stepped out onto a landing so highly polished it was as if they were walking on a mirror.

'No great surprise,' remarked Clinton, admiring his reflection in the floor. 'This is the finest apartment block in the whole of Brokenshire. The monthly rent alone would keep me in shampoo, conditioner and styling mousse for the rest of my career.' He patted his bouffant. 'Our Russian friend is a mature student, to my knowledge. Curious that she can afford it.'

'Either she's from a very rich family, inspector, or someone else is paying the rent – the Russian secret service, for example.'

'Ah. Yes. Erm, actually, I was just about to suggest that.'

'Of course you were, inspector. What number is the flat?'

'It's 1917. Dickie laughed when he gave it to me – said it was highly appropriate. Not sure why.'

'Maybe because it's the year of the Russian revolution?'

'Possibly. But Dickie has a very odd sense of humour. So maybe not.'

'What tactics will you use with Svetlana?'

'Haven't given it much thought, to be honest. I've not dealt with any Russian spies before.' He sifted through his mental case files. 'I once took a statement from a Ukrainian bodybuilder whose eyes were a bit too close together for my liking and reminded me of a villain from a Keanu Reeves movie. But that's the closest I've come.'

'Shall we put our heads together and agree the best approach?'

'No need. I'll just bluff my way in there and hope for the best. It often works. Especially if you're as good-looking, intelligent and well-spoken as I am.' He clapped his hands. 'Now, let's get to work.' He strode up to the door of flat 1917. But there didn't appear to be a bell, so he rapped on the door with his knuckles. 'Ms Kalashnikov!' he called. 'It's Inspector Trump. Please open up.'

'Erm, inspector,' whispered Josephine. 'You used her real surname.'

'Did I?'

'Yes, you did.'

'You're right. I don't know Svetlana's fake surname. I forgot to ask Dickie. Do you know what it is?'

'We're not even on first name terms, so no. Probably best to stick with her first name.'

'Good thinking.' He took a breath and addressed the door. 'Natasha, could you come out, please?'

'No, inspector. That's her real –'

The door swung open. It was Svetlana – dressed in black silk shirt, shiny black leather trousers and black combat boots, with a black belt to elegantly tie the whole foreign-assassin ensemble together. 'No Natasha live here. Only me – Svetlana.'

Clinton gulped for air. 'My apologies. I'm terrible with names. Can I come in?'

'What you want, inspector?' growled Svetlana, blocking the doorway with her arm.

His brain clicked into bluffing mode. 'Erm, I know Dickie stores a lot of his sporting gear in your spare bedroom and he said I could borrow his golf-club warmers for tomorrow's tournament – seeing as he's not playing.'

'You make mistake. I use Dickie's golf-club warmers on Saturday.'

He shook his head to try and urge bluffing mode to work properly. 'Oh. But I, erm, believe he promised his golf-club warmers to me first.'

'You his girlfriend?'

'Obviously not.'

'Then I use golf-club warmers.'

Clinton rebooted the bluffing part of his brain. 'His golf balls. They're the best money can buy. He said I could come inside and take my pick.'

'I using Dickie's balls.'

'What, all of them?'

'Yes. Dickie's balls mine now.'

'Oh. Um. Ah. What about his Nick Faldo biography? He offered to lend me that.'

'I reading it. I big Faldo fan.'

'Really? So you're watching his exploits down the Amazon on the Golfing Channel?'

Svetlana shook her head.

'I understand. Sporting documentaries aren't your bag. Mine neither. But I really must gain access to your apartment.'

'Why?'

'Because, erm, Dickie's been telling me how wonderful it is. He mentioned a walk-in shower with non-slip floor tiles the last time I saw him and I've thought of nothing else for the past forty-eight hours.'

Svetlana didn't seem convinced about Clinton's shower obsession. 'Why you bring woman with Master's in Advanced Criminology with you?'

'I'm very interested in modern architecture,' squeaked Josephine, not realising how nervous she was until she spoke.

'Are you alright, Ms Savage?' asked Clinton.

'Fine,' she squeaked again. 'Perfectly fine,' she added, three octaves deeper.

'I have a pear drop in my jacket pocket if you'd like something to suck on.' He beamed at the Russian. 'Or maybe an offering of a boiled sweet is the secret to opening this Aladdin's cave of golfing accessories?'

Svetlana's right hand darted into her jacket pocket, pulled out a handgun and pointed it at them. 'Enough golf bluff.'

'Is that a genuine handgun?' asked Josephine. 'Or some hi-tech golfing equipment to enable the correct distance to the flag to be determined when shooting from the fairway?'

'It real gun. Just like Natasha Kalashnikov my real name.'

'Your name's Natasha Kalashnikov?' gasped Clinton with fake surprise. 'What an incredible coincidence that I should accidentally call you Natasha Kalashnikov just now, when I hadn't the foggiest inkling that was your actual name. Must have been some form of extra-sensory perception.' He fake-chuckled. 'I must remember to play the National Lottery this week.'

'You talk too much, Inspector Trump.'

Clinton spun round to address Ms Savage. 'Do I talk too much? Because, in my highly regarded opinion, I'm firmly on the middle ground between loquacious and taciturn.'

'Shut up or I shut you up!' shouted Svetlana, waving the gun in his direction.

The inspector did his best to ignore the gun pointing at him, banished all thoughts of a Clinton Trump memorial trophy being announced at Goosing golf club on Monday, and determined to charm his way out of this rough spot. 'Come on. Let's not fall out over knitted golf-club warmers. And I know you Russians are fond of your firearms.' He nodded at her handgun. 'You were probably just cleaning yours, forgot you were holding it, answered the door and whipped it out in front of us when you simply meant to offer a hand in greeting. A simple mistake to make and not one we shall hold against you.'

'I know why you here, English man.'

'To borrow Dickie's golfing bits and bobs. Now, please, put down that weapon and we'll go inside. You can make a pot of Earl Grey – tea first, milk second, don't forget – and I'll have a root around and see what golfing goodies I can unearth.'

Svetlana jabbed the gun nearer Clinton's stomach. 'Gun stay with me. But we not stay here. We go to my car.'

Josephine attempted to defuse the situation. 'This has all escalated rather quickly, Natasha. Or would you prefer I call you Svetlana? They're both very charming names. And Kalashnikov – that's erm, very redolent of the, um, Russian, erm, I mean, it reminds me of the time I went to Moscow – beautiful place – and, erm, the name is ...'

'It's a gun, Ms Savage,' interrupted Clinton. 'One of the most deadly on the planet. I would expect you to know that.'

Svetlana grimaced. 'I not interested in English chit-chat. I know you here to interrogate me about Jepson murder. Interrogate, arrest, charge. It only explanation for you coming here.'

Clinton forced a hearty laugh. 'I think there's been a terrible misunderstanding. One that I hope we can all laugh about tomorrow in the clubhouse when I've soundly thrashed you at golf, Svetlana. You see, I really have no investigative interest in Russians with aliases who own firearms which they enjoy polishing at home and accidentally pointing at cold-callers.'

'Your clever talk not fool Svetlana. You genius, Mr Trump. Greatest detective in South East England.'

Clinton blushed. 'It's very generous of you to say so, Svetlana.'

'It only matter of time before you discover truth.'

'The truth? Erm, yes. I've discovered the, um, truth.' He scratched his chin. 'Remind me what that is again.'

'I drown butler in mango chutney at Peculiar Manor!' declared Svetlana, with a dramatic swish of her red hair.

Clinton went into flabbergasted mode. 'You really did it?'

The muscles in Svetlana's neck tensed. 'I really did it.'

'Because, if I'm honest, I didn't really think you had anything to do with Jepson's murder. It was more a case of needing to arrest and charge someone to free up my weekend.' He raised a finger. 'Ah. Are you doing this to avoid the embarrassment of losing to me tomorrow? If so, you don't have to go to all the trouble of falsely confessing. You can simply withdraw from the tournament with your reputation moderately bruised and your golfing honour slightly battered.'

Svetlana's voice was now deeper than Clinton's. 'I repeat – I really did it.'

'If you're sure.' He took a brilliant breath, struck his another-case-solved-by-South-East-England's-greatest-detective   pose, and tossed his head magnificently. 'Then we have our killer!'

Josephine smiled weakly. 'I suppose we do.'

Clinton wobbled his bouffant in triumph. 'Now, Svetlana or Natasha or whatever you want us to call you today, because you've confessed, it's a whole new ball game.'

'I not see anyone with balls,' snarled Svetlana.

He straightened his tie. 'Allow me to explain, it's an old Upper Goosing tradition for murderers to come quietly and without fuss once South East England's greatest detective has identified them. I really don't care whether you're a Russian spy or not. As far as I know, it's not directly relevant to the Jepson case, so no further discussion is needed between us on that point. Therefore, I'd appreciate it very much if, as a guest in our wonderful village, you'd fully immerse yourself in our particular brand of rural-law-enforcement culture by agreeing to accompany me to the police station without a struggle, any unnecessary language or derogatory remarks about how we do things around here.'

Svetlana studied his face. 'You serious?'

'Deadly serious. Now, did you say you had a car?'

'Yes. I have car. And I have trip planned for us.'

'Ah, excellent! You're ahead of me. I can give you directions to the police station.'

Josephine clasped his arm. 'I don't think she's taking us there, inspector.'

Clinton's bright eyes dimmed. 'We're not going to the police station?'

Svetlana put both hands on the gun. 'No. Get moving to lifts. And no talk to anyone.'

Clinton huffed in annoyance. 'I'm British, born and bred. I never talk to people in lifts. So you have nothing to worry about on that score.'

'Come on,' snarled Svetlana. 'We go to golf course.'

'Golf first, police station second – sounds good to me!' whooped Clinton.

'But not to me,' added Josephine, clutching his arm tighter.

Clinton's joy was short-lived. 'Ah. But it's closed this afternoon – so they can freshen up the greens for tomorrow's tournament. They don't water them until the evening, so I have no idea why they shut the course early, but there you are. It'll be deserted. The greenkeeper and his assistant will be in the Goosing Arms all afternoon. There won't be a soul around apart from the three of us.' He had a thought. 'But, if we are going, there's a handy little space close to the thirteenth green where you can park your car behind an oak tree at the end of a service road. Nobody will see it from the dual carriageway. Then you can gain access to the course via the gate in the fence that's bolted shut but never padlocked.'

'Aren't we being a little too helpful?' whispered Josephine.

'You can never be too helpful to a fellow golfer, Ms Savage.'

Svetlana grinned. 'Thank you. Thirteen hole exactly where I plan to take you.'

'Unlucky for some,' muttered Josephine, as the gun-toting Russian ushered them to the lifts.

Chapter 32

Superintendent Block was stomping to his office. After futile trips to the executive coffee machine, non-executive coffee machine and communal kitchens, he was preparing to enter the kind of foul mood he normally reserved for the second Monday in January.

'Nothing works in this flaming police station,' he muttered to himself as he kicked open the door. 'And that includes a certain detective inspector I haven't seen for the best part of two days.' He flopped furiously into his chair, picked up a pencil from his desk and snapped it in two. 'When that no-good excuse for a law enforcer comes waltzing back here, he is not going to know what hit him.'

Constable Dinkel poked his head around the door. 'Everything alright, sir? I heard a crash.'

'That crash was perfectly in order, constable. Both coffee machines are on the blink. And none of you junior officers had the foresight to buy any instant coffee in case one of your senior officers was in desperate need of a caffeine fix but wasn't able to get his hands on any proper stuff. I know because I checked all the kitchen cupboards – three times.'

'I could pop home in a police car, fix you an espresso and whizz it back here, sir – siren blaring and blue lights flashing all the way.'

'No. Don't worry, constable. I've got bigger problems. Trump being the main one. Have you seen him since yesterday morning?

'No, sir.'

'Hmm. I'm beginning to wonder what he's up to.'

'Like I said yesterday, superintendent, he's been investigating.'

Block picked up the two pieces of snapped pencil and fitted them together. 'You said something else to me yesterday. I dismissed it as ridiculous. But now I'm wondering if you might have been barking up the right tree.'

'What was that, sir?'

'That Trump could be on the golf course. I'm making him work the weekend if he hasn't unmasked the Peculiar Manor murderer by the end of today. You know how golfers can be – it's an addiction for most of them.' He separated the pencil pieces. 'My brother-in-law – a golfer – broke his index finger last month. Nurses had to sedate him for three days after telling him swinging a club was off the agenda for a month. He nearly headbutted the matron.'

'There's no doubt about it, sir. Golf is the crystal meth of the sporting world.'

'Absolutely. And my sixth sense is telling me this particular addict might have resigned himself to weekend working and be satisfying his urges as we speak. And when you're dealing with an addict, it's best to outnumber them. You and I are taking a trip to Goosing golf course, constable.'

'Right you are, sir.'

'But, before we head out, tell me how your latest meeting with Lady Peculiar went.'

'My main observation was that she wasn't drinking Earl Grey. She was drinking top-quality Russian vodka – possibly the Kremlin's brand of choice.'

'So what?'

'It's just I met an American tourist who used to work for the CIA. And he told me there might be a Russian spy operating in Upper Goosing.'

'Right now, I don't care if half the Kremlin is over here – unless it's them who've been sabotaging our ruddy coffee machines.'

'Automated-caffeine sabotage? Doesn't sound like the kind of international espionage the Russians usually indulge in, sir.'

'I was being facetious,' groaned Block. 'Is that all you got from this meeting – that her ladyship owns a bottle of Russian vodka?'

'Yes, sir. But I just got this feeling it was significant. Maybe I'm developing my own sixth sense, superintendent.'

'If it was your sixth sense, it's badly misfiring, Dinkel. Because I ate beluga caviar last week. And that doesn't mean I'm a double-agent for the Russians, Iranians or anyone else.'

'Don't suppose it does, sir.'

Block stood up. 'Now come on, Dinkel. I want your first five senses firing on all cylinders because you're driving us to the golf course. And we'll be stopping at a coffee shop on the way.'

Chapter 33

The dual carriageway that led to Goosing golf course was clear in both directions. Only Svetlana's anonymous battered brown car – which was cruising along at thirty miles per hour – graced the tarmac.

'A hundred metres further on, past the layby, and you should see a lane running off to the left,' called Clinton from the back seat footwell. His hands were bound behind his back and his ankles tied together with garden twine, but he was managing to crane his neck and see out the far window. 'It's actually a service road but it's not really worthy of the name. More a dirt track these days, so drive carefully. Travel up it for fifty metres or so, and you can't miss the oak tree.'

Without acknowledging him, Svetlana made the left turn onto the narrow side road.

'Inspector,' whispered Josephine, who was sporting matching hand and leg restraints, 'why are you being so helpful? Is it all part of some cunning master plan?'

'What? Oh. No, I'm just assuming she's got her golf clubs stashed in the boot and wants to play a few holes before I take her into custody. She can start at the thirteenth and finish on the eighteenth. Probably wants me to carry her clubs and you to keep score.'

'So why are we tied up and sitting in the rear footwell?'

'For our own safety, I presume. There are no seatbelts in this rickety old thing. Far safer to jam us in here nice and tight. Svetlana will untie us once we've arrived safely, and we'll crack on with the golf.'

'And why has she brought the gun with her?'

'Those blasted squirrels must have returned. Little blighters have run off with my ball on more than one occasion. As it'll be her last swing of a club for a while, better not let a bushy-tailed, ball-robbing rodent spoil the occasion.'

Josephine tried unsuccessfully to wriggle her hands free. 'I hate to disagree with you, inspector, but I doubt Svetlana wants to play golf.'

'I beg to differ. She's driving us to a golf course. What else could she have in mind?'

'Another two murders, perhaps?'

'But there's nobody on the course. I told you – it's closed this afternoon.'

'I mean us. With you and me out of the picture, she'll be able to get away with murder. And we'll probably end up stuffed and on display at that ghoulish local museum.'

Clinton's eyes glazed over. 'South East England's greatest detective – immortalised for future generations in the Getting Away With Murder museum. Not the worst legacy to leave behind.' He was lost in self-admiration for a moment. 'But it's the stuff of fantasy. I'm supremely confident our Russian friend will do the right thing and, at the end of the day, recognise how important it is to comply with English law-enforcement etiquette, hand over the gun once she's holed out on the eighteenth, and come quietly.'

The car had reached the oak tree and Svetlana was manoeuvring it into a spot where it wasn't visible from the dual carriageway.

Once the car was parked, Svetlana turned round to address her captives. 'No more talking. I open doors, bring you out, untie legs, you come to golf course with me.'

'You see,' whispered Clinton to Josephine. 'She's going to untie us.'

'Only our legs.'

'The most important limbs when it comes to walking. We can worry about our hands when we're on the thirteenth tee.'

Svetlana checked her gun was in her jacket pocket, got out, jerked open the right rear door, yanked Clinton out by the scruff of his jacket and hauled him to the back of the car.

'Steady on!' cried Clinton. 'I almost banged my bouffant there!'

Svetlana ignored him, walked round to the left rear door and dragged Josephine to the back of the car with even less ceremony. The Russian pushed her female captive to the ground, sat on top of her, untied her legs and ordered her to stay where she was for the moment. Then she walked over to Clinton.

'I do hope you're not planning to sit on top of me, Ms Kalashnikov. There is already a considerable amount of dirt on this top-quality Marks & Spencer suit. Any further soiling and I shall be forced to ask you for a contribution to the dry-cleaning costs.'

'You not have to worry about dry cleaning,' snarled Svetlana, whipping off his leg ties with alarming dexterity.

Clinton smiled with relief. 'You're covering the full cost. That's very kind.'

'Enough chit-chat. Get up – both of you. Start walking to fence. I open gate and you go through. Then walk to big bunker near green.'

'You mean Big Bertha?' asked Clinton. 'The mother of all sand traps? The sandpit of doom? The largest stretch of sand between here and Dover?'

'I said no more chit-chat. Just do it.'

'If you insist.' And he started moving.

Josephine stumbled forward. 'This isn't looking promising, inspector.'

'No. We'll probably get sand in our shoes. But she probably just wants a bit of bunker practice before she tees off. And I don't blame her. Big Bertha has swallowed more balls than a National Lottery machine.'

They all trudged to the fence. Svetlana unbolted the gate and they advanced through it – Clinton leading, Josephine following and Svetlana bringing up the rear, her gun at the ready.

The thirteenth green came into view. To its left, as they looked at it, were the treacherous slopes of Big Bertha – and a huge bag of sand sat nearby.

When he was a few metres away, Clinton swivelled round to address Svetlana. 'Shall we get these hand ties off now, young lady? Because I don't intend dragging your golf bag around by my teeth.' He noticed the Russian's hands were empty apart from the gun. 'You forgot to bring your golf clubs.'

'I not need them,' growled Svetlana. 'I have gun.'

Clinton twitched with confusion. 'That's not going to be any good to you if your ball's wedged in the bowels of Big Bertha. Firing a bullet at it will just bury it even further.'

'I not here to bury golf ball.'

'No? Then kindly explain what's going on. Because I have a deadline for bringing Jepson's killer to justice and this little sojourn is delaying my moment of glory.'

Josephine gulped for air. 'She's not burying a golf ball.' She glanced at the giant bag of sand. 'Svetlana's burying an inspector and a woman with a Master's Degree in Advanced Criminology.'

The Russian cracked a smile. 'You clever lady. Kind of lady who could get away with murder – one time, two time … maybe three time.'

'What's she talking about, Ms Savage?'

'I've no idea,' croaked Josephine.

After retying their ankles with garden twine, Svetlana marched over to the bag of sand and started slowly dragging it towards Big Bertha.

Chapter 34

Superintendent Block was savouring the aroma of his super-mega-jumbo espresso at a small table in the Death By Chocolate café – a couple of miles from Goosing golf course – while Constable Dinkel nursed a regular latte.

'Brilliant idea of mine, Dinkel – coming here.'

'Undoubtedly one of your best caffeine-related decisions of the decade, sir.'

'How's your latte?'

'Better than the ones our non-executive coffee machine dishes out.'

'Mind if I try?'

'Go ahead, sir.'

Block sipped a healthy mouthful. 'Not quite up to the standards of the station's executive coffee machine, but it's not far off.' He sipped from his own cup. 'But this stuff is the best I've ever tasted. And, after the week I've had, I'm sorely tempted to treat myself to another.'

'What about our visit to the golf course, sir? Shouldn't we get moving?'

'Ah, yes. I was reflecting upon that on the journey here. It's going to be one hell of a trek to walk all the way round it to see if Trump is bunking off work.' He smirked. 'Or bunkering off, you might say.'

'Bunkering off! Very good, sir. There's not many amusing things you can say about golf. But you've managed to dig one out from the rough.'

'I certainly have, constable. Now, to get back to our golfing trip, I was wondering whether you should just pop along on your lonesome.'

'Go on my own?' asked Dinkel, his voice shooting up two octaves.

'Yes. I can stay in this café. It's got everything I need – coffee, doughnuts, a loyalty card enabling me to qualify for a free espresso if I buy ten of them by the end of the month, and decent Wi-Fi. I can mastermind operations from here.'

'Won't it take me twice as long, though, sir? Because if it was both of us, I could check holes one to nine and you could check holes ten to eighteen.'

'I take your point, Dinkel. However, if you double your normal walking speed there won't be a problem. And if, or most probably when, you find Trump on that golf course, tell him to quit his round and come straight here.'

'But the inspector is my senior officer, sir. He won't take any orders from me.'

'Then tell him I've sent you.'

'That doesn't work. He always says he won't take orders from a stable boy. He has to hear it straight from the horse's mouth. Then he gallops off.'

Block harrumphed. 'Refers to me as a horse, does he?'

'Amongst other things, yes, sir.'

The superintendent's lip curled. 'Maybe I'd better come along with you, after all.' His stomach rumbled noisily. 'But only after I've had a doughnut.'

Chapter 35

Svetlana had finally dragged the bulky bag to the bunker's edge and was now using the rake that had been lying nearby to scrape away at the sand in the middle of Big Bertha. Clinton was standing with Josephine on the edge of the sand trap, watching proceedings. Their wrists and ankles were still tied.

'What's she doing, Ms Savage?'

'Digging our golfing grave.'

He blinked rapidly. 'I thought you were making a poor-taste joke when you said Svetlana wanted to bury us.'

'It was the poor-taste truth, inspector. That Russian plans to bury us alive or dead – I'm not sure which, but we'll soon find out – and then make her escape.'

'You mean … she's not coming quietly?'

'No. I think it's more a case of us *going* quietly.'

'She's going to bury us in Big Bertha?'

'It would seem that way.'

'But I'll miss tomorrow's tournament!'

'Yes. And I'll miss the rest of my life.'

Clinton's face contorted. 'This is awful. How did we ever get into this predicament?'

Josephine collected her thoughts. 'Well, you took the decision to surprise a Russian spy in her apartment without informing anyone of what we were doing or where we were going. Then you gave our Russian assassin here direction on how she could best bring us to a place where she could dispose of us without any witnesses.'

Clinton's nose twitched. 'I hope we're not playing the blame game here, Ms Savage. Because I must warn you, I am one of the highest-ranked British players when it comes to the blame game. And I am taking no responsibility whatsoever for this

Russian woman's skulduggery. We are simply innocent victims who could never have foreseen our fate. And that's my final word on the matter.'

The advanced criminologist stared into his eyes without accusation. 'If you say so, inspector.'

Svetlana triple-checked there were no potential witnesses in sight – not even a squirrel – and strolled over to them with the gun clutched firmly in her right hand. 'So, my friends, this nearly end of road for you.' She jerked the corner of her mouth in a way that James Bond villains might do instead of laughing. 'Or maybe better to say, as we on golf course – it end of round for you.'

'You mean you're planning to bury us in Big Bertha?' asked Clinton.

'I not bury you just yet. First, I reveal to you, inspector, how this Russian spy outsmart genius detective. Then I kill you.'

'What's the point if we'll be dead in five minutes? When I reach the pearly gates, I certainly shan't be boring Saint Peter with your murderous monologue.'

Josephine discreetly bumped her hands into his – in an effort to indicate she was in the process of freeing her hands and needed all the extra seconds they could wrangle out of this situation to complete the job and try to mount a surprise attack.

'Why are you bumping my hands, Ms Savage?'

'I w-w-wasn't,' stuttered Josephine.

'Yes, you were. Are you losing circulation? Or are you having another giddy spell?' An idea came to him. 'Ah, maybe you're trying to break free from your bonds? Because I wouldn't bother. I've already tried several times without success. Don't waste your energy. Save it for your death throes.'

Her hands were almost free. 'No, I'm fine. All tightly bound and awaiting my fate with a combination of dread ...' She twisted her right hand. '... and despair.' She twisted her left hand. 'But also an overwhelming sense of having achieved what I want to achieve in this life ...' The last loop of twine round her wrists was almost off. '… and an expectation that I shall achieve even more in the next.'

'Show me wrists,' grunted Svetlana, keeping the gun pointing at her female captive as she walked round behind her. It only took a second for the Russian to see the loosened hand ties. 'Oh, Miss Master's-in-Advanced-Criminology even smarter than I thought. Her hands almost free. But not quite.' And she stashed the gun in her jacket pocket, whipped out the garden twine and began tying their wrists even more securely.

Chapter 36

Superintendent Block and Constable Dinkel were still in the Death By Chocolate café and showing no signs of shifting.

Block jabbed a fork at his doughnut. 'I could stay here till midnight, constable. I really could.' He shovelled a chunk into his mouth. 'Who knows? Maybe I will.'

Dinkel frowned. 'But I thought you changed your mind about staying here, sir?'

'It's the doughnut, constable. Once it's safely nestled inside your stomach, and all those vitamins and minerals are surging through your system, it gives you a whole new perspective on the world. It sharpens your senses. Gives a man a clearer appreciation of his environment.' He looked over his shoulder at the serving area. 'As an example, I've just noticed a four-cream-cakes-for-the-price-of-three offer that I didn't spot on my first trip to the serving counter. If I'd just plumped for the garrotte cake, I probably would've missed that completely.'

Dinkel glanced at the clock on the wall – they'd been here twenty-five minutes now. 'Extremely perceptive of you, sir.'

'Yes. And my heightened senses are suggesting I'd be better off seeing Friday afternoon out right here, using my doughnut-fuelled temporary superpowers to think of innovative ways to increase the productivity of my staff.' He sipped his second espresso. 'Many of whom seem to grab any opportunity to slope off to places like this and waste valuable police time stuffing their faces with cake and slurping coffee.'

Dinkel couldn't think of anything to say that wouldn't sound sarcastic. So he kept his mouth shut.

The superintendent carved another slice off his doughnut. 'They call this one "crime-scene surprise". The shape's supposed to be a dead body lying prostrate, the strawberry jam covering it is meant to give an authentic blood-spatter effect and the head's been bashed in to show the brain-coloured fondant inside. They've even punctured the torso multiple times with this dark-chocolate dagger. Very creative.'

'I suppose so – if death-themed cakes are your thing.'

'Very much so. I was tempted to go for the Swiss death roll or the morgue-marble slab cake, but I'm glad I stuck with my crime-scene surprise. Want to try a piece?'

'No, thanks, sir. I don't eat doughnuts.'

The superintendent froze mid-chew. 'You *don't* eat doughnuts?'

'I don't. They're not healthy, the sugar gets all over the investigation files and everyone who eats them in the office – apart from your good self, sir – is chronically obese.'

Block slammed a fist on the table. 'How the hell did you pass detective training school with that kind of killjoy attitude?'

'I'm not being a killjoy. I'm just stating facts, sir.'

'There's a time and a place for facts, constable. And right here, right now, I don't need facts getting in the way of my doughnut consumption.'

'My apologies, sir. Minor judgement failure. I'm just a bit concerned about the time. We've been here nearly half an hour now.'

Block's cheeks were crimson now. 'Word of advice, constable – never time-pressure a senior officer with a half-eaten doughnut.'

'Sorry, sir.'

The superintendent pushed away his plate. 'You've made me lose my appetite.' He curled the edge of his lip. 'I'll be making a mental note of this for your yearly appraisal.' He checked his hands. They were covered in sugar crumbs. 'I need to visit the little boys' room.'

Dinkel stood up. 'See you in the car park, sir?'

Block snorted so hard, the napkin tucked into his shirt collar flapped. 'Yes. I'll see you in the car park, Constable Killjoy.'

Chapter 37

Back at Goosing golf course, Clinton and Josephine's wrists were being bound with enough twine to last most gardeners a whole English summer.

'That's really biting into my wrists,' protested Clinton.

The Russian finished her binding and took a step back into the bunker. 'Shut up and listen to South East England's greatest Russian spy.' She puffed out her chest. 'Before I reveal detail of my master plan, tell me, inspector – why you think I kill butler?'

'I was recently told that Russians don't confess everything at the end before they kill you. They just kill you. I was badly misinformed.'

'This Russian different. I big fan of James Bond film. Villain always explain plan at end.'

'Yes. But they never kill James Bond.' He glanced at Josephine. 'Quite often they shoot his lady friends.' He turned back. 'But never 007.'

'Never say never, inspector. Now answer my question – why I kill Jepson?'

Clinton shrugged. 'Did he spill mango chutney down your cleavage? Serve you a soggy poppadom? Or tell you an extremely unfunny joke about an Englishman, an Irishman and a Russian?'

'No. I kill him because I need murder for you to investigate.'

Clinton digested this revelation. 'For *me* to investigate?'

'Yes, you. Detective Inspector Clinton Bush Trump.'

The inspector flinched. 'How the devil did you discover my middle name is Bush? It's a closely guarded secret only known to blood relatives, HR departments and the golf club treasurer who wangled it out of me after four white-wine spritzers.'

Svetlana's tone was triumphant. 'I know lot about you, Mr Trump. I know you have two cats – Columbo and Clouseau. I know they eat chicken, beef, lamb and rabbit cat food. And, of course, I know they recently lose testicles.'

Clinton gasped. 'You mean … there's a Russian secret-service file on my tomcats?'

'No. I use Google. You join cat forum on internet. And Clinton Bush Trump your username.'

'Is it? I didn't realise I'd filled in the middle-name field when I registered. It must have been one of those blasted forms that pre-populate themselves with information you've previously provided to other websites. Probably picked it up from the online police-expenses form.' He would have put his head in his hands at this point – had they not been tied together. 'How could I have been so foolish?'

Svetlana allowed herself a sly smile. 'A fatal mistake, Mr Trump. Because we Russian secret agents have saying: "When you know man's middle name, you can see into his soul."'

'Then you'll know I have one of the sturdiest souls in South East England and I won't be intimidated by Russians who know what flavour cat food I buy in Waitrose. Or Lidl, if Waitrose is closed. Occasionally, I pop to Tesco's but that's a bit of a trek. And there's no Sainsbury's round here, which is a shame because they're usually a few pence cheaper than—'

Josephine interjected. 'Erm, aren't we drifting slightly off-topic here?'

'Yes,' snorted Svetlana. 'I go back a bit.'

'Oh, no,' groaned Clinton. 'We'll be here all night!'

Svetlana mentally ran through her monologue so far. 'Ah, yes. I tell you I murder Jepson so you investigate.'

'I remember,' sighed Clinton. 'But why go to all the trouble of committing a murder in Upper Goosing when we have plenty already? And I investigate them all.'

'You not understand. I need to be murderer so I in control.'

'Alright. But why Jepson?'

'He easy target. We go for drink two or three time. He think Svetlana like him. He complain about working in kitchen on curry night. I already invited, so I see chance. I sit nearest door at dinner party – behind fat woman who run diet club – and visit kitchen during meal. Nobody see me leave during ladyship talk about poppadom. Jepson pleased to see me. He sweet. He say he have strong feeling for me. He come close. I drown him in mango chutney. I go back to dining room. Nobody see me return.'

'Fascinating,' huffed Clinton. 'But it's always a lot snappier in the James Bond films.'

'Be quiet or I start from beginning again.' She collected her evil thoughts. 'I know you investigate all murders in Upper Goosing. And I leave lot of false clues, so you fooled.'

Clinton tutted. 'Red herrings, Svetlana. We don't say "false clues" in England. We say "red herrings". As a master criminal, I would expect you to know that.'

'You interrupt. I start from beginning.'

He shook his head. 'No, no, no. I can't face hearing it all again – even though it would give me a few more precious minutes of life. Just pick it up from the red herrings.'

'Okay. There red herrings everywhere. Pages ripped from joke book I know Jepson create for big comedy competition. There story written by Agatha Twisty with dinner-party murder of butler in country manor. And I leave bad reviews for author under false name.'

'So you're Goosing Jeeves?'

'Yes. I big fan of Wodehouse. That why I chosen for this mission.'

'Mission?' asked Josephine. 'What mission?'

Svetlana raised a finger. 'One second.' And she removed a piece of paper from her jacket and started reading in an even more stilted way than usual. 'My mission is to strike at the heart of rural English society by infiltrating treasured institutions, controlling key infrastructure and creating internal disharmony with the ultimate goal of destabilising the country.' She put away the paper. 'That make sense? I use Google translate for some of it.'

Clinton and Josephine stared at each other in astonished silence.

Svetlana continued. 'In Lower Goosing, we already control biggest village car park in Western Europe. And we have plan for fast-food chain. We will call it Beetroot King.'

Josephine struggled with her new hand ties but it was useless. 'So the new Russian-oligarch-funded easy-access car park in Lower Goosing was only the beginning?'

'Yes. It coded statement to world of our intentions. Why you think our president open it, huh?'

Clinton would have rubbed his chin at this point, had his hands been free. 'So, what treasured institution was your target in Upper Goosing?'

'First, I try to damage confidence in Tourist Trap café. I complain many times about thickness of meat-pie crust, and cream in cream horn, in front of American tourist. Then I inject chocolate éclair with salmonella. But that not work – because English lady who own café eat whole box. So I choose new target.'

'Peculiar Manor!' gasped Josephine. 'With her ladyship a fifth cousin four times removed of Her Majesty Queen Elizabeth II, it's the obvious choice.'

Svetlana frowned. 'No. It not come up when I google "treasured institution in Upper Goosing". Instead, number one search result was Goosing golf club.' Svetlana pointed at the flag on the green. 'I kill butler, so I win Goosing Golf Open and Russian flag fly from clubhouse for next twelve month!'

The inspector's bouffant wilted a little. 'Sorry, you've completely lost me. How would killing Jepson lead to you winning tomorrow's tournament?'

'I explain. I plan for Jepson killing to be perfect murder just before golf tournament – so you must work weekend, inspector, and miss it. There more. I make friend with your superintendent in post-office queue, suggest you work on day of competition –

218

just to make sure. I also tell boyfriend Dickie he not fit to play. And I visit Getting Away With Murder museum and see man face down in bowl. So, I set up murder scene like this. Another, erm, red heron.'

'It's red herring!' squealed Clinton. 'There may be red herons in Moscow but not in rural England!'

Svetlana smiled with evil satisfaction. 'Heron, herring, who care, huh?' Her smile vanished. 'But even with red herrings and herons, genius detective discover my real identity and my plan change now.'

'Sorry, but why not just kill Clinton, fool your boyfriend into not playing – like you did – and win the tournament that way?' asked Josephine, as the inspector gave her a funny look. 'It would make a lot more sense. It's certainly how I would have done it.' She checked herself. 'If I were a cold-hearted killer.' She beamed at Clinton. 'Which, of course, I'm not.'

The Russian nodded at the inspector. 'Kill policeman, it national news. Kill butler, nobody care.'

Clinton raised an eyebrow in acknowledgement. 'That's a very good point.'

'But your plan has changed now?' asked Josephine. 'And you *are* going to kill a policeman?'

'Yes. I kill policeman to protect my true identity. And I kill you, lady. You not listen to my warning to stay away from investigation. Your deaths necessary now. And I leave country on Sunday morning for Moscow. And I not come back.'

'What about Dickie?' asked Clinton. 'Have you employed your Eastern European charms to persuade him to become a Russian spy?'

'No. Dickie hate beetroot. But I use him to find out information about you, inspector – how you love golf more than job. I let Dickie live. He quite boring man. But maybe he useful in future, if Russia need information on other quite boring man in village. There lots of them.'

'I hope you're not suggesting *I'm* quite boring,' hissed Clinton. 'Because, believe me, my biography will make Nick Faldo's look *very* tame indeed.'

'Enough of your English games. That end of my formal criminal confession.'

Clinton shook his head. 'Well, all I can say is, you haven't watched many Bond films. Because that is one of the most convoluted, overcomplicated, ridiculous criminal monologues I've ever had the misfortune of listening to.' He waggled his cheeks. 'If it were a movie, you'd have cinema audiences leaving in droves and demanding their money back. If it were a novel, even Agatha Twisty would blush at such a longwinded denouement.'

'Maybe if it was a spoof detective story it might work?' suggested Josephine.

'I'm not so sure,' muttered Clinton. 'Take my advice, Svetlana – when it comes to murder, keep it simple. It's a lot less work for everyone – victims, murderers, detectives, authors, editors and readers.'

'Thank you for advice,' grunted Svetlana.

'Hang on,' interrupted Josephine. 'If you're going to bury us in this bunker, the greenkeeper will find our bodies tomorrow morning and the tournament will be cancelled.'

'Not if I dig deep enough.' Svetlana looked behind them. 'I hide big spade in those bushes. And I champion Siberian snow-shoveller for last three year.'

Chapter 38

Block and Dinkel's police car was currently stuck at the front of a traffic jam caused by a lorry fifty metres ahead that had spilt its entire load of fresh lemons onto the dual carriageway – blocking it completely.

'Would you believe it?' groaned the superintendent, flicking a switch on the dashboard to turn off the car's blue lights and siren. 'If we'd set off thirty seconds earlier, we would've passed that flaming lorry and be heading for the golf club.'

Dinkel tapped the steering wheel and eyed the doughnut crumbs on his superior officer's trousers. 'Yes, sir. Absolutely nothing we could have done about it.'

'If it was a doughnut lorry, we could have offered to help clear the carriageway. But I'm not sucking my way through ten thousand lemons.'

'No, sir. And I can't see anyone else coming to our lemon aid.'

'Was that a lemon joke, constable?' asked Block, ironically looking like a man who was sucking ten thousand lemons.

'My attempt at one, sir. Hope you're not bitter.'

'Why would I be bitter?'

'My second attempt at a lemon joke, sir – to pass the time. We played this game when I was a kid and we were stuck in traffic. Picked a topic and kept telling funnies about it.'

'Sounds like comedy hell.'

'That's what my dad called it. Do you want to hear another lemon joke? It's my funniest.'

'If you must,' sighed the superintendent. 'But if you're thinking of entering that Big Titter competition, I wouldn't waste your money.'

'Twenty lemons walk into a restaurant.'

'Walk? Got legs now, have they?'

'For the purposes of the joke, yes, sir. They ask for a table.'

'They're walking, talking lemons?'

'That's right. The waiter checks availability and tells them all that's available is a booth for four. So, the chief lemon says—'

'Chief lemon? What's a chief lemon?'

'The senior lemon in charge, sir.'

Block now looked as if he was sucking fifty thousand lemons. 'You're not suggesting all senior officers are lemons, are you, constable?'

'No, sir. The status of the lemon isn't actually important for the purposes of the joke. It could be any member of the lemon group. But it sounds a little more comical if you say "chief lemon" because, of course, lemons have no hierarchical societal structure. At least, not that I'm aware of. Although I'm sure if they could walk and talk, a system of social norms would develop similar to those seen amongst *Homo sapiens* and other higher species in the natural—'

'Yes, alright. We're doing this to pass some time. Not the whole of eternity. Proceed to the punchline, constable.'

'Okay.' He gulped for air. 'The chief lemon says "Twenty lemons in a booth for four? We'll take it. But it'll be one hell of a lemon squash."'

Block paused for five seconds. 'Then what happened?'

'Erm, that's it, sir. Lemon squash – like the drink.'

The superintendent uttered a noise Dinkel had only ever heard his neighbour's dog make during a full moon. 'Telling jokes that bad should carry a minimum five-year jail sentence.'

'I've got a couple more lemon funnies, if you're—'

'Can we save the rest of your dreadful lemon jokes for an occasion when we're not trapped behind several tonnes of citrus fruit?'

'As you wish, sir.' Dinkel wiped the inside of the windscreen with a cloth and peered out. 'Even the hard shoulder is blocked.'

'Great. We're going to be stuck here like a pair of lemons.'

'Very good, sir. Although I thought they were off the agenda.'

'You thought what were off the agenda?'

'Lemon jokes.'

'That particular lemon joke wasn't intentional, constable.' The superintendent banged his fist on the passenger window. 'This is all thanks to Trump. He *is* a lemon.'

The car's satnav system bleeped and a message came up on the screen in the middle of the dashboard:

Road ahead blocked

'That's very helpful, you stupid computer,' growled Block. Another message appeared:

Possible access to golf course via service road 250 metres on left

'That's no flaming use to us!' shouted the superintendent.

Dinkel had an idea. 'It might be, sir. If we walk.'

'Walk?'

'Yes, sir – walk. Like the lemons in my joke. We don't have to talk, though, if you don't want to.'

'Stop jabbering about lemons. You're making my head hurt.'

'We can lock up the car and wander over.' Dinkel stared out of the windscreen again. 'Looks as if we can get past the fruity obstruction if we walk along the grass verge.'

Block wiped some sugar from his mouth. 'I'm not sure it's worth all the hassle. It's only Trump, after all. And I may have jumped to a hasty conclusion about him spending all day on the golf course.'

'Where else would he have disappeared to, sir? Inspector Trump's not in a relationship, to my knowledge – he's too in love with himself. He's got no other hobbies, apart from feeding his cats and telling me what to do all the time. And there's a big golf tournament at the weekend. He's probably practising.'

'I told you – he won't be playing if he hasn't solved this case by the end of today.'

'I remember, sir. But I was thinking. Maybe he'll be allowed to play in the late evening after work – it's a full moon tomorrow and you can buy luminous golf balls. When it comes to golf, the inspector can always find a way.'

Block gazed out at the lemony horizon. 'You're right. And when I get hold of Trump, I'm going to squeeze him until his pips pop out.' He bared his lemon-yellow teeth. 'And that wasn't a joke.'

The superintendent left the police car and was swiftly followed by the constable, who locked the vehicle and followed his senior officer along the verge.

Chapter 39

Clinton's gut instinct had just persuaded him that, now he had been informed of his imminent demise, it was time to start begging for his life – especially as the hole in the middle of Big Bertha was growing by the second.

'I say, Svetlana,' he called. 'Do you have a minute?'

'I digging,' puffed Svetlana. 'Not talking.'

'You don't need to talk – just listen. I want to plead for my life.'

'What about mine?' whispered Josephine.

'One life at a time, Ms Savage. We don't want to overburden her conscience.'

'Oh. Of course.'

'I say, Svetlana,' he called again. 'I was thinking about joining the Russian secret service. We could team up. Like a modern-day Sherlock Holmes and Doctor Watson – me being Sherlock, of course. You playing a supporting but much less significant Watson-esque role.'

Svetlana didn't appear to be listening, so Clinton increased the volume.

'A detective genius such as myself could be very useful to you. You know the sort of thing – I could pass you all the gossip from the post-office queue, share the latest goings-on at the golf club, and keep you up-to-date with the cat food situation at all the local supermarkets. Even establish the middle name of every man in the village if it would help further your cause.'

Josephine nudged him. 'Inspector, you're not seriously offering to work for the Russians?'

Clinton pouted. 'On a long-term basis, no. I'd insist on it being a short-term arrangement until I had a proper understanding of the benefits on offer – annual leave, pension plan, opportunities for overseas golfing junkets. That sort of thing.'

'Not possible, inspector,' yelled Svetlana. 'You not born in Russia.'

'No. But I did accompany my mother to the Crimea for her seventieth birthday in 2011. Admittedly, it was still part of Ukraine then – and we spent most of the time in the hotel due to me spraining my ankle after slipping on a cocktail cherry – but it's part of your country now. So, technically, I have visited your great nation and it was a lovely part of the world. If I was a world leader looking to extend my country's borders, I couldn't think of better place to annex.'

Svetlana's digging continued at an impressive pace.

Clinton ploughed on. 'Maybe you could arrange for me to stay a few nights in Moscow so I can familiarise myself with my new working environment? Minimum four-star hotel. Preferably with a view of the Kremlin. Serving continental breakfast. And with a sauna where it's not obligatory to remove all of one's clothes. Jacuzzi would be lovely, too. And complimentary bottled water – still, not sparkling – a working trouser press and a fluffy dressing gown and slippers. Those last three are non-negotiable.'

The Russian was now one hundred per cent focused on her shovelling. And she was past the sand now, into the soil and launching dirt into the air at a frenetic rate.

Clinton projected his voice even more. 'And please ensure it's an original Corby trouser press and not a sub-standard Russian replica.'

Josephine jerked her ear. 'What was that, inspector?'

'What was what?'

'I thought I heard a voice.'

'A man's voice?'

'I think so. Did you hear it, too?'

'Yes. It was my voice. I was stipulating my trouser-press requirements.' He shouted in her ear. 'Is everything alright with your hearing?'

'It's functioning normally,' replied Josephine, trying not to wince. 'What I meant was I heard a distant voice. Barely audible – but definitely a voice.'

'Did it have a rather annoying nasal twang? If so, that'll be the jobsworth that patrols the car park. His whines about not paying and displaying can carry for miles.'

'It was a deep voice.' She cocked her ear and they both listened. Apart from twittering birds, there was nothing for their hopes to cling to.

'I can't hear anything, Ms Savage. Maybe the voice you heard carried on the wind from the dual carriageway.'

'Possibly.' Her nose twitched. 'What's that smell? Is it … lemons?'

Clinton snuffled. 'My finely tuned detective's nose can indeed confirm there is a citrusy smell wafting our way and the fruit in question is almost certainly of the lemony variety.'

Josephine's head flicked to the fence. 'I think I just saw somebody, inspector.' She screwed up her eyes. 'Actually, it's two people.'

'Where?'

'By the gate we came through.'

'The gate?' His head bobbed as he checked. 'You're absolutely right. What a turn-up for the books. I wonder what they're doing here.'

'I've no idea. But I know what they could do.'

'Put a new bolt on that gate? It's been crying out for one for months.'

'No, if there's any bolting to be done, it'll be done by us.'

'Ah. You mean these chaps could investigate the source of that curious lemony smell? It's not exactly the kind of scent one wants lingering in one's nostrils when being buried alive.'

'That's not what I meant.'

'You're saying they could cut down that oak tree so Russian spies planning dastardly deeds on the thirteenth green at Goosing golf club can't conceal their cars from view?'

'No, I mean they could rescue us.'

'Ah. Yes. Erm, exactly what I meant by those previous three comments – but in a cleverly cryptic, sub-textual way.'

'Whoever they are, those two individuals are our only hope.' She took a breath. 'What should we do? I don't want to blow this chance of rescue – if it is a chance.'

'Fret not, Ms Savage. This phenomenal brain of mine has already processed all the possibilities, analysed the optimum outcomes, and devised a fiendishly simple masterplan.'

'What's that?'

'We do absolutely nothing and – faced with overwhelming odds and the prospect of near-certain death – we cross our fingers and hope for the best. It's worked for me before and it'll work for me again.' He licked his lips. 'Probably.'

And they crossed their fingers tighter than they'd ever crossed them before.

Chapter 40

Superintendent Block and Constable Dinkel had strolled to the end of the dusty service road identified by the satnav. They'd inspected the bashed-up brown car parked behind the oak tree and quickly decided it had been abandoned long ago – there was nothing of obvious interest inside so the motoring wreck was best left for their uniformed colleagues to eventually stumble upon. Now the senior officer was peering through the fence that enclosed Goosing golf course, his face pressed to its black metal railings.

'Do you see what I see, constable?'

'What do you see, sir?' asked Dinkel, who was admiring the thick wrinkly trunk of the oak tree.

'No. I want you to use your eyes and tell me what you see. Then I'll compare it to what I'm seeing.'

'I see.'

'No, you don't see. You're facing the wrong direction. Stop bothering that oak tree and come over here.'

'Right you are, sir.' He did as ordered. 'Is that … Inspector Trump standing just off the green?'

'That's what I thought.'

'The blond bouffant is unmistakeable, sir – even from this distance. And he's standing next to a woman.'

'Any idea who she is, constable?'

'No, sir. Could be anybody.'

Block peered some more. 'Why aren't they moving?'

'No idea, sir.'

'I mean, I know golf can be a bit dull. But the players usually move around a bit, don't they?'

'I'm no sporting expert, but I believe forward motion is a key component of golf, sir.'

'Are their hands behind their backs?'

'Hmm. Seem to be.'

'Strange. And … hang on. What's going on in that massive bunker?'

'It's difficult to see exactly, sir. But I think a woman's head and shoulders bobbed up from it just now.'

'She's not much cop at golf, because there's no ball flying out – just a load of sand and earth.' The superintendent tapped his chin. 'No, she can't be taking shots that quickly. She must be digging.'

'That's one way to get your ball out of the bunker, I suppose. Though I've never seen Nick Faldo trying it.'

'There's something very odd going on. And my sixth sense tells me it's probably not good news for the two of us.'

'You mean there could be trouble, sir?'

'Trump is *always* trouble. You should've learnt that by now.'

'You think we should investigate further?'

'I think *you* should investigate further, constable. It'll be a good learning experience. I'll stay here and keep a senior officer's strategic eye on proceedings while you push on to the front line.'

'If you're sure, sir.'

'More sure than I've been since I fried that extra sausage for breakfast this morning. Step to it.'

Dinkel pushed open the unbolted gate and wandered down the gentle slope towards the green. His mind was struggling to comprehend the puzzling scene but, despite the warnings of his superintendent's sixth sense, he wasn't unduly worried about what might await him. Within a minute, he would be within conversing distance and then his senior officer would be able to explain exactly why he and his companion were so captivated by a bunker digger – if that was the correct label for such a person. Yes. Perhaps the course was undergoing minor refurbishment before tomorrow's tournament and the inspector was overseeing the works, along with a female official from the golf course. That would be a logical explanation.

His mental meandering was interrupted when he saw the inspector briefly glance across at him, jerk his head towards the bunker a couple of times and then return it to its previous orientation. *Very odd*, Dinkel thought, as he continued his approach. It was almost as if he was trying to tell him something. Or, then again, he could be batting away a wasp. Probably the latter.

The head and shoulders of the woman in the bunker had now completely disappeared from view and he could hear the sound of a shovel hitting rocky ground every few seconds. But the steep sides of the bunker prevented visual confirmation of this.

As he moved nearer, he could see a rake on the ground in front of him. His eyes focused. This was a top-quality piece of equipment. The type a professional gardener might even be prepared to kill for. And, while he had only recently been converted to the gardening cause, its shiny prongs, sleek contoured shaft and ergonomic handle were enough to make him want to pick it up and experience it in all its raking glory. So he grasped the opportunity – quite literally – with both hands.

The thrill of holding it was everything he'd expected and more. He gasped for breath. It was incredible. The laws of physics didn't seem to apply to it: the rake felt both light and sturdy; it was nimble but heavy-duty; user-friendly but … potentially lethal if it got into the wrong hands. It was a marvel of sediment-smoothing creation. Rakes didn't get much better than this.

The inspector was gesturing again with his head, so Dinkel proceeded – still clutching the phenomenal rake – to where his boss was standing.

'Thank goodness you're here, Dinkel,' whispered Clinton. 'A little earlier would have been preferable but I won't quibble about that now. My companion and I are about to be murdered in cold golfing blood.'

The noise from the bunker was getting louder – allowing them to speak at somewhere near normal volume.

Dinkel looked confused. 'Are you joking?'

'No, we're not,' spluttered Josephine. 'A Russian spy armed with a gun, shovel and extensive knowledge of the inspector's cat-food purchasing habits is on the verge of burying us in that bunker as part of a plan to strike at the heart of rural English society by infiltrating treasured institutions, controlling key infrastructure and creating internal disharmony with the ultimate goal of destabilising the country.' She gulped a massive breath and composed herself. 'Apologies for not introducing myself. I'm Ms Josephine Savage. Mrs Josephine Savage until my husband accidentally toppled into his own mincing machine completely by accident without me, or anyone else, giving him a helping hand.'

'And I'm Constable Dinkel.' He went to shake hands but after a few seconds realised both of hers were tied behind her back. 'I used to buy your late husband's tripe for my mum's dogs. They couldn't get enough of it. Can't find any tripe quite like it now. It's a tragic loss to the tripe-buying community.'

The inspector rolled his eyes. 'I would think your mouth comes out with enough tripe to feed every hound within a ten-mile radius. Now, go and tackle that Russian spy.'

'Shouldn't I untie you first, inspector, so you can help?'

'Yes, you can untie me. And Ms Savage, if you have the time. But I'm not going to help you. It will be a valuable learning experience for you to tackle an armed and dangerous foreign secret-service operative with no backup, no firearm and the limited brains God gave you.'

'So, you're not coming with me, sir?'

'Of course not. That Russian's got a gun.'

'Very good, sir.' He stared at the bunker. 'What exactly shall I do after I untie you?'

'Well, you've a top-quality rake in your hot little hands, so you can try and incapacitate her with that.'

Dinkel admired the rake. 'Yes, it's beautiful. I bet it's a pleasure to rake over your footprints after you've played out of the bunker.'

'It most certainly is. Only the best raking equipment for our sand traps.'

'Where does the club buy them, sir? Only I wouldn't mind getting my hands on one myself.'

'Erm, I'm not entirely sure. I can ask the facilities secretary for you.'

'That would be very kind of you, sir. I've been renting an allotment since the start of the year.'

'Really? I don't suppose you're growing cherry tomatoes?'

Josephine butted in. 'Aren't we veering slightly off track here? We need you to save the day, constable.'

The inspector coughed. 'If I might correct you there, Ms Savage, it would be South East England's greatest detective Clinton Trump saving the day – the constable would merely be carrying out my day-saving orders.'

'Yes, of course. How silly of me to suggest otherwise.'

Dinkel untied their hands and feet and held the rake aloft. 'Right, let's see how much of the day can be saved.'

As the freed duo began to hurry to the gate, Constable Dinkel edged tentatively towards the lip of the bunker. He could see the dirt flying to his left in an arc and hear the woman's grunts but he still couldn't see her. He continued his tentative edging – even more tentatively than before.

After a few seconds, the back of her head came into view. With both his eyes firmly on the target, he deftly moved the rake horizontally in the way Jackie Chan might if he had an allotment. Time seemed to slow down. Dinkel had never swung a rake at anyone's head before. The closest he'd come was at training school when he'd aimed a police truncheon at a watermelon stuck on top of a large sandbag. But a watermelon provided a much bigger target than this female's head. And, while she was probably knee deep in more sand than his training-school mock-up could boast, she would be a lot more mobile. He felt a lump in his throat. He wasn't sure he could do this.

But when the woman's head came within striking distance he felt a surge of rake-swinging confidence and he didn't hesitate. He swung his makeshift weapon with all the skill of a veteran baseball player and it made a satisfying clonk as it connected with her cranium. Fortunately, her head was made of stronger stuff than his training-school watermelon so it didn't explode on contact. Instead, the Russian toppled forward and rolled over into the freshly dug hole.

The constable took a few deep breaths to calm himself and heard a magpie caw, as if in recognition of his achievement. He laid down the rake, carefully descended into the bunker, retrieved the gun from the woman's jacket and checked to see if she had a pulse. She did. Then he checked her breathing. It was shallow but regular. Satisfied that no urgent medical intervention was required, he climbed out of the bunker, picked up the rake, trotted back in the direction of the fence and caught up with Clinton and Josephine.

'Entire day saved,' announced Dinkel, quickly adding, 'by you, of course, sir.'

The inspector eased his brisk pace and barely nodded. 'That was quick.'

'Yes, sir. If I'm honest, I was expecting a dramatic finale where she and I faced off in a duel of village-policing good against rogue-foreign-power evil – possibly involving me being de-raked at gunpoint, the Russian spy temporarily gaining the upper hand and revealing all the details of her dastardly plan before she attempted to kill me.'

Clinton huffed. 'Don't worry. She's already described her plan at length. You didn't miss much.'

'And with me,' continued Dinkel, ignoring the interruption, 'ultimately gaining the upper hand and bringing her into custody along the River Sticks on a high-powered executive speedboat.'

'Speedboat?' queried Clinton. 'This golf club doesn't have any speedboats.'

'Imagination running away with me, sir.'

'Where's the gun, constable?'

'Here it is, sir.' He handed the weapon to the inspector.

Clinton stashed it in his jacket pocket. 'Is our former captor out for the count?'

'Yes, sir. She'll be like a Russian bear with a sore head when she wakes up.'

'Good. And the rake?'

Dinkel checked. 'Not a scratch on it, as far as I can see.'

'Excellent. You have permission to congratulate me, constable.'

'Erm … congratulations, sir.'

'And congratulations from me!' cooed Ms Savage.

Superintendent Block had already squeezed through the gate and was stomping over to meet them. 'Well, Trump, what have you been up to? Or don't I want to know?'

'Oh, nothing much,' chirped Clinton. 'I've captured an undercover Russian spy who confessed – to both myself and Ms Savage here – to killing Jepson as part of an elaborate plot to undermine this wonderful country of ours.' He jabbed a thumb over his shoulder. 'The lady in question is currently out cold in that giant bunker. I have her firearm in my jacket pocket for evidential purposes – and, of course, the obligatory media photographs of me posing with it à la James Bond.' A thought occurred to him. 'Actually, I believe you and she are acquainted, sir. It's Svetlana – Dickie Blinder's other half. She mentioned your friendship during her tedious confession. But I'm sure nobody will hold that against you. You weren't to know you were matey with a Moscow mole on a murderous mission. Although you may want to think twice before you befriend a foreigner in the post-office queue in future.' Block remained tight-lipped. 'Now, will there be anything else, sir? Because I was thinking of popping to Waitrose for some cat food.' He raised his finger. 'Ah. One more thing – the good news is no premium raking equipment was damaged in the process of capturing your friend the spy. That means there'll be no additional expenses – other than the thirty-six holes of golf I played yesterday to enable me to solve this crime, two plates of fruit tartlets, a full-price copy of the *Goosing Times* and a few other sundries I may throw into the magnificent mix. Cat food from Waitrose being one of them.'

Block closed his gaping mouth and turned to the constable. 'Is any of that half-baked excuse for a fairy story true, constable?'

Dinkel nodded. 'I can confirm everything apart from the legitimate expenses, sir. In fact, it was me who swung the rake and brought Svetlana to just—'

'Alright, Dinkel,' huffed Clinton. 'That's enough own-trumpet blowing from you. The records will show I saved the day and your name, if it appears in the records at all, will be a four-point, single-spaced, Times New Roman footnote.'

'Will I receive a mention in the records, inspector?' asked Josephine, with a gentle squeeze of his shoulder.

Clinton shook his head. 'Not in official police records, Ms Savage. You may, of course, note it in your personal diary.'

'That's very generous of you, inspector. Thank you.'

The inspector preened in acknowledgement. 'Now, all that remains is for the superintendent to call in the uniformed troops to retrieve our murderer because she's covered in sand and I don't want anyone here ruining their white clothing – not even you, Dinkel, given your cameo role in this detective drama.'

Dinkel smoothed his shirt. 'Very magnanimous of you to recognise my contribution, sir.'

'The uniforms can restore the bunker to its former glory and rake over their boot prints before they leave. The superintendent can grant me – and only me – six months' access to the police station's executive coffee machine ...'

Dinkel's face fell.

'... and inform the British security services of my heroism so they can alert Her Majesty and the media. Then, once the public has been informed, the country can toast yours truly as a national hero and start a campaign to have me nominated for a knighthood. Possibly even raise a petition for a statue of me to be erected in the village.'

'Anything else I can do for you?' snarled the sarcastic superintendent.

'Oh, yes. When you're on the phone to Dickie Blinder, giving him an extensive quote about my day-saving activities for next week's front-page story about South East England's greatest detective, please tell him his girlfriend is a Russian spy – no point sugar-coating it, just come out with it – and that there's nothing wrong with his leg – the injury was a Russian misinformation campaign – so he and the Major can once again pair up tomorrow to do battle at the Goosing Golf Open and allow me to play solo without fear of being bombarded by military anecdotes.'

'That all, is it?' growled Block, managing to sound even more sarcastic.

'Oh, no. Ask if I can borrow his golf-club warmers. And his best golf ball. Oh, and his Nick Faldo biography.'

While the superintendent's face flushed pink – the result of what Clinton assumed was a rush of admiration – Constable Dinkel tapped the grass with his rake to get everyone's attention. 'I was thinking – it's been a very funny murder mystery, hasn't it?'

Clinton grimaced. 'What's your point, Dinkel?'

'I wonder if we could get Agatha Twisty, or someone else, to write a book about it?'

'With me as the lead character?' asked the inspector.

Dinkel hesitated. 'Of course, sir.'

'I don't want to be in it,' snorted Block.

'You'll have to be, sir,' explained Dinkel. 'You're one of the key characters in the whole adventure.'

'No, no, no. I know what writers are like. They'll make a mockery of my seniority. If anyone does decide to write a novel about all this, you can tell them from me to keep the superintendent out of it.'

A tall, shaven-headed man appeared out of nowhere.

'Excuse me, ladies and gents. I don't know if you can help. I'm on my way to surprise the cast of *Murder at Dress Rehearsal* and I've had to bail out of my taxi due to a traffic jam. The Goosing Players rehearse in a hall next to the golf course, and the taxi driver said I could get there by walking this way, but I haven't got a clue which way to go.'

'Who are you, then?' grunted the superintendent. 'A Russian spy?'

'No. Even worse. I'm a comedy novelist.'

Dinkel's ears seemed to enlarge. 'A comedy writer? What? A real one?'

'No, a pretend one.'

Dinkel's ears shrunk back down. 'Oh.'

'That was a joke. Of course I'm a real comedy writer.'

The constable's ears inflated again. 'Great! I can show you the way.'

'You're still on duty, remember,' barked the superintendent.

'I know, sir, but policing isn't just about saving the day.'

'You didn't save the day,' snorted Clinton. 'I did.'

'Saved the day?' asked the writer. 'Sounds interesting. What's been going on? I'm always looking for real-life inspiration for my novels.'

Block placed himself between the writer and the bunker. 'There's nothing to see here, sir.'

Clinton swished a carefree hand. 'That's right, my curious friend. There are no foreign assassins lying in that sand trap after being knocked unconscious by top-quality raking equipment.'

The superintendent flashed a scowl at the inspector then turned to the constable. 'You get going with this literary gentleman, Dinkel. Show him the way to the rehearsal.'

'Will do, sir.'

So, as the superintendent called for uniformed backup on his work mobile and the inspector stood admiring himself, the constable escorted the comedy writer across the golf course.

'You write novels?' asked Dinkel, sounding completely star-struck.

'Yeah – why?'

'Don't tell anyone I told you …' The constable grinned like a schoolboy in a sweetshop. '… but I've just helped solve a very funny murder mystery.'

Other novels by Paul Mathews:

The Blood Moon Of Doom
To Kill A Shocking Bard
Clinton Trump Detective Genius **series**

An Accidental Royal Kidnap
The Royal Wedding Saboteurs
Royal Wedding in Vegas
Royally Funny **series**

We Have Lost The President
We Have Lost The Pelicans
We Have Lost The Coffee
We Have Lost The Chihuahuas
We Have Lost The Plot
We Have Lost **series**

Discover more about author Paul Mathews –
South East England's greatest comedy novelist –
and his tremendous novels by visiting his
website at www.quitefunnyguy.com and signing
up for his Very Funny Newsletter

P.S. Congratulations, dear reader! You're now
officially a literary genius!

Printed in Great Britain
by Amazon

11939416R00140